Terror-Olympic Size

To Nicole -

A very fine care-giver. Hope you enjoy reading this fictional adventure.

George L. Hoffman

Terror-Olympic Size

George L Hoffman

Library of Congress Control Number:		2009902739
ISBN:	Hardcover	978-1-4415-2201-6
	Softcover	978-1-4415-2200-9

This is a work of fiction. Names, characters, places and incidents either are the product of the author's imagination or are used fictitiously, and any resemblance to any actual persons, living or dead, events, or locales is entirely coincidental.

This book was printed in the United States of America.

To order additional copies of this book, contact:
Xlibris Corporation
1-888-795-4274
www.Xlibris.com
Orders@Xlibris.com
36387

Contents

George L. Hoffman, Jr.
BAZEBALLC@AOL.COM

About the Author

The author, after thirty-seven years of service, retired as a lieutenant from an Empire State police department. He then took on the challenging task of teacher and baseball coach at a Florida high school.

While so engaged, he published two books in the how-to category: *Pitching Tips I thru V* and *So You Want to Be a Catcher.*

This book, as well, started out in theory as another how-to book, relative to establishing the means to handle a large public gathering. The event selected was the International Games for the Disabled, where the author was site commander, charged with protecting more than two thousand world-class athletes, their coaches and handlers for the duration of the competition

Almost immediately, however, the book morphed into the fiction genre of violence, betrayal, and mystery.

Not for the faint of heart, the adventure involves sex, terrorist attacks, murder, and feuding within the PD. If you are easily offended by street talk, this book is not for you. Language is strong in places, and there are adult situations involved.

The ending, however, is surprising and satisfying.

George L. Hoffman

Acknowledgments

When this book, my first in this genre, neared completion, my feelings were ambivalent relative to its entertainment value. It was my decision, therefore, to submit the roughest manuscript to a Florida literary society for their evaluation. The seven members who read the manuscript wish to remain anonymous. Their recommendations and praise encouraged me to complete the effort. I thank them, one and all.

No less heartfelt thanks go to Jeanette Williams and Marge Day, both of whom urged me to continue. Jeanette was invaluable in her help in research, and Marge proofread and critiqued every page. Thank you both very much.

Finally, I want to thank my wife, Joyce, for not reading one single word of the book. Her pious upbringing would have caused her to discourage and impede the completion of this effort.

Prologue

Uniondale, New York

Throughout the assignment and particularly for the past two months, the tension had been building and building. By the time the first tour of duty of the housing site security staff was in readiness, the pressure had reached a wild crescendo.

All the meetings and the accompanying heavy discussions that led up to the first day were in the past. The parameters had been established, posts determined, and personnel assigned.

Protocol had been agreed upon and was in the background, general ground rules thrashed out, and housing mix underway.

However, the most important item—execution—still remained untested.

Could a group of terrorists infiltrate the perimeter fencing unobserved by the roving patrol officers? Could the terrorists swarm over the six-foot-high chain-link fence topped with barbed wire? Then once having accessed the inside of the compound, could they, with their automatic weapons, gain entry into a high-rise dormitory and brutally take as hostages the athletes of their choice?

They did in Munich, Germany, in 1972, when on September 5th at 4:00 AM, eight armed Black September terrorists scaled a six-foot-high wire fence at the Olympic compound and committed a crime so grievous that it staggers the imagination. These fedayeen (Arab word for "men of sacrifice") set into motion one of the bloodiest and most horrifying spectacles ever covered *live* on television—the murder of eleven members of the Israel Olympic team!

After all the intelligence-gathering and preparation, could that happen here in New York because of the failure of someone to execute his/her responsibilities?

Most certainly it could!

Thus, the stage was set for the largest single public event ever to be held in Nassau County, New York. And the most dangerous!

Before that first twelve-hour tour on duty would end, there would be an explosion of major proportions within one-fourth mile of the housing site complex and the first intrusion through the security perimeter would be accomplished.

Introduction

Lieutenant George Hollister, despite the chaos and confusion of battle reverberating around him, lay full length on his back uncharacteristically quiet on the floor of the housing site command post. His systematic and orderly command post had, in minutes, become a pile of wreckage, destroyed during the swiftness of the initial assault.

Large chunks had been bitten out of doors, walls, and windows by the monstrous concentration of rocket and automatic weapons fire. Shards of glass were everywhere.

The darkness in which he lay was suddenly erased by the unexpected start-up of Hofstra University's independent generating system. What few lightbulbs remained unbroken sprang into existence, putting a dim and spooky appearance on the devastation around him and his bloodied body.

The AK-47s being fired nearby were making their distinctive low-pitch *chuk-chuk-chuk* sounds, answered by the high-pitch sound of M15s set on rapid fire.

Frenzied voices shouting unintelligible words came in a rush of noise back to Hollister's ears.

Out of the disorder and debris, his peripheral vision picked up a tiny lick of flame flickering to life from a severed electrical cable. Fed by this rubble, it would be a full-blown fire in no time at all!

"My god . . . I can't move my legs . . . I'm going to burn to death!" he said as the horror struck him.

He had to fight the panic.

He could make out the sharp crack of the police .38s and hoped that perhaps they were coming to help him.

"C'mon you guys, find me fast," he urged.

The back of his head and neck were jammed grotesquely against the top of his overturned desk. With his chin thus forced downward toward his chest, he had difficulty in focusing his eyes on objects merely a few feet away. In the newly created dimness, he could barely discern the crimson stain spreading from his chest through his white shirt, through his uniform jacket, and down to the floor next to him.

As the warm and sticky blood flowed slowly, his thoughts conversely raced wildly and without reason through his mind.

Shit! What a waste of a perfectly good white shirt!

Strange. I always thought being shot would cause unbelievable pain. What I feel instead is heat—a very sharp burning sensation!

Does the absence of real pain mean that I'm dying?

Jeez—what a way to go—shot but dying from the loss of blood. Not really going out in a hail of bullets hero-style the way I thought I'd go, but rather slowly, lying on the floor with my body refusing to function.

"Ridiculous!" he said aloud.

He somehow found the energy to laugh wryly, but the chuckle only caused him to cough, and he could see a pink spray of blood and saliva leave his mouth.

He stopped laughing abruptly and tried to concentrate on fighting off the feeling of hysteria that threatened him.

Then he felt the anger growing in him as the uproar of the firefight seemed to be moving away from him. His emotions were covering all the highs and lows imaginable.

Where the hell is everybody? Why doesn't someone stop that goddamn shooting and come help me!

"Hey!" he screamed as loudly as he could. "Over here! Give me a hand, dammit! Where the hell are you guys!"

He was astonished to find that his voice was nothing more than a feeble, hoarse whisper. He received no response, only more blood in his mouth along with the sudden realization that gunshot wounds *do* hurt like a son of a bitch!

Weakened by that effort, he refocused his eyes to his lower body stretched out in front of him, and he could see another puddle of blood forming along the side of his left leg.

Is that mine, or is it coming from the poor bastard lying across my legs?

How long does it take to bleed to death?

How'd that guy get there?

How the hell did I get here?

He tried mightily to move his legs and dislodge the body lying across him. Despite the energy surge, the effort failed and only served to weaken him even more. His vision started to cloud up, and the dark grey sensation deep in his brain began to creep over him.

How the fuck did I get myself into this damned situation anyway?

Should have had my head examined however it was started!

Above the tumultuous sound of renewed sporadic gunfire close by, Hollister became aware of the telephone lying on the floor next to him.

The handset had been knocked off its cradle when the desk was so unceremoniously overturned by grenade concussions during the first bizarre minutes of the attack. The five extension buttons were blinking urgently, and the telephone company's recorded scratchy voice message was being played.

"If you are making a call, please hang up and dial again. If you need assistance, hang up and dial your operator," said the mechanical voice at the end of the cord.

That familiar high-pitched wavering tone then screeched out, demanding attention.

Unable to gather the strength to shout out his insult, he merely thought, *I would if I could, you dumb bitch! Oh God, I wish I were back in Florida. Hey! That's how it all started, dammit! The lousy telephone, that's how!*

Completely exhausted by this simple thought process, Hollister permitted his eyes to slowly drop closed.

The last sound Hollister could distinguish was . . . *a freight train?*

The grey fog turned to blackness and took over his whole being—all tension left him as his body collapsed.

"Aw, guys, where are you?" he sobbed weakly.

The gunfire resumed with new intensity, but Hollister heard none of it.

Chapter 1

Recruitment or Retirement

The events leading up to the terrorism that follows on these pages really began in January 1984. Lieutenant George Hollister was on vacation but working long and hard hours clearing land at his close-to-complete retirement home in Florida.

On this fateful day, he was engaged in what he termed his labor of love—driving stakes into the ground in the rear of the home and stretching a cord, designing a uniquely shaped swimming pool for construction later in the year.

His daydreams were interrupted by the slightly husky voice of his wife, Joy, calling, "Babe!"

"Yo," he replied over his shoulder.

"Telephone," she said, and he detected urgency in her voice. "Chief Gerlich!"

"Gerlich? From New York?" he said, turning to face her wary stare. "What the hell could he want!"

She didn't reply but held the telephone out to him in silence. He crossed the yard to the patio with quick strides and snatched the phone roughly from her hand in mock anger, causing her to break into a smile.

"Helllll-o," Hollister said lightly.

"Hi, Rackets," said Deputy Chief Oscar Gerlich, a very solicitous tone to his voice.

Hollister was suspicious of this tone since he and Gerlich were never ever on really good terms. The greeting even brought Hollister's eyebrows together in anticipation of some distasteful subject. That had been his most recent history with Deputy Chief Oscar Gerlich.

Hollister, as CO of a group of special enforcement teams, knew that Gerlich was always waiting for the unit to step over the line so that Gerlich could impose discipline on them. Hollister not only knew that his highly successful people were many times just inside the legal limits, but also knew that it was the only way they could operate, given the type of criminals with whom they had to deal.

"Hi, Chief, what's wrong now?" was Hollister's matter-of-fact response.

"Oh, c'mon, what makes you think there's something wrong?"

Hollister thought to himself, *You sphincter muscle*, but instead chuckled his reply. "Thirty-six years with the PD, that's what. The deputy chief doesn't call up a lieutenant vacationing in Florida unless there is something definitely wrong, and the chief just can't wait to get at this lieutenant's ass and chew him out!"

Hollister was savoring this moment—thirty days from now, he was planning on putting his papers in and retiring. How much damage could Gerlich do to him in that period of time?

Whatever it is, Hollister thought, *I can do it standing on my head*.

He decided, however, to play this conversation out with a touch of sarcasm instead of the outright disrespect he would like to show for the man.

"Go ahead, Chief. I'm hanging on your every word," he replied quietly, meanwhile turning to casually watch Joy as she moved around in the kitchen.

Good-looking lady, he commented to himself. *Looks great in shorts*.

His voyeurism was interrupted, and he winced silently as Gerlich embarked on an obviously carefully prepared lecture, true in form to the manner in which the chief prepared all his assignments.

"This involves an assignment to the 1984 International Games for the Disabled to be conducted in the new Mitchel Park Complex, Nassau Community College, Hofstra University, and other surrounding facilities."

Gerlich's voice was annoying background noise to Hollister's inner thoughts. *International Games for the Disabled. Did this guy think that I'm going to postpone* again *a hard-earned retirement to babysit a bunch of gimps.* And a grin appeared on his face.

He began waiting for a momentary break in Gerlich's voice so that he could jump in and say "no way."

Joy drifted by again, and Hollister delayed her with a touch on her arm. He motioned with his head to the scratch pad lying on the table and printed, "Stop! Pay toll!"

She giggled slightly and, leaning close, planted a kiss on his cheek. Hollister smiled and shook his head. Lifting his mouth from the phone, he took this second kiss on the lips.

She was considerably younger than he, but it was not apparent. He was in excellent shape, worked out regularly, and was gifted with a youthful appearance and exuberance. She loved him totally and emotionally, and at times, they played like a couple of kids. Life was good together, and they agreed that they had a good thing going. The teasing and touching were still fun for both and actual sex acts frequent and rewarding. Truly in love, they showed it often to each other and reveled in their happiness.

During Hollister's conversation, though, Joy tried to keep her mind on the impending retirement, assuring herself that Hollister would never, never be convinced again to postpone it. She (and he) had been through enough for that damned job that very often possessed him entirely.

It was very difficult being a wife to a policeman who lived and loved his job with such fervor. The job to her was at times "the other woman," and during those times, she hated it as though it *were* another woman.

Hollister had taken an oath years ago as a police academy recruit to protect others. Joy found it difficult to accept the fact that he was still, after all these years, firmly committed to that oath, even at the risk of his own life.

She tried desperately to block out the things he was doing as Commanding Officer of the special enforcement teams—a sort of street crime entity—dealing most often with the lowest forms of humanity, drug pushers, pickpockets, muggers, rapists.

She had been told many stories by members of the teams, despite Hollister's protestations to the contrary, relating that he was always in the middle of things, running down dark alleys, or grappling with a pusher when need be. He could play it safe as the commanding officer, but she knew he loved the job too much to do that.

Police psychologists have spoken to police wives often in the past in an attempt to keep couples together when the gap between them inevitably began to widen. The psychologists advised wives to urge heir husbands to talk about their work, to communicate their stressful emotions, to pull themselves closer together by sharing the experiences and trauma.

Joy found this particularly difficult to accomplish because Hollister, long ago and early in their marriage, told her, "Talking about some of the things that happen on the job would be like bringing the dirt from the street into our living room. I don't want it there to contaminate you. There are things going on out there that normal people never get to see, and the police stand protectively between those normal people and the slugs on the street."

She deeply loved this man who could deal all night with the worst scum, then come home and, for the most part, be the most loving, tender, and considerate person you could find.

Indeed, he was a most unusual person, and she was heartened by his approaching retirement from the pressure and danger, which she perceived as a definite threat to their relationship.

She hated not knowing whether or not he was going to return home after leaving in response to one of those middle-of-the-night emergency calls.

She took great pains to conceal from him her worst recurrent nightmare. That was the one in which she watched a television news bulletin covering the shooting death of a policeman whom they would not identify "pending notification of the next of kin."

Her nightmare would then flash to the dreaded arrival at her front door of a police car occupied by a deputy inspector and the police chaplain—the customary "notification to the next of kin" people.

She involuntarily shuddered as the thought of the nightmare persisted in her mind.

Joy knew that Hollister was disturbed by the drop in morale on the job, brought about by an Affirmative Action Decree imposed on the police department by the justice department. The far-reaching effects of the plan had not yet reached his unit, but he knew that it was unavoidable and that they soon would.

She had heard Hollister state many times that he wanted to retire from the job while he still loved it and while he still respected the efforts put forth by the vast majority of the men. However, in his opinion, the actions decreed by the Department of Justice were destroying the very fiber of the job.

Promotions had been directed to be made not via the competitive examination method used so successfully in the past, but were to be made based upon the finding that there were insufficient minorities in supervisory capacities and in special assignments. In other words, the allegation was that these assignments currently were slanted heavily away from the percentage of minorities residing in the county.

In addition, the county was directed to actively recruit minorities in an effort to correct the imbalance. This, Hollister believed, was a step in the right direction; however, he did not approve of a special-test preparation class held for the recruited minorities only.

This was reverse discrimination.

To the cop on the street, it seemed that the most damaging thing was that it also mandated that minorities be placed at the top of a promotion list, regardless of their competitive standing. This led the nonminority employees of the police department to start searching their family trees for some sign of a minority, real or invented, in their background, whether it be American Indian, Spanish, or whatever—anything to eliminate what was viewed as an unearned advantage and to compete on a more even basis again.

What he disapproved of even more, if that were possible, was the production of a so-called "Dream sheet" to be completed by the minorities on the job. This dream sheet asked that they list the assignments they most wanted in the police department.

He was of the opinion that the commissioner, not a very dominant personality, caved in too easily to the minority demands.

Already, Commissioner's Orders were beginning to appear, making choice assignments based on these dream sheet wishes, rather than being based upon dedicated and loyal performance. He said that he could feel the pride of the job crumbling down around him.

Joy knew that these things bothered Hollister a great deal because he was a firm believer in competitive examination and promotions gained by merit evaluation and on performance. She was, therefore, delighted with his decision to retire following this vacation.

1984 would be their best year yet!

While he continued his conversation with Gerlich, Joy poured a glass of iced tea (it was a little too early in the day for anything else), brought it to Hollister, and absently started rubbing his back and shoulders lightly. Whenever she thought he was annoyed or angry, she would quietly soothe him by performing that tender act. It always worked!

Hollister had a slightly silly smile on his face while Joy performed her ritual rub.

Boy, does she know me, he thought, while thoroughly enjoying it.

Gerlich's voice suddenly came back into focus in his ear with the words, "And that means lots of overtime pay for you in your final year's average salary."

Hollister, thinking now in dollar signs, was attentive to Gerlich's next words as he explained that traditionally the games are held in the country that hosts the "able-bodied Olympics." The 1976 version was held in Toronto, Canada, and the 1980 Games were held in Arnhem, Holland. Thus, the United States would be host for 1984—with Nassau County bidding for and winning the right to have them held in the County. The 1988 Games were tentatively scheduled for Korea.

Hollister jumped in, "What the hell kind of events could be involved in Olympics for the disabled?"

Oscar Gerlich was now in full swing and warming to his task. Hollister thought, *He probably rehearsed this bullshit all night*, as Gerlich continued.

"Competition is an Olympic type. Events will include track and field, swimming, weight lifting, archery, soccer, wheelchair soccer, bocci-ball, wrestling, volleyball, riflery, goal ball, table tennis, horseback riding, and cycling, to name some. They tell me the athletes participating in the games are just that—athletes! They are world-class performers who have been selected to represent their homelands based on qualifying contests held in their own nation's national championships."

Gerlich was really rolling now. "Would you believe that there are blind athletes who run the hundred-meters in eleven seconds? How about an amputee high jumper with one leg, from Canada I think, who will probably jump seven feet during this meet? Or a cerebral-palsied light-heavyweight lifter who can bench-press 450 pounds? These are world-class athletes! We expect athletes from maybe sixty countries, like Russia, East Germany, and Poland; from Sweden, Denmark, and Italy; from Scotland, Japan, and Korea; from Israel, Mexico, and Brazil. There will be more than two thousand of the world's top athletes under our protection from early June through the Fourth of July!"

Gerlich was now raising the volume of his voice as he became more and more excited.

Just like the little politician he is, Hollister thought. *But it is beginning to sound . . . well, challenging.*

Gerlich practically shouted the next sentence, his voice becoming distorted by the telephone, "The 1984 International Games for the Disabled will demonstrate to Long Island, the United States and, yes, the world, the top-notch athletic talents of these athletes!"

Then in an almost confidential tone, "We anticipate that these games will receive a lot of local, regional, national, and international media coverage with lots of television exposure. The economy of the county can only prosper during this period."

"Obviously there's a lot more to this thing that I originally considered," Hollister interjected. "But where do I fit in? I'm about to put this battleship in mothballs. Why me?"

At this statement of his, he heard a sharp intake of breath and turned to see a quizzical look on Joy's face, accompanied by a small forced, nervous smile.

He winked at her as reassuringly as he could.

"George," Gerlich continued, once again sounding very sincere and back in control of his enthusiasm, "you've been around the block more than once, and we all know of your reputation as a tough, knowledgeable, and fair boss. Beyond that, you can organize a unit and knit it together better than anyone I know. There are some very challenging problems that go along with this caper, requiring that we put the very best people in charge.

"Security of the athletes and support staff would mean close cooperation and association with top officials from the State Department, Central Intelligence Agency, Federal Bureau of Investigation, Secret Service, and Hofstra University Security, among others.

"Despite all our personal disagreements in the past, you are undoubtedly the best man for the job of Site Commander for the housing unit, the most difficult unit to set up and the one most likely to be hit by a terrorist attack."

Hollister, with the words "overtime pay" still in the forefront of his consciousness, was beginning to fall into the trap, if that's what this conversation was designed to do.

"Hofstra University Security?" he growled. "What the hell will the rent-a-cops have to do with this?"

"We plan to use the university's dormitories to house the athletes, trainers, coaches, and staff."

Hollister, showing interest, inquired, "Why the call here? Why not wait until I get back to New York next week sometime?"

"Schooling" was Gerlich's terse reply.

"Schooling?"

Gerlich then switched gears to phase II of his pitch, "You handpick your men, and I will arrange for attendance at a school, instructing attendees on terrorists, their beliefs, practices, weapons, and goals. They will be instructed by the FBI and other agencies knowledgeable in the field. We must start setting up the course of instruction right away."

The concept was very intriguing to Hollister, and he suddenly heard an enthusiastic voice say, "Enroll me—you have a Site Commander." It was only then that he realized that it was his voice!

That's how this fiasco started!

Good or bad, Hollister was *in*!

* * *

At the other end of the telephone in his study at home in Baldwin, New York, Deputy Chief Oscar Gerlich turned to the heavyset swarthy man seated across the desk from him and said with a satisfied smile, "Got him!"

The man removed the sloppy, wet stub of a cigar from his mouth, flashing a flamboyant diamond pinky ring as he did so. He nodded a vigorous "Good!" tumbling cigar ashes down the front of his suit and onto his ample stomach.

* * *

At the same moment back in Florida, a different and serious problem faced Hollister.

How to convince Joy that a few more months was worth the extra retirement money that would be forthcoming from this venture. He put the phone back on the wall hanger and folded a waiting Joy into his arms. Her eyes were glistening and wet—probably from the bright Florida sunshine.

Her first words, muffled by her face buried in his chest, were "You promised!"

"But listen, hon . . . ," he started lamely.

"But you promised!" Her voice was heavy with controlled emotion.

"You said that this was your last year on the job. You were going to file for retirement after this vacation!"

Her words started coming with a rush. "We were finally going to spend time together without planning everything around that stupid job."

She leaned backward slightly, still in his grasp, and looked up at his face. Hollister saw distress in her eyes, along with the tears that were welling up and cascading down her cheeks.

"You promised," she said weakly.

Hollister reached out and cupped her tear-stained cheeks in his hands and kissed her gently—first on one eyelid and then on the other. Her tears were slightly salty.

"We will, hon. We will do all the things we talked about," Hollister soothed. "Let me explain . . . uh . . . let me tell you what this is all about."

"I don't care," she said firmly, "what it's all about. You intend to stay on that job until it gets the best of you—until you die. You don't care about *us*, you only care about *them*. Judging from what I heard of that conversation, you have no intention of quitting that job. OK"—she sobbed—"go do your thing in New York, if that's what makes you happy. But I'm not going with you!"

She wrenched herself completely free of his embrace and looked defiantly up at him. "I'm going to stay here in Florida. I'm going to visit with Mom and Dad in Stuart, and I'll stay there until you come to your senses and decide to keep your promise!"

Hollister looked on in utter disbelief. These were the first real angry words she had spoken to him in their ten years together. Oh sure, minor skirmishes over missing family outings or a wedding reception, things like that—but that was because that's the way the job is. Nothing as serious as this encounter though.

"Sweetheart . . . ," he started again, brushing her blonde hair away from her cheeks. "That overtime money makes a lot of sense. We'll be able to do many more things together with the extra money coming in. A part of every working day on this assignment will be on overtime. Be practical. Think about the cash flow. Think about . . ."

In control again, but still tearful, she said, "I am thinking. Thinking about how you were going to retire last year. Thinking about how at the last minute they talked you into putting together a street crime unit. Thinking about how these special assignment guys took all your time with their nighttime capers. Thinking about the telephone calls in the middle of the night from people called Mr. Dirt and Animal and Chris Vicious and . . . and . . . other horrible names. Thinking about how you would scramble out of bed and dash out after some of these calls. And yes . . . thinking about how much you loved it."

Her emotions gained the upper hand again, and she blurted, "What do you want from the job—an inspector's funeral? Get off now while you can. I want you off this caper. No! I want you off the job!"

With a catch in his voice, which sounded foreign to him, Hollister said, "Please, hon, don't cry. I don't know what to do when you cry. It makes me feel so bad . . . but this is what I do best . . . what I know . . . this is who I am . . . ," and his voice trailed off.

"Then be who you are by yourself! You look down on anyone who is not a cop!"

"Being a cop is my job."

"There are other jobs! You have an obligation to me too . . . not just to the job."

They looked at each other for several long seconds, each trying to comprehend what was taking place here.

Hollister broke the silence.

"Look," he said, "I promise that as soon as this assignment is over, I'll throw the papers in gladly and retire. Just don't do anything like not going back north with me. Don't do that to us!"

Joy countered with, "You know what to do to stop it from happening. I love you, babe. You are my world and always have been. I want to do things for you and with you. I want us together for the rest of our lives. I don't want to worry anymore every night about having one of the lowlifes you have to deal with hurting you, or worse—being notified that you were lying in some stinking alley somewhere!"

Shaking her head from side to side in a "no more" gesture, she gasped, "I just can't take any more of it, babe. I want us to be together!"

"But that's what I want too." His mind was spinning.

Christ, Hollister thought. *She's right—I really do love it!*

He sincerely believed that it was important for him and his boys to go to work every day. He and Holly's Boys, as they were known on the job, were the last bastion between the slime of the streets and the good guys. Their presence was important to keep that slime from ruthlessly attacking the weak, meek, and elderly—the easy targets of our society. Every day was productive and rewarding to the community as well as to the self-esteem of the teams. Esprit de corps was sky-high. They worked together like a precision-made clock and were close enough that they hung together socially, family with family.

It was universally accepted that Hollister had teamed them up admirably, considering personalities and physical attributes in putting together each team.

Every team had what he termed a runner—a man with excellent mobility and unusual endurance.

Each team also had a man well versed in police procedure and in law since important decisions were necessarily made on the spot, routinely.

Often, more than one member of the team possessed all of these qualities.

Damn it! He did love it, and it was important!

The next days were days of quiet discussion and difficult decisions.

Chapter 2

The Assignment

Alone on Eastern Airline's flight from Daytona Beach Regional Airport to John F. Kennedy International Airport, New York, Hollister thought back to the tearless good-byes at the new house. There were no tears left. He had watched as Joy slowly and deliberately put her things together for her visit to Stuart, Florida.

He watched sadly but was determined to carry out what was to be his last detail with the Police Department to the best of his ability. His ego would permit nothing less.

* * *

"Welcome to John F. Kennedy International Airport, New York. The weather is currently overcast and the temperature is twenty-eight degrees. The Captain requests that you please remain seated until the aircraft has come to a compete stop in the terminal. Thank you for choosing Eastern and please enjoy your stay in New York," intoned the flight attendant.

Hollister shivered involuntarily at the words, "Twenty-eight degrees." Three hours ago he was enjoying seventy-four degrees in a lightweight shirt. Now he was reaching into the overhead luggage compartment for the lined strap-collared jacket that he frequently used on these short flights.

He joined the cattle drive out of the aircraft and through the terminal toward the baggage carousel. There was no doubt that he was back in New York. So eager were the people that they began to orbit the baggage carousel, which was already in motion transporting luggage, trying to be the first person to grab his or her luggage.

Hundreds of people were dodging and scurrying in all directions, crisscrossing almost recklessly. As he looked down from the top of the escalator, the fabled craziness of New York City was emphasized by the seemingly unstructured high-speed movement of the masses below. The scene reminded him of the herky-jerky movie speed of a Mack Sennett Keystone Kops comedy from 1900. The most amazing thing, however, was that in spite of the pandemonium, people seemed to reach their destinations, all the while experiencing a minimum of body and eye contact.

The flight was on time and he hoped that the special enforcement team that was to meet him was also on time.

As Dame Fortune would have it, his single luggage bag was one of the first to be propelled along the winding rubber track toward the impatient passengers. He quickly grabbed it and headed for the automatic doors that led to the curb, the meeting place.

The conditions outside the terminal had worsened to a light drizzle, which seemed to freeze immediately upon reaching the ground.

It seemed even more dark and foreboding without Joy at his side, a fact that was not lost on this unhappy man.

No sooner had he reached the doors when he heard a familiar voice call, "Hey boss!"

There they were—two of his finest.

Pat Connors was a huge man, six feet three inches tall, 260 pounds of sinew and muscle; but beyond that, he possessed a linebacker's attitude. He was adorned in what the other team members called his "Sunday Go-to-Church Clothes." Today's wardrobe consisted of a pair of faded dungarees, a blue plaid shirt and a tan sleeveless insulated vest. His scuffed shoes looked as though they had been picked out of a trash can on the way to the airport, or worse, stolen from a derelict along the way. He wore a full beard, topped off with a crop of unruly dark curly hair that would put a Zulu warrior's headdress to shame.

Even the sophisticated New York travelers skirted warily around him.

This was the Hammer—recipient of the department's highest award for bravery, the Medal of Valor—earned by his actions in a shooting incident.

His medal was one of the few that was not awarded posthumously. Pat was probably the bravest man Hollister had ever known and he had personally recommended him for several other citations for his actions while assigned to the special enforcement teams.

The second man was much smaller all around and was often accused, jokingly, of buying his way on to the job because of what appeared to be a short stature. He was wearing a blue-grey sport jacket over a pale blue V-neck sweater, grey slacks and dark felony shoes. He too was fully bearded, although his was trimmed very closely. The hair on top of his head was beginning to permit his scalp to peek through. He had most unusual cheeks in that he resembled a gerbil or perhaps a squirrel with a full winter's supply of goodies stashed in them.

This was Animal. He was not named for his appearance, but for the manner in which he handled the "sleaze bags" on the street. Unmercifully! He was the so-called "runner" on this team; and Pat, who studied constantly, was the "procedure man."

Animal, straight name Tom Egan, was not sure what he wanted out of life except a good time.

The Hammer, on the other hand, wanted a promotion to sergeant more than anything else. His father had been a railroad police department sergeant. Pat was secure and solid and usually measured his words carefully before speaking for officialdom.

Hollister characterized their approach to the job as, "Pat breaks down the doors and Tom sprints through the opening."

Animal was flamboyant and impulsive and had the "gift of gab" that the females of the species seemed to love. It is said of Animal that he "gets more ass than a toilet seat."

He was at this moment involved with an airport security guard who had the audacity to question Animal's right to park in a "No Stopping" zone. With his detective's shield held overhead in the palm of his left hand, he was yelling at the hapless man, "Where the hell is your supervisor. Can't you see that this is official police business!"

Turning toward Hollister, he completed his bluff by saying, "You'll have to come with us, sir, downtown!"

Hollister went along with the hoax and tossed his bag into the rear seat of the unmarked Chrysler LeBaron assigned to him by the department. He followed the luggage into the car, which was parked illegally curbside, and with a sardonic grin said, "Yes, sir!"

The other two clambered into the front seat of the car. With Animal driving, they moved out into the chaotic traffic mess surrounding the airport, cutting off two cars in the process. This left the security guard standing there staring after them, mouth agape, and the drivers of the cars that had been cut-off slamming on their brakes and swearing at the disappearing LeBaron.

"Jeez-uz H. Christ," Hollister said. "Can't leave you guys alone for ten minutes without you getting into some kind of trouble. I sometimes think that I was put on this earth just to keep you from screwing up!"

"You don't know the half of it yet, boss," deadpanned Animal.

"Uh oh. You'd better be kidding, Tom," said Hollister, calling Animal by his true name. "I'm not going to be around to save you for much longer. I'm moving into another assignment."

"Yeah," offered Pat Connors. "We heard. There are a zillion rumors goin' around. You're going to be the Site Commander for the International Games, right?"

"And you're taking us with you, right?" interjected Tom Egan in the most earnest tone he could muster.

"Boy," Hollister said, "it didn't take long for the old bullshit to start, did it? I just heard about it myself a few days ago. I really don't know all the ground rules yet."

Reverting to expected form, Tom said, "I'm sure you'll want your crack troops with you on this detail. I've got my locker all cleaned out, my bag packed and I'm ready to move out!"

"Uh huh, and that's his house the asshole is talking about," said an annoyed Pat.

"Oh no! Don't tell me you've gotten Carol mad at you again," said Hollister, recalling that he had counseled a dispute between Tom and his wife a while ago.

Hollister thought highly of Carol, a very young, pretty, and obviously tolerant lady. She was a quiet homebody, while Tom was anything but quiet, and was in fact a carouser of wide reputation.

"Not 'again'," laughed Tom. "Still, but we'll work it out, we always do."

"Only because Carol is such a nice girl," said Pat, still annoyed at his partner's obvious lack of concern over a situation, which Pat considered to be very serious.

Hollister sensed Pat's concern and putting on his police face, said, "I made it clear to you last time, Thomas, that if your extra-curricular activities begin to interfere with this job, you are history as far as this unit is concerned. I don't want your tongue playing tonsil hockey with every female you meet! I mean it; if Carol starts bitching to me about long hours that you are not really working, Pat will have a new partner and you'll be back in the 'bag' the next day. I kid you not!"

Egan knew from watching Hollister work in the past with his "iron hand" that he could be back in uniform in a New York heartbeat should Hollister get angry enough.

"Hey, boss," he pleaded, "there's nothing to it. Everything is OK," meanwhile giving Pat a sideways glance.

Catching the look from his vantage point, Hollister said, "Just keep your eyes on the road. We'll continue this in the 'rubber room' if it becomes necessary!"

This statement caused Egan to gasp, in a half-whisper, "Oh shit! Nothing good has ever happened to me in that room!"

At this point Hollister was trying very hard to conceal a grin that was about to break through his stern countenance.

All of the special enforcement members and many of the uniformed people were well aware of the so-called "rubber room," and became apprehensive when "it" was spoken about. "It" was nothing more than the deputy chief's office, vacant most evenings, but utilized by Hollister when he wanted complete privacy with a subject. Being called to such a confidential meeting with Hollister usually meant big trouble for the conferee, since Hollister believed in reprimanding in private.

He never embarrassed them in public and permitted them to maintain their dignity in front of their peers. His reputation, however, had him expert at private reprimands.

Thus, being bounced from one assignment to a lesser important one often took place after a conference in the "rubber room" and was feared by many. Hollister, a "salty long-timer" had a great deal of power and influence and wielded it with that well-known iron hand. His philosophy was that workers would be rewarded and shirkers hounded.

It followed then that if you didn't love Hollister, chances are that you hated him. These emotions then also categorized you as a "worker" or a "shirker."

Hollister decided not to pursue Animal's domestic trials at this moment since Animal was busy fighting the traffic leaving the airport proper. The traffic situation was not much better when they came to the Belt Parkway and so they jumped off and cut to Linden Boulevard as soon as they could. Their conversation soon became centered on the latest rumor focus, the International Games.

Policemen, traditionally, are great rumormongers and some even relish their ability to start an outlandish rumor and then wait for it to travel throughout the precinct and return to them as an accredited fact. That, according to this special enforcement team, was the situation all over the county. The grapevine was rampant with wild conceptions of what the assignment would be like and the manner to be pursued to get assigned to it.

Everyone was concerned about who would be assigned to the Games, and the overwhelming number wanted the assignment.

They are a proud bunch, police officers, and assignment to the Games was looked upon as choice and challenging. Many of them wanted to be where the action was and this certainly looked promising for plenty of action and not incidentally—overtime money.

* * *

Their arrival at the precinct was long after dark, fortunately, which saved Hollister from having to listen to a million questions. Questions for which, at this point, he had no answers.

He dropped off Pat and Tom, who transferred to the "taxi," one of the other vehicles used in their undercover assignments and then left for home.

He drove slowly, not relishing the thought of opening up the house in Uniondale and trying to conduct "business and usual" without Joy. He only half-listened to the emergency calls being broadcast over the police band in the car by the female dispatchers in the Communications Bureau.

Hollister knew that this was going to be a very difficult time for him and wished Joy could have agreed with his viewpoint and returned to New York with him. He could use her quiet, steady support very much in the weeks and months to come.

Once at home he dialed the Florida house. He let the phone ring ten times.

There was no answer.

These were going to be difficult times, indeed.

* * *

Hollister experienced a rather fitful night and rose very early the next morning. Without his usual enthusiasm, he rode a couple of miles on the exercise bike and did a few "sets" on the weight bench. After a shower and shave, he left the house and stopped at a little restaurant a block away from his home.

"Henry's Wife's Place" announced the sign in front. He strolled inside and, passing up the tables, sat at the small counter near the grill.

Elaine, Henry's wife, who was attending the counter, looked behind Hollister expectantly. "No 'Joy' in Uniondale today?" she quipped.

"No. And not for awhile," he growled. "She's staying in Florida for a bit."

Laughing, she said, "A bit of what?"

Hollister shook his head and grumbled, "Look, it's seven o'clock in the morning, I've got a big deal meeting coming up on my first day back from vacation, I didn't sleep well, I haven't had a cup of coffee yet, and you want to act like it's the *Lucy Show* in here. Gimme a break . . . and a cuppa coffee!"

"Sheesh! Boy, do you get grouchy when you're horny! One coffee, black and sweet, on the way!"

Henry, Elaine's husband, was a firefighter who was pressured by her into buying this small restaurant to give her something interesting to do because he spent so much time at the firehouse. She kept the place open only during the daylight hours for breakfast and lunch customers. By dinner time the place was closed down; the neighborhood was beginning to get a little risky at night. Hank was a long-standing friend of Hollister's, going back to Hollister's bachelor days before Joy entered his life.

After a difficult divorce, Hollister almost went sour. He began dating at every opportunity, not being very selective at all, looking for . . . what . . . he didn't know. Perhaps someone to fill the void suddenly created in his life.

There was a problem with the women available to him. They were mostly very young or recently divorced people, and after a second date, he had the feeling that they were planning the honeymoon trip. That meant that he had to move on to another companion. No more mistakes for him. Oh no! No one was going to get "close" to him.

So, instead of looking for "Miss Right"—he settled for a succession of "Miss Right Now"!

One night, out with Hank and some other friends for an evening of good-natured bowling and a few drinks, Elaine showed up with a friend from school days—Joy. After some hours in her company, Hollister began to rethink his philosophy.

It takes a very special lady to be a policeman's wife and perhaps there was one out there for him after all.

No longer was he intent on trying to see how many ladies he could "do" quickly . . . he decided that he wanted to spend some time with this one.

The four of them—Hank and Elaine and Hollister and Joy—had remained close friends over the years and dined out together frequently; at least as frequently as the men's unusual occupations permitted.

"You need tea leaves for that," he was startled to hear Elaine say.

"What?" he said, breaking out of his reverie.

"The way you're staring into that cup, I thought you were trying to 'read' the leaves. You need tea for that," she repeated.

"Very cute."

She leaned over the counter on her elbow, chin in hand. "Want to tell me about it? Maybe I can help."

"Nope," said Hollister as he reached into his pocket. "And showing me a lot of cleavage will not make me talkative either!"

She straightened up, suddenly self-conscious.

"That's OK," she said, smiling again. "Cops drink coffee here on the arm."

He dropped a dollar bill on the counter and said, "Not this one," as he headed for the door. "See you later, love."

He slid into the LeBaron and headed for the Station House.

The weather, unpredictable as usual, had warmed considerably from the previous evening.

Hollister had traveled along the same route for so many years that the trip to the Southern State Parkway was automatic. Once on the six-lane express roadway, however, his attention was focused on driving. The commuter traffic at this hour of the morning was heavy and some drivers seemed almost to be intentionally aiming at others.

Unfortunately, New Yorkers are known nationwide for their aggressive driving habits and this morning was no exception. Demolition derby time. Twenty-five action-filled minutes later he pulled into the police parking field at the station house and parked near the rear door in the parking spot reserved for his vehicle.

Entering the locked security door with a key, he strode down the hall, through a set of double doors to the main desk area. As was his custom, despite the fact that he was in civilian clothing, he saluted the flag of the United States on its stand behind the desk officer and requested a "line in," meaning that the blotter recorder should sign him present and on duty.

This formality accomplished, he retraced his steps through the double doors, turned left at the sign "Detective Division" and was about to mount the stairs to the second floor where his office was located, when he heard loud voices.

He found that they belonged to two very frustrated and angry police officers attempting to interrogate one of the low-echelon street drug pushers, who was not being cooperative at all.

Hollister stood in the doorway of the Arrest Processing Room for a few moments until one of the officers acknowledged him.

"Hi, Loo. We're just killing time waiting for the dicks on call to arrive and talk to this joker," he said apologetically.

"No problem," Hollister smiled. "Perhaps I can prime the pump a little. Mind if I take a crack at him before the 'squeal team' gets here?"

"Hell no. We're not making any progress with the asshole anyway."

Hollister sauntered into the room and leaned over the "pusher." "What's your first name, Bud?"

"James," was the sullen reply.

"James," Hollister asked quietly, "did you ever play tag when you were younger?"

The suspect looked up at Hollister, surprised for a moment and said, "Hey man, are you for fuckin' real!"

Hollister patiently replied, "Of course I'm for real. I'll repeat my question and this time you think carefully before you answer.

Did you ever play tag when you were younger?"

The pusher grimaced and stole a quick glance at both uniformed officers standing nearby.

The two uniforms looked questioningly at each other.

Finally, Jim, averting his eyes, mumbled, "Yeah, I guess I played fuckin' tag."

Hollister continued his scam quietly. "Just in case you don't remember how it works, let's go over it one time.

"One guy is 'it' until he tags someone else. Right? Then that person is 'it' until he tags someone. Isn't that the way the game is played?"

He waited a moment for his statement to sink in.

James looked up again a Hollister, disbelief in his eyes. "So? What's your fuckin' point?"

"My point is that we really don't want a small-time piss-ant like you. We want the slimeball who supplies you! So, stop running your mouth for a second and really listen carefully to me this time, Jim."

Hollister proceeded evenly, "You see, that's what we're doing right now . . . playing a game of tag . . . and you're 'it'.

"These officers have tagged you, so you'll have to keep on being 'it' until you tag someone else.

"If you don't want to play my game, it's all right. Just say so and we'll drop you in a detention cell until your hearing. I'm sure some big, ugly, horny bastard would love to have a young tight-ass like you for a cellmate and girlfriend."

He watched the muscles in Jim's jaw convulse before he continued.

"Does my game sound any better to you now?"

"I think so," Jim replied, thoughtfully this time.

He studied the lieutenant carefully, furrowing his brow in concentration before saying, "OK, I don't think I want to be 'it' anymore, man. What now?"

"OK," continued Hollister. "Now you understand the rules of my game. If you really don't want to be 'it' anymore, then you have to 'tag' someone else. Then that guy becomes 'it'. *Comprende*?"

"I getcha," answered James, very attentive now. "What's the rest of this fuckin' game?"

"The rest of the 'fuckin' game' is that you need to tell these officers, and they're playing too, who it is that supplies you with your 'nose candy' and then he will be 'it'.

"I have to leave now, but you do what we just talked about and you won't have to play the game anymore. Sound good?"

"Terrif! Sounds like a plan, man!" nodded the low-level pusher. "Makes a lot of fuckin' sense the way you put it, man!"

Hollister straightened up from his position in the pusher's face and turned to the two officers and said, "He's ready to play the game. You guys take over and finish the game."

With a big grin and pat on the young officer's back, Hollister continued on his way to his office. On the way up the stairs, Hollister recalled his "rookie" days when "old timers" wouldn't even talk to the recruits, much less help them.

The clerical staff was arriving for their days work, and the second story of the old brick building was coming to life.

All of the action for the past fifteen hours or so had taken place on the first floor where defendants were booked, complainants interviewed and the myriad of problems brought to the precinct's attention were resolved.

More than a few blood drops on the floor, and the offensive grousing of the elderly laborer cleaning up a mess bore mute testimony as to the kind of night it had been inside the building as well as outside. Now the focus shifted to the second floor.

The several female clerks chirped "Good morning, Lieutenant" one after the other as he drew close to his officer. "How was your vacation?"

He acknowledged each greeting with a smile and a brief comment.

All of these second-floor people liked Hollister. Whatever their work problems might be, they were resolved by Hollister with Solomon-like logic, and he never turned one away.

Several of the young girls gazed admiringly at this good-looking man, standing six feet two inches tall and carrying 215 athletic pounds. He wore a light brown mustache groomed to end at the corners of his mouth and neatly trimmed along the vermillion of his upper lip. His confident air and thorough knowledge of the job encouraged people to talk to him, and he never violated a confidential trust. As a result, he knew just about everything that was going on in the precinct.

Conversely, however, and not unexpectedly, there were a number of people who were jealous of Hollister's station in life and preferred to label his confident air as cockiness.

The farther up the ladder you go, the more your ass is exposed.

Upon reaching the office, he was greeted by a police officer who said, "Hi, Loo," and in a lower voice added, "It's cloudy inside this morning."

Hollister smiled and nodded his acknowledgement.

To those with more than a few months on the job, the word "cloudy" was meant as a caution that a very high-ranking officer was in the vicinity.

It was one of those "fun" traditions that were fast disappearing from the police department though.

Sure enough, it was cloudy inside. Deputy Chief Inspector Oscar Gerlich sat in his private office, one of four similar offices he egotistically maintained throughout the county. (Every station house on the south shore that he may have reason to visit during his workday was required to allocate private office space for Deputy Chief Gerlich.)

During the night, however, this one was utilized by Hollister as the "rubber room" in which he conducted disciplinary meetings and which had caused Animal so much concern the previous evening on the way back from Kennedy Airport.

Hollister had to pass Gerlich's office in order to get to his own. He quickened his pace, hoping to get to his own desk first before Gerlich cornered him.

Unfortunately, his luck ran out.

Chapter 3

Deputy Chief Inspector Oscar Gerlich

Deputy Chief Gerlich hung up his phone as Hollister passed his office.

"Come on in, George," Gerlich called as he waved vaguely in the direction of several chairs in the room. "Sit."

Hollister resisted the urge to reply, "Woof," but instead hastily grabbed a notepad off a clerk's desk and pulled a chair up close to Gerlich's ornate desk. His experience with Gerlich in the past taught him that copious notes would have to be taken so that Gerlich could not readily recant any statements he made.

"How was your vacation?" Gerlich asked absently without looking up.

Slowly and deliberately, Hollister answered, "Terrible! It was completely ruined by a phone call!"

"That's too bad," mumbled Gerlich, preoccupied with himself.

Great sense of humor, thought Hollister. *Completely missed the point of my thrust!*

"A few more seconds now," muttered Gerlich, "while I organize these things."

Hollister watched as Gerlich shuffled his paperwork, arranging it in what he considered the most impressive sequence.

His desk was so organized that it made Hollister want to reach over and mess it up a bit!

Gerlich had close-cropped, almost crew-cut silver hair, touched with dark tones here and there—what could be described as salt-and-pepper. He was impeccably dressed in uniform and had enough gold in prominence to rival a Mexican army general. Nameplate, buttons, badge and the stars, his shoulder insignia of rank—all shown brightly. Even his navy blue uniform cap bore a gold cap device. Embroidered on the peak of his Pershing style hat were gold "scrambled eggs."

He was obviously in very good physical condition—slim and trim. Impressive.

Unfortunately, Gerlich was too impressed with himself and in what he believed was his superior intelligence. During conversations, he often belabored a single point for minutes, unnecessarily talking "down" to all present. Being interrupted by some vassal during one of his interminable dissertations seemed to bother him to no end. His ego barely fit into the room with him; it was so huge.

Everything about him breathed inflexibility and seemed to be rigorously measured. His black necktie filled the space completely between the edges of his white shirt collar, permitting only sufficient room for the knot. He was the only person Hollister had ever seen who tucked the ends of his shoelaces inside his shoes so that no floppy ends showed.

You had to hand it to him, however, that despite his inability to communicate with personnel one-on-one without turning them off, the man was a master at paperwork.

As Hollister watched and waited, his mind flashed back to an incident involving Deputy Chief Oscar Gerlich and himself, and there have been many.

As Hollister recalled, a few months earlier, Gerlich and he had been assigned to investigate a complaint regarding an alleged illegal search conducted by one of the precinct's uniformed men. The complaint came through the American Civil Liberties Union from a local resident-neighbor.

It was not considered a serious violation of rights at first, but took on an air of importance because of the involvement of the ACLU, who, in Hollister's view, were radical, left-wing liberals intent on promoting controversy and unrest.

As a result, some spineless headquarters underling agreed to an investigation, coupled with an interview of the complainant.

Gerlich had been assigned because of his rank and because the incident took place within his Division.

Hollister, on the other hand, was assigned by Chief Inspector William Wildig because the lieutenant was reputed to be so smooth at times that he could charm the chrome off a bumper—if that was what the "squeal" required. Obviously, Wildig thought that this was one of those times and thus assigned his longtime friend, Hollister, to achieve some sort of balance in handling this complaint.

Briefly, the incident involved a bicycle theft from in front of a local store. The young owner of the bike reported the theft immediately, and since it was not much more than two hundred feet from the station house, a police officer responded very quickly. Because of the short response time, the conscientious officer began a canvass of the people walking nearby. As he talked to adults and children alike, he felt that he was getting closer to the thief, whose trail led to a residential area.

As circumstance would have it, another teenage boy informed the officer that he had seen a boy, with a bicycle fitting the description of the stolen bike, enter the garage of a nearby house.

The officer went to the garage pointed out, peered briefly through one of its small windows. Finding it unoccupied, he then knocked on the front door of the house. A young girl, perhaps fourteen or fifteen years of age, answered the officer's knock, at which time he asked if he could look in the garage for the bicycle alleged to have been stolen. The girl replied that the garage was unlocked.

The officer then went to the garage again and pulled up the overhead door. Inside was a bicycle very close in appearance to the one that was stolen—but not in fact the stolen bike.

A few days later, the complaint from ACLU was received, and the investigation instituted.

There came a time when the complainant was to be interviewed and informed of the findings of the investigation. Hollister made telephone contact with the complainant, and she stated that since her separation from her husband, she worked a part-time job. To accommodate her, a late afternoon meeting was set up at her convenience between Gerlich, Hollister, and her.

Upon arriving at her house and being invited inside, Hollister observed the complainant to be a very attractive blonde in her midthirties. She was wearing, barely, a pair of white terry cloth short shorts that were so tight that they could have been painted on her body. The accompanying top was a navy blue T-shirt that appeared probably two sizes too small for her.

Hollister could not help but notice that she was "bumped out pretty good, front and rear"—as he was to relate later at the chuckling prompting of Chief Wildig, who, in retrospect, thought this incident was hilarious.

Hollister, by prearrangement with Gerlich, broke the ice with the story of how the incident was provoked—with a stolen bicycle from a nearby store—and so on through the peek into the garage.

About two minutes into the tale of the stolen bike, and hearing it described aloud for the first time, the young woman obviously suddenly realized how ridiculous her complaint really was and started smiling and nodding her head in slow exaggerated moves, signaling, "Oh, I see. I understand."

Hollister picked up on her change in manner, returned the smiles, and made his presentation light, friendly, and brief.

Gerlich, oblivious to the change in atmosphere, had his legalese rehearsed and quickly launched into an involved technical examination of the laws concerning illegal search and civil rights. He went on and on for more than thirty minutes—first, citing case law and then examples framed in layman's terms. No number of hard looks by Hollister or the upward rolling of her eyes by the complainant could slow him down. Gerlich was Clarence Darrow reincarnated—and droned on!

It was apparent that this complaint was satisfactorily resolved in the very first minutes of the explanation by Hollister, but the complainant was forced to endure a lecture on law in which she no longer had any interest.

As Gerlich continued and referred frequently to pages of notes, Hollister and the complainant started eye games. She began to look him over carefully with undisguised curiosity, smiling frequently and permitting Hollister to see that she was a friendly native.

Hollister began playing the same game, deliberately getting caught looking at her breasts and nipples straining against the T-shirt. She began moving around slowly, doing small things, like moving a vase from here to there—and back again—any bending, stretching, attention-getting movements she could find to do in the area of Hollister's view.

At the same time, Gerlich was still busily impressing the hell out of himself with his "expertise," completely unaware of the "spectator sport" going on in front of him.

No wonder I love this job! This uniform attracts more than just lint!

At long last, Gerlich used up all his examples and technical phrases and came to the end of his dissertation, uninterrupted.

On this particular evening, Hollister was disappointed that Gerlich did not have more to say. The pleasurable interview was drawing to a close too quickly.

The poor lady never had a chance to tell Gerlich that she had been satisfied with the explanation thirty to thirty-five minutes earlier, and so just meekly surrendered by saying something about never having been overly concerned with the incident. She had been encouraged by a helpful and protective neighbor (*and who could fault him*) who called the ACLU on her behalf.

Based on the complainant's tempting behavior, Hollister believed that had this incident occurred BJ (before Joy) the outcome would have had an even more satisfying conclusion.

A few parting words and a very warm handshake, held by the complainant for an overly long time, left Hollister with the feeling that further overtures on his part would have definitely been well received by this lady.

He was right!

Gerlich and Hollister headed back toward the station house in the chief's car.

Once underway, a puffed-up Gerlich beamed victoriously at Hollister and said, "How'd I do, George? Won that one, eh?"

Hollister, maintaining a deadpan and staring straight ahead at the roadway, said, "You won by default, Chief."

"Default? Default? What the hell is that supposed to mean?"

"It means that you won because you bored her to death!" And Hollister laughed out loud, not being able to contain it any longer.

The remainder of the trip to the station house was accomplished in silence, except for a snicker from time to time that Hollister could not completely suppress and which was answered by a very hard-set jaw by Gerlich.

Hollister's flashback was ended by Gerlich's paper shuffling and he hoped that Gerlich didn't see the big smile on his face that his recollection of the incident had prompted. He braced himself for what he knew was to follow. Gerlich was not one for polite small talk.

Gerlich took a deep breath. "George, I have been charged with the responsibility of presenting the overview regarding the preparation for the International Games. I have started a management plan and have put together a mission statement. Here, take a look at this," and he thrust some papers forward.

Hollister reached for the proffered document and read:

> "This mission statement reflects the fundamental reasons why the 1984 International Games for the Disabled were conceived, planned and are soon to be implemented.

> "Therefore as a result of the initial decision to bring the Games to Nassau County, New York, United States of America, achievement of the following goals is anticipated:
>
> > "To bring together for the first time in the United States world-class amputee, blind, cerebral palsied and Les Autres athletes, representing nations in a variety of Olympic athletic events."

Hollister continued reading this three page mission statement which had twelve or thirteen paragraphs stating such things as:

> "To provide a superior, safe and friendly environment for all participating athletes and staff.
>
> "To bring together in a unique partnership, the extensive resources of Nassau County's public, private and voluntary organizations, committed to the successful and cost-efficient achievement of the Games.
>
> "To provide new and significant social and cultural experiences for the participating athletes and their aides during their stay in Nassau County.
>
> "To enrich the . . ." and so it went for seven more paragraphs.

Well written, thought Hollister. *This portion is playing to Gerlich's strength—paperwork.*

Hollister had been to in-service training courses at the same time as Chief Gerlich and had seen him take pages of notes. These notes were often rewritten as many as four times before finalization.

Man, that's thorough!

"Well, what do you think?" asked Gerlich, when he saw that Hollister had finished reading his dissertation.

"Frankly, I'm impressed, Chief. Some very lofty goals were expressed there."

"Thank you. Now let's get to things a little more substantial," said Gerlich, going through still more papers on his desk. "As I see this taking shape, it will be the commencement of the most complex security problem ever faced by our department. Our actions must indicate the commitment we have made to ensure the complete safety of the participants as well as that of the more than 250,000 spectators who are estimated to attend the games."

"That is to say nothing of the continuing commitment to the rest of the county residents," Hollister interjected.

Gerlich looked up sharply from his paperwork at that 'interruption," but went on. "I visualize certain units being formed to be responsible for clearly drawn actions.

"One—and probably most important—the Housing Unit. This unit will be the first to be implemented. Some sixty nations will be sending athletes and aides and coaches, all arriving well before the start of the Games themselves. They will have access to the various facilities for the purpose of training and practice. The Games Committee anticipates that there will be 2,500 people to be housed for the contests.

"That's the job I mentioned to you on the phone. Security for these varied nationals is going to be the most difficult phase of the operation. I want you to spend as much time as possible at Hofstra University. Get to know every inch of the dormitories and surrounding buildings and grounds.

"Look into the existing security measures and suggest any modification to the way the place is managed. Remember, a successful terrorist attack on us would be a disaster."

Hollister interrupted again with, "Do you really believe that a terrorist group would attack people like this—cripples, I mean?"

"Yes, I do," said Gerlich solemnly. "What better way is there to gain notoriety and publicity and embarrass the United States all at one time?!"

"I'm not so sure," said Hollister skeptically, "it seems that world opinion would be firmly united against any terrorist force that tried any such atrocious act against disabled people."

Gerlich countered with, "Since when did any terrorist group worry about world opinion? The more outrageous the incident, the more worldwide attention they would get. After all, isn't that what their immediate goal is? In my view, this would be a perfect situation for them. As a matter of fact, the FBI is of like opinion. Further, they believe that if an incident is created, it would be at the housing site. That is where the largest number of persons from any nation would be at risk."

"Two," continued Gerlich, "a Command Post for the Games themselves will be set up at the Olympic Plaza. They will be responsible for the athletes after they are transported from the housing site to the competitions. Traffic around the Games area will also be their responsibility."

"Three, Crises Response Teams will be established. They will reenforce any routine patrols and respond as the need arises.

"Four, the Escort Detail will assist in moving the athletes from the housing unit to the Games site and back to the housing unit after competition is completed for the day.

"Naturally, there are a lot of details to be explored yet and changes will undoubtedly be made. These are all preliminary ideas and refinement is in order. As you proceed with arrangements, I would appreciate any input at all on any segments of this project. You and I will have many opportunities to converse. I insist upon it!"

"Sounds reasonable and sound to me right now," said Hollister. "When do I get started?"

"Immediately," Gerlich replied curtly.

Hollister inquired, "Has my CO been apprised of these developments and my assignment? You know that I'll need precinct personnel to be assigned by him."

Gerlich, leafing through more papers replied, "Forget the CO, you take your orders on this thing directly from me. The CO will have very limited involvement. Besides, I know that you have more to say about the day-to-day operation here than he does!"

Annoyed at that remark, Hollister exploded, "That's bullshit, Chief! The CO and I are personal friends but have a fine mutual working agreement. Granted, I make recommendations based on my perspective, but he implements them or not, depending on how he views them. He is the boss!"

Gerlich glared at Hollister and snorted, "You'll never convince me that you don't run this place, so let's not kid each other. Let's just get on with this assignment. He'll have to try to get along without you!"

Warming up for a grand argument, Hollister demanded, "Are you saying that I'm relieved of my normal duties today to start on this housing unit phase?!"

"No," retorted Gerlich. "This is in addition to your normal duties."

"That's in conflict with your last statement, Chief," exclaimed Hollister, still baiting Gerlich. "You just finished telling me how important this assignment is, and in the next breath you tell me to do it on a part-time basis. What kind of nonsense is that?!"

"It's not nonsense, Lieutenant," said Gerlich with a scowl. "You've jumped all over me without good reason, as usual. My next sentence was to tell you that you'll have to get someone broken in on your routine matters and then go full-time on this one. The sooner the better, incidentally. You'll have no time left for that Enforcement group of yours!

"The first thing I want you to do is to evaluate the precinct's personnel. I'd like a prioritized list of the people you want assigned to this detail. I want the best. Remember, this takes precedence over your capers with the Enforcement teams!"

"You realize, of course," offered Hollister as a trial balloon, "I'll want all of my special enforcement people assigned!"

Gerlich continued to glare at Hollister, but the battle was a draw as Hollister steadily returned the glare.

Gerlich broke the short silence with, "You realize, in turn, that the beards and dirtbag clothes have to go, don't you? Everyone assigned to the detail, including you and your 'boys' will have to wear the Uniform of the Day. Perhaps when they find out they will have to behave like solid citizens again, they may not volunteer for this detail. No beards, no boots, no nonsense!"

The thought of that turned Hollister's glare into a grin. "Boy, this ought to be fun. I can hardly remember what some of these guys look like without beards. We may all be sorry!"

Gerlich smiled and infrequent smile and said, "Oh yes, one more thing you have to know. The Terrorism Schooling I spoke about will commence on April 16 and run for two weeks.

"I would like to be able to announce to the attendees at that time the plans for the security of these athletes. That gives you a little more than two months to whip it into shape. That's not very much time for a thing of this size, but I'm sure you can handle it.

"I'll want it all in writing, naturally."

"Naturally."

"So get busy," said Gerlich. "You are on your own, but keep in touch."

"OK, Chief. I'll get back to you," said Hollister as he rose to leave. "Keep the faith."

Chapter 4

The Campus

Hollister didn't wait for a response from Gerlich but quickly made his way directly to the clerical office. There he approached the same officer who had warned him of the "cloudiness" inside the office.

"Hey J. B.," he said over the noise of several typewriters clacking away there, "I need some things from you right away."

Police Officer John Barclay was the man directly supervising the many civilian clerks who worked in the precinct. It was an extremely sensitive and important position.

"Sure," he replied. "Name it and it's yours."

"Get on your computer terminal and pull out a precinct roster of personnel. Everybody. Make it first by alpha and then by squad assignment. Better give me two prints of each."

"Big doings, eh, Loo," said Barclay, again using the traditional police abridgement for lieutenant.

"Yep, and I'll probably be bothering the hell out of you for awhile. I can foresee lots of computer terminal work for you and lots of typing for the girls. Most of the stuff I ask for will be things I needed 'the day before yesterday,' so be prepared for some pressure from me."

"So what else is new," rejoined Barclay with a resigned shrug. "I'll just get out my ulcer medicine again—LT Hollister is back!"

That evoked a grin from Hollister since he knew it was true. He and his Enforcement people certainly generated a lot of work for the clerical staff. He also knew that Barclay did, in reality, have a bad stomach and was probably not joking about his medicine.

J. B., as Hollister called him (among other not-so-nice names) was a veteran of Vietnam and had seen lots of fierce and bloody action.

Just prior to entering the service, John had done a stint in a prep seminary. After his discharge from the service and upon his return to civilian life, J.B. had become a staunch atheist, having left all his religious faith back in the jungle with Viet Cong.

John's agnosticism or atheism notwithstanding, Hollister liked Barclay and defended him when he got himself into an uncomfortable situation. Most of the time it was because of his explosive nature. It seems that when his control did slip, the room was usually filled with expletives and red-faced female civilian clerks. He always apologized to the ladies later and after a few episodes the clerks pretended not to hear. That gave everyone an easy out.

J. B. was a valued man who had complete knowledge and control of the many programs and features of the recently acquired computer system.

At that moment, Barclay called out to him, "Hey Loo, some cop is on the horn for you. He wants to talk to you for a second from the arrest room extension."

Hollister picked up a nearby telephone and answered, "Lieutenant Hollister."

The voice at the other end identified himself as the officer Hollister had spoken with earlier upon his arrival at the station house.

"That game of tag you started before has paid off. This scuzz bag has given us some pretty good information. From what originally started as a bullshit arrest, you turned it into something promising. We just wanted to say thanks for the help."

Hollister replied, "You're welcome, bub. You know, of course, that you can run the same game on the next guy in line and so on, depending upon how many times the junk has been stepped on. You can end the game of tag whenever you want to. That's the beauty of it!

"When you get to that point, you can ask my soft-clothes guys for some help. The 'bust' will be yours when the time comes and I'll tell my people to be sure to cut you in. You guys developed the lead, so the collar is yours when the time is ripe.

"One more little tip. A good cop has got to have a large cadre of informants. He is only as effective as his informants . . . who are, incidentally, the most aggravating bunch of people with whom we have to deal. Play it right and get some more parasites off the street! Good luck."

The young cop responded enthusiastically, "Thanks a lot Loo. Now I know why they pay you guys the big bucks!"

Hollister chuckled a "keep in touch" as he replaced the receiver, glad that he had encouraged the young man to "get into the game."

Leaving Barclay to dig out the information he required, Hollister went to his own desk and began clearing up matters that had been suspended while he was vacationing. Many phone calls had to be returned . . . Hollister was meticulous about returning telephone calls. That custom, plus the fact that some new circumstances had come to light while he was away put him right back into full swing as he scheduled his Enforcement people to cover new investigations throughout the week.

Questions about the assignments to the Games were starting to pour in as police officers became aware of Hollister's involvement. All incoming calls were always initially answered by either Patty, a young, shapely and pretty female civilian clerk-typist who did the bulk of Hollister's typing, or by J. B. Both were adept at sidestepping unwanted queries and only permitted calls of a substantive nature to come through to him.

The only exception was that if the call was from an irate citizen. In that case they couldn't get rid of the call fast enough and promptly transferred the problem to Hollister, who had an uncanny ability to soothe irate complainers.

He could foresee, however, that handling this assignment to the Games was going to take more and more of his time. Reluctantly, he decided to temporarily give up the handling of his "baby," the special enforcement teams.

The job, he decided, should go to Sergeant Tom Wesson, one of the more capable and cooperative sergeants in the precinct.

It didn't take much persuasion to have Sergeant Wesson agree to the assignment. As a matter of fact, Tom was eager for the opportunity since it was considered to be a prime assignment by most supervisors.

Now Hollister was reasonably free of one assignment. Although he could not emotionally give up special enforcement, he could at least get started with the Games assignment.

His first intention was to set up a liaison with the security staff at Hofstra University. Accordingly, he made telephone contact with the college's Director of Public Safety, one Robert McCauley, who immediately proposed a luncheon meeting at their University Club.

Already this assignment was getting interesting.

The Club was one of the finest restaurants in the area, quite exclusive and very expensive!

The meeting went very well after the initial discomfort that occurred when the waiter asked if either of them wanted a cocktail before lunch. Both men hemmed and hesitated, not wanting the other to think less of him because he ordered a cocktail at this early hour of the day.

Finally, it was Hollister who said, "Oh hell, give me a scotch sour, rocks."

McCauley, relieved, said, "Martini for me."

McCauley and Hollister hit it off well from the beginning and they were to meet very frequently over the next months.

McCauley had recently retired from the New York City Police Department, coincidentally enough as a lieutenant. The timely retirement of the college's former Director of Public Safety, a good resume and a "hook," (the facilities manager was a relative) and McCauley was hired. That is not to say that McCauley was not qualified. He definitely was.

As time went on and their contacts became more frequent, Hollister and McCauley were to become good friends. McCauley had the inherited Irish humor and a million stories. He handled his large staff of private guards with the same self-assured easy manner that Hollister employed with his staff of sworn police officers.

McCauley said that he decided to retire because one night, as he was working the booking desk, a young recruit marched into the station house with a man in tow.

"Lieutenant, I've got a man with a gun," the rookie announced to McCauley.

McCauley's natural response was, "Great! Gimme the gun."

The recruit turned to the defendant and said, "You heard the lieutenant—give him the gun!"

Ouch!

"That showed me it was time to retire," said McCauley; and he did.

After enjoying the delicious lunch, paid for by an insistent Bob McCauley, the two went on a tour of Hofstra's campus. The complex was huge and the buildings complicated, requiring Hollister to prepare many pages of descriptive material for Gerlich.

McCauley was an attentive host and filled the afternoon with stories that only an Irish retired police lieutenant could tell effectively.

Since classes were still in session, the grounds were filled with students, some hurrying from building to building and some just lounging on the grass in the bright sixty degree sunshine. It was a glorious one day break after too many months of grey, dismal Long Island weather.

The two men, both clean-cut in appearance and striking in suits, shirts and ties, attracted a lot of curious coed attention as they walked through the student center.

The basement Rathskeller was jammed with students munching lunch as was the main dining hall on the street level.

The halls as well were filled with apprentice scholars hurrying somewhere. The mode of dress was very casual, ranging from sweatpants to shorts and from sweatshirts to T-shirts, sans bras. This latter observation prompted McCauley to make the observation that the females attending Hofstra from various states, were of the healthiest variety.

That, coupled with the inviting smiles and flirtatious looks, caused Hollister to retort, "And the friendliest too!"

Entrances, exits, rooms, and corridors were everywhere—a veritable maze. Floor-to-ceiling glass panels encouraged a view of the expansive grounds outside.

The faculty dining room, divided into sections by folding doors on tracks, seemed to be the only available spot for the housing unit's command post.

It was located at the student center and right over the central power station. Readily divided into three sections for use by the sliding units, it would nevertheless be completely accessible to all.

One of the problems of which Hollister took special note was that this area had towering glass walls on two sides, which exposed the interior of the room to view from the outside. Closely manicured grass and beautifully landscaped plots extended for two hundred feet from the glass partitions, farther increasing the sight distance.

The ends of the A-frame roof sloped sharply downward and ended a scant four feet from the ground. Very attractive architecturally, but a distinct invitation to a terrorist to scamper up the A-frame and gain a commanding position high above, overlooking the student center.

This brief initial walk-through showed the beauty of the campus to advantage, but it was evident that it was a security nightmare.

After all, the place was designed for aesthetic beauty and not to be a fortress.

That appeared to be Hollister's challenge—to *make* it a fortress without having it *appear* as one.

McCauley arranged for Hollister to be photographed and issued him a permanent pass (as opposed to a visitor's pass, which was good only for one day). A sticker was also issued to Hollister's car to permit him to park anywhere on campus. Both these items, whether by design or not, also served to alert the campus cops to Hollister's presence.

Campus security people were sensitive about outside law enforcement finding, perhaps, some drug activity and taking unilateral action.

Instructions were left with the security desk that should Hollister request a guide, a knowledgeable guard would be assigned; otherwise, for the next two months, Hollister would roam at will, poking, peering, and examining all aspects of the grounds.

At the end of that period, Hollister knew the operation of the area, which was to accommodate the housing site command post as well as anyone involved in the administration of the university.

This knowledge was to prove its value later during the troublesome times ahead during the International Games!

* * *

Hollister, now armed with some preliminary knowledge of the difficulties that will face the people to be assigned to the security detail, spent the following day in the station house evaluating personnel, just as Deputy Chief Gerlich had ordered.

JB had provided the lists of police officers just as Hollister had ordered, and the site commander went through the lists, using his personal knowledge of each member to formulate a prioritized compilation.

He had already satisfied himself that full-sized vehicles could not easily maneuver through the maze of chain-link security fences he was to propose. He, therefore, chose the complete complement of the motorcycle summons detail of the precinct to be assigned.

These ten police officers, in his view, were to be utilized as roving patrols and, as such, would be ultimately important to the success of this operation. He would recommend that their three-wheeled motorcycles, small enough to fit through proposed pedestrian checkpoints yet powerful enough to cover quickly the grassy rises throughout the campus, be commandeered for assignment to the detail. A few golf carts that could utilize the sidewalks would also be requested for those shorter trips between dormitories.

Next, he listed ten of his special enforcement members, leaving poor Sergeant Tom Wesson with only half the enforcement complement to handle the day-to-day complaints.

Fisherman Frank, Swede, Surfer, Animal, and Hammer would have to be directed to get haircuts and/or shaves in order to be able to report for this detail when it commenced. The remainder of the enforcement group looked reasonably human, including the Chris Vicious, whose name alone was enough to frighten Joy!

Hollister then had to telephone the commanding officer of the uniform section and prepare the lieutenant for the parade of strange-looking detectives he was going to send over for uniform fittings. This action, he was sure, would prompt a great deal of pissin' and moanin' from the unit's members, but he was also sure that they were looking forward to the detail in spite of the fact that they would have to wear the feared "bag" again and, what's even worse, *shave*.

Then taking extra care so as to avoid making any single squad short of personnel, he listed in priority order the remaining 180 of the precinct's available personnel.

Particular note was made to include the female officers in the first grouping. They, he believed, would have to be spread throughout the housing site assignments to cover certain eventualities, that is, search of female prisoners or suspects and casual public relations contact with the female population of the international teams.

He inwardly chuckled when he remembered comments that were made by some civilian tailors after they had measured female police officers for new uniforms. The comment, said as a joke, was that a few female officers, when walking in uniform trousers and gun belts, had asses that bobbed and bounced like two puppies fighting under a wool blanket.

He also recalled being tipped off that one or two others have round heels and fall on their backs at little urging.

His own experience, however, was that the vast majority were capable, dedicated officers, and would be invaluable to the success of the detail.

*   *   *

For the next several weeks, Hollister's days and evenings were crammed with activity.

Mornings, since he resided so close to the campus, were spent prowling around the buildings and grounds at Hofstra—sometimes accompanied by a security person, sometimes alone.

Late afternoons and evenings were spent keeping on top of the activities of the special enforcement teams in such a manner as to keep Deputy Chief Gerlich from finding out about it.

At the end of those few weeks, Hollister was beginning to formulate some definite plans for the security of the visitors from many nations. Pages and pages of notations began to take form, and Hollister was ready to begin submitting preliminary reports to Gerlich.

His first one, to point up his perception of the area for which he was to be responsible, was given to Patty for preparation, and went:

"In order to separate the housing site security responsibility from those of other segments of the games, this report and those to follow will confine themselves specifically to the area described as follows:

> "Beginning at a point where North Oak Street meets Oak Street, east along the south curbline of Oak Street to the east curbline of Hofstra Boulevard; then south along the east curbline of Parking Field Number 6A; then east along the north curbline of Parking Field Number 6A to a point opposite the east curbline of Hofstra Boulevard; then south to the California Avenue entrance gate to the university; then west along the north curbline of Hempstead Turnpike to the point west of Oak Street, where the west fence line of the Netherlands Residence Halls meets Hempstead Turnpike; then north along this fence to the north fence line of the Netherlands Residence Hall; then east along the north fence line to Oak Street; then north along the east curbline of Oak Street to the point of beginning.
>
> "It is strongly recommended and imperative that a six-foot-high chain-link fence topped with barbed wire inserts be erected to surround that area not already fenced. A diagram of these sections is attached hereto.
>
> "In addition, a walking tour of the perimeter of the university's grounds has revealed that a large number of broken sections of chain-link fences are in dire need of repair before our security of the area can be undertaken. A list of the locations requiring repair is also attached, along with notations of area containing

> such heavy growth of underbrush, as to prevent any security people from viewing the fence.
>
> "It is requested that the old fence be repaired and the underbrush cut back to provide us with a buffer zone prior to the commencement of our security responsibilities.
>
> End of report."

Hollister smiled inwardly because he knew this preliminary report would please Gerlich. First, because of its wordiness and then by the fact that it placed the burden squarely on Hofstra University to repair some very serious possible security breaches.

"Excuse me, Loo," said Patty softly. "Will you take a look at this, please?" and leaned over his shoulder from close behind him, immediately getting his attention.

The warmth radiating from her body was pleasant on his neck and shoulders.

She placed a bookbinder in front of him on his desk and, with one hand on his shoulder, leafed through a couple of pages in the book with the other.

"I have started a separate three-ring binder in which to file all communications between you and Deputy Chief Gerlich.

"Is that all right? There can be no misunderstanding of directives or recommendations that way."

Boy, does she ever smell nice. She's a smart cookie also. She knows how Gerlich operates, and this is a good way to protect the ol' lieutenant.

Hollister responded aloud with, "Hey, that's a fine idea. The file can then be used as a sort of manual of procedure for the housing site command post."

Her record could feasibly settle some major disagreements between Hollister and Gerlich who, it seemed, were natural adversaries.

I love loyalty in secretaries!

Little did Hollister suspect at this time that there was something more than loyalty involved.

He continued to work long after the office staff had left for the day.

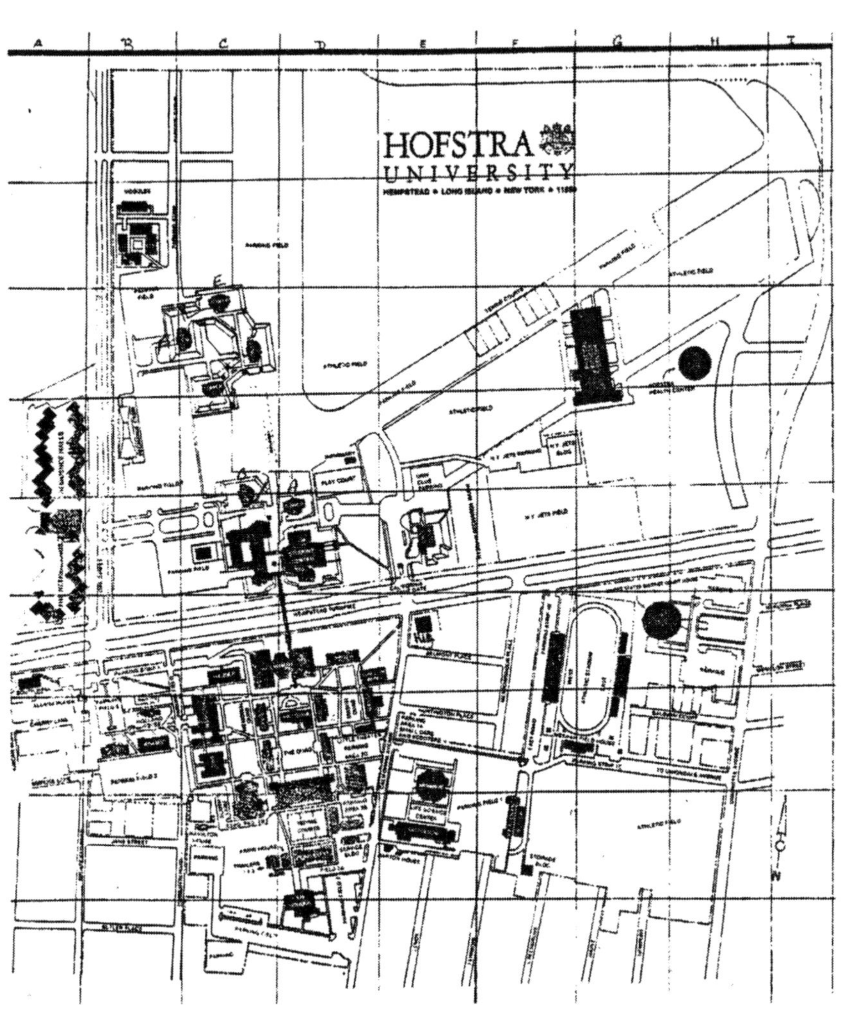
A B C D E F G H I
HOFSTRA
UNIVERSITY

Chapter 5

Party Time

It was almost midnight when his telephone extension rang just as he was about to leave the office for home.

"Lieutenant Hollister," he sighed into the mouthpiece.

"Hey, boss," said the hyper Animal's voice at the other end. "I've got some people down here who want to see you."

"Where? Downstairs?"

"No, no. We're at the Green Tree Restaurant in Green Acres shopping mall. Joe Martin's been promoted and they are having a celebration or him down here. Great time! Hammer is here and Greenie and Swede. Haise and Henderson will be here after they sign off duty. Come on down. Great time."

"Sounds to me as though you have a head start on everyone. Are you sure you didn't have a few before the party started?"

"No, really. It's just getting started now that the mall is closing. C'mon, Lissen' a' me, Joe and all the big wheels are here and asking for you," pleaded Tom.

Hollister took a deep breath, held it for a second or two and then let it escape slowly.

"Well, OK. I'll stop for a bit to eat anyway and shake Joe's hand. See you in a bit."

"Great time," repeated Animal. "'bye."

Hollister went downstairs to the locker room and jumped into the shower to shake the cobwebs of fatigue. Fifteen minutes later, he was on his way to the watering hole, which, according to recent reports, served elegant food.

The mall was one of the more spacious ones on the east coast and held some 210 stores under its roof. The inside was newly refurbished and brand new construction provided waterfalls and large planters as well as tinted glass enclosed elevators and long escalators between floors. The place was beautiful.

The parking fields held over 8,000 automobiles, but despite the fact that the fields were monitored by rooftop television security cameras, one of which could zoom in and read a license place, an average of twelve cars per week were reported stolen from them every week of the year.

Private security inside the mall was considered horrendous and only when the public outcry was so loud that special enforcement teams were "permitted" to be sent in did it improve. This was another one of the sore points in Gerlich and Hollister's relationship.

Gerlich vehemently forbid the use of special enforcement teams in the huge shopping complex except on very rare occasions when Hollister unilaterally ordered them in.

"We are not in competition with private security," was one of Gerlich's favorite sayings.

Hollister, on the other hand, believed that they, the teams, should be utilized wherever the crime was most severe. He could see no significant difference between a mugging in Green Acres parking field and a mugging on Hempstead Turnpike in West Hempstead. Both areas deserved the best police coverage available.

Most recently, Gerlich turned down flatly and without other comment, a proposition to establish, cost free, a Community Relations Booth to be placed in an alcove of the mall.

It was designed to house, temporarily, the large number of arrestees processed every day at the busy shopping mall.

The mall even proposed constructing a "holding cell', the cost of which would be borne by the mall's owners, which would negate the too frequent transportation jobs to the station house by the sector car.

Complaints and reports could be handled right here at the place of occurrence eliminating the necessity of pulling other sector cars from their areas to respond to the mall.

Further, it could be utilized in other ways to include the dissemination of information to the public, covering a wide variety of subjects (i.e., missing persons, wanted persons, safety hints, and others) and would be absolutely cost free to the department.

Hollister, drawing from experiences in the mall, knew most of the owners, managers and security people throughout the complex and for the most part, had their respect and admiration.

The restaurant he was heading for had only recently opened and was still pretty much of an unknown factor. Information provided to Hollister, however, indicated that perhaps the owners of the restaurant and disco-bar liked to stretch the closing hours somewhat. At any rate, he was prepared to keep and eye on it.

He parked the LeBaron in the near-empty mall parking lot (it was 12:45 AM) and walked across the lot to the entrance of the restaurant. He could already hear the sounds of a loud party in progress.

Immediately upon entering the bar area he was sighted by Tom Egan and Pat Connors.

"Here he is! Hey, boss, over here!" they called.

Hollister strolled over to the bar and was greeted warmly by Joe Martin, the newly promoted Operations Manager and his own people. The bar was crowded with people from every segment of the mall and most of the girls from the Mall Management office were in attendance.

Thing were really rocking with the band thumping out an unintelligible musical arrangement while bodies bounced around as mere shadows in the dim light of the dance floor. The squirming bodies were lighted momentarily by the flashing disco lights before disappearing into weird shadows and then suddenly reappearing in a brightness that assaulted your eyes. Over and over this dizzying scene was repeated with bewildering speed in the strobe lights.

"Dewar's and water, twist," Hollister ordered in response to the bartender's mouthed question.

As soon as he was served, Hollister started a slow maneuver along the bar, designed to permit him to greet everyone and at the same time slip farther away from the raucous band and their huge amplifiers, obviously intended to house a family of four. He found respite from most of the noise at the far end of the bar and also found a seat.

The high stool provided a base for the small talk with Joe Martin and in a few minutes a knot of owners, managers and employees were gathered around discussing, as usual, the crime rate in the vicinity. The conversation switched to how much the Enforcement people and Hollister would be missed when he mentioned the possibility that neither would be available for the duration of the Games.

The owners and their people were quite eloquent in protesting this set of circumstances. They were just as eloquently assured by Hollister that precinct cooperation from Sergeant Tom Wesson would continue throughout the time that Hollister was occupied with his new assignment.

Animal appeared again and, bumping his way through the people gathered around Hollister, ordered the bartender, "Give the boss the best scotch you've got back there!"

Hollister smiled, "Thanks, Tom, but I just got a fresh drink. I'll have one with you as soon as I get to the bottom of this one." Then laughing, "You don't have to suck up to me."

Animal, swaying slightly replied, "Oh yes I do." Then he reached into his mouth and removed his chewing gum.

Holding it between his right thumb and forefinger, he held it uncertainly above Hollister's glass, saying, "Hey, whaddaya know, I think I see something' floatin' in there. You surely need a fresh drink now!"

That remark brought a laugh from everyone standing nearby and Hollister warned, "You drop that in there, Animal, and it's going to cost you. I'll stick it right in your ear!"

Encouraged by the laughter from the group, Animal's response was to open his fingers very deliberately and drop the gum right into the full glass held by Hollister.

"You asked for it, Tom," said a calm Hollister as he placed the glass on the bar and carefully fished the gum out.

Realizing at that very moment that he was in deep shit, Animal made an attempt to escape but was caught around the neck by Hollister, who quickly stabbed the gum toward Tom's ear. The gum, however, went awry during Egan's struggle to escape the tight headlock and embedded itself firmly in the hair behind his left ear!

He panicked and grabbed feverishly at the gum, which only served o squeeze it more firmly into his hair. All the while he bellowed loudly, "Oh no! Oh shit! Fahcrissake!"

Pat Connors, hearing his partner's cries of anguish, shouldered his big frame into the middle of the convulsed group and demanded, "What the hell's going on?"

Tom blurted out what had transpired. Pat's laughing response was, "I told you not to do it. I told you he'd fuck you somehow if you messed with him. You're no match for the boss."

He walked away, shaking his head. "Some guys never learn."

For the remainder of the night, Tom was the center of attention from every unescorted girl at the bar, and there were many.

Various home remedies were suggested and tried one by one from ice to alcohol, to combs and picks, all without success. General consensus dictated that the only solution remaining was . . . the deadly scissors treatment!

The operation was undertaken amid sufficiently loud moans from Tom and a facetious ceremonial chant by the group watching. "Cut it off! Cut it off! Cut it all off!"

At the conclusion of the ritual, Tom Egan was left with a bald spot behind his ear.

He tottered away to enjoy his newly acquired charisma with a few groupies, while an unperturbed Hollister resumed his conversations.

Sometime later in the evening, Egan again offered o replace Hollister's drink, which by now was virtually empty.

This time, Tom approached, exhibiting a hangdog demeanor, saying, "Christ, I'm sorry for what I did before, El General. Pat warned me that you're a master at one-upmanship and would sure as hell beat me somehow."

Hollister, although a little suspicious, found it easy to be gracious in victory and accepted his third drink of the night apparently without incident.

The party continued to rage on into the early morning with everyone having a 'great time,' according to Animal.

At one point, during a trip to the men's room, Hollister passed the front entrance door and heard a coarse voice raised in anger outside. He paused to take a look. There, parked in the fire lane, was a big shiny Lincoln Town Car. Just to the rear of the vehicle was a motorcycle officer, assigned to the area of the mall, in the process of writing out a ticket for the violation.

Standing there on the sidewalk was this very large man, yelling. "I've got your boss inside and half of the detective squad eatin' and drinkin' an' you're out here writin' out that damned chickenshit ticket! Don't you know who that car belongs to?!"

Hollister reached out a grabbed passing stranger by the elbow and motioning with his head, demanded, "Who's the fat guy?"

The man took a darting glance and said, "Sal Tamarago, the Manager here," before pulling free of Hollister's grasp and continuing his dash to the men's room.

"Thanks."

Hollister took a hard look at Tamarago. He was fat. Very fat. The top of his head was bald, but he had some dark hair around his temples and ears that extended back to the nape of his neck. He was pacing, or was it waddling, agitatedly on the sidewalk.

Hollister observed the motorcycle officer lift his pen in momentary uncertainty and so he stepped out on the sidewalk. When Sal, in his pacing, crossed in front of Hollister, the air behind him smelled strongly of stale cigar smoke.

"Don't worry about who that car belongs to, Jim," Hollister said, recognizing the officer. "If it's in violation, write the ticket. Don't worry about who's inside either. We pay our way everywhere we go, but you can bet your ass we won't be back here again!"

Sal Tamarago's demeanor was getting Hollister angry.

"I knew you'd say that, Loo. Thanks," and Jim resumed writing the ticket.

"Listen you," said Hollister, thrusting his forefinger into the chest of the indignant bar manager, "you can't pull that shit with these officers and expect to get away with it. You'd be much better off watching the clock for closing time instead of mouthing off. Take this as a warning, we'll be watching the operation of this place from now on!"

"Oh yeah? Well that car . . ." started the still belligerent Sal.

"I don't give a hairy rat's ass about who the car belongs to," interrupted Hollister firmly. "And furthermore, I don't care if you own a dozen discos somewhere, you can't throw your weight around here. Regardless of your treatment in other areas, these guys do their jobs! I'll be seeing you around Sal, that's for sure!"

"Yeah, Lieutenant, that's for dam' sure," returned Sal as he jammed his cigar back in his mouth, causing his ornate diamond pinky ring to glint brightly for an instant in the parking field floodlights. "That's for goddamn sure!"

Hollister spun around and reentered the restaurant, permitting the door to swing closed in Sal's face.

"Creep!"

He made his way back to his spot at the bar and to the new Mall Operations Manager, Joe Martin.

Joe took one glimpse at Hollister as he returned and said, "What's the matter, George? You looked pissed-off!"

"I really am, Joe. That Sal whats-his-name who owns or manages this joint is a real shithead. He's out front shouting at one of the uniforms who's writing a ticket for a vehicle parked in the fire lane. It's a block-long Lincoln and probably belongs to some hotshot friend of his whom he's trying to impress. That's bullshit! Who does he think he's dealing with?! These cops do a helluva job and certainly don't need interference from some self-styled big shot!"

Joe looked cautiously over his shoulder and leaned closer to Hollister's ear so he would not have to shout to be heard above the never decreasing din in the room.

"Sal is supposed to be very well connected . . . with the mob, I mean. He manages several of these operations and the word in the office is that he fronts for some family' members."

"Joe," said Hollister, showing some interest, "I want to know more about this guy. I'd appreciate anything you know about him, and I'll check my own sources too. He's got more nerve than brains, though."

Hollister recalled his exposure to some organized crime bosses when, as a newly promoted young detective, he was assigned to bodyguard a wise guy, deemed a possible States' witness in an attempted murder incident. The witness was Frank Costello!

In those days they knew what was important and what was bullshit!

That recollection caused him to add, "The mob, if they are involved, usually keeps a lower profile on minor crap than this guy is exhibiting. Imagine a real mobster making a scene over a parking ticket!"

Hollister shook his head in disbelief.

"OK," Joe responded. "I'll check with the home office in King of Prussia, Pennsylvania and get back to you with anything I pick up."

"Swell, Joe, that would be fine," said Hollister. "I've got to make a break right now. Congratulations on your promotion. You certainly deserve it—you do a helluva job here. Don't forget, if you need something special, give me or Sergeant Wesson a call. We'll do what we can for you!"

On the way toward the front door, Hollister stopped momentarily at the spot where Tom Egan was standing, still swaying, in front of a high bar stool. On the stool, naturally, was a dark-haired girl showing a great expanse of leg. Tom was at this best with chatter and wisecracks and the girl was enjoying the attention.

"Tom," yelled Hollister in competition with the band. "Give me a call late this afternoon . . . got something for you and Pat to handle."

"OK, boss. I'll call as soon as I get finished at the barber shop." Then added, "You're not mad at me, are you?" reaching up to put his hand on Hollister's shoulder.

"No, but I think you'd better leave too before you get into trouble."

Placing his other hand on the girl's bare upper thigh, Animal" turned toward the girl and asked, "Is your name, Trouble, darlin'?"

She snickered and shook her head, "No, Sandra."

"There you are, boss. I'm not getting into 'Trouble'," winked Tom. "Everythin's gonna be aaalll right!"

"I give up," said Hollister, throwing both arms up in mock despair as he turned to leave, making one more momentary stop with Pat Connors to mention Tom's apparent condition.

Pat's response was an explanation. "He's not that bad off, boss. He's play-acting. Says that it helps with the ladies and besides, people are not too careful what they say in front of a 'drunk.' Claims he gets good info that way sometimes. Don't worry, with my bad stomach I'm not drinking so I'll keep him straight. Talk to you later."

Once outside and near the LeBaron again, he put his hand into his coat pocket for the car keys.

With an exclamation, "What the hell . . ." He quickly yanked his hand out again.

This time, very slowly, he slid his hand back into the coat pocket and cautiously removed . . . a ball of chewing gum, covered with hair!

Laughing out loud he said, "That little son of a bitch!" and started his long-legged stride back toward the bar.

No wonder he was being so friendly—arm on my shoulder and all!

Suddenly he stopped as a better idea for revenge struck him. He whirled around and this time left for home, still laughing.

Chapter 6

Reports and Reports

The next day, just before the noon rush, Hollister made another stop at Henry's Wife's Place, not being in the mood to prepare his own coffee at home.

As usual, the owner, Elaine, was there and gabbing to anyone who wanted to converse.

"Well look who has decided to pay his old friends a visit, finally," she said at Hollister's approach.

"Sorry, Pal, but I've been busy, busy, busy," Hollister smiled as he dropped himself onto a seat at the counter. "How's Hank?"

Grimacing, she said, "He's in the 'Big Apple' fighting fires instead of being here, lighting my fire! Coffee?"

"Yes," he responded—"and the works; two eggs over easy, bacon, home fries and a toasted English."

"My, we're hungry today, aren't we? That's a good sign," and she turned to pour the coffee. "Someone's been asking for you already this morning. Couldn't reach you last night at all."

"Oh?" he replied, knowing it was probably Joy.

"Don't deadpan me," she laughed. "You know damned well who it is. She has called me several times in the past few days because she gets no answer at the house. Been out a lot, eh?"

"Been out a lot . . . working," he corrected pointedly. "This detail I'm on takes an awful lot of time and energy."

"Joy's worried about you, George . . . really worried. Why don't you give her a call," Elaine said with feeling.

Hollister shook his head. "I've tried the Florida number several times, but she's not staying there. We didn't part on the best of terms, either . . . but I'll call again today."

Elaine's response was, "Call in the evening, though. She's working during the day."

"Working?"

"Yes," she shrugged. "She's working in a bank in Stuart to keep from being bored to death, like me. We both have men who spend entirely too much time on the job. Here's the new number at her mom's house," and handed him a piece of paper already prepared with the telephone number.

"All right," Hollister said. "I'll try her tonight after I finish."

"Sounds good," she said and went about preparing the breakfast Hollister had ordered and continued to chatter on. "According to the cops who stop in here, this thing's a real big deal. All those foreign countries sending people here for a couple of weeks puts Uniondale on the map and on the spot! Do you think there will be any problems?"

Grinning, Hollister shot back, "There will be plenty of problems, kiddo. For instance, Uniondale and the whole surrounding area will be up to their kimonos in traffic. Motorists may be lost in the back streets for days. They may even find your restaurant!"

"Jeez, I hope not," she replied. "I don't want any more business than I have now. I know everybody who comes in here and their problems. I don't need any new ones. What about some screwballs from Iran or wherever causing trouble?"

Hollister smiled, "We'll probably get more problems from the local dissident groups who find a reason to demonstrate against almost anything than we will from foreigners!"

She put the plate amply filled with food in front of Hollister. "Don't kid me," she said earnestly. "If it were no big deal, you wouldn't be assigned and putting so much time into it."

"Relax," he said chuckling. "It's only a big thing because we've never done it before. As far as assigning me to this job, they need a fall guy if it gets screwed up . . . and a guy who's retired and gone from the area is easy to blame. Now, will you leave me alone so that I can eat in peace?"

"Enjoy," she huffed and bounced away to start another conversation farther down the counter.

As he ate, Hollister remembered the wonderfully relaxing meals with Joy on the screened patio of the Florida house and yearned for those times again. He ate with good appetite though, and scraped the plate clean.

After a few moments he rose and sauntered over to the cash register and waited for Elaine to come over.

She looked down at her pad and said, "$3.98."

Hollister pointed back at his plate and said, "Don't I get a discount? You won't have to wash that plate."

"No, smart ass," she grinned. "$3.98!"

"OK, OK."

He counted out five single dollar bills from a money clip and handed them to her. "The tip is for your sparkling conversation. Catch you on the rebound, love."

"Try to make that call, OK?" was her parting shot.

"Yeah, yeah, I'll do it tonight, you nag," he grated as he reached the door and went out . . . turning to grin back at her as he passed the front window.

She responded to his jibe with a sour grimace with extended tongue!

* * *

This time the ride to the station house was uneventful . . . commuter time had long passed.

Hollister parked in his reserved spot by the rear door and went through the same ritual he had for so many years. Down the hall . . . salute the flag . . . retrace back up the hall . . . up the stairs . . . to his office.

"Good afternoon . . . good afternoon . . . good afternoon . . ." and on to his desk.

"Patty!" he called. "Are you terribly busy right now?"

Steno-clerk-typist Pat smiled her sweet smile, "Never too busy for you, Lieutenant."

That was followed immediately by John Barclay making loud, smacking sounds with his lips and mimicking in a high falsetto, "Never too busy for you, Lieutenant," followed by more smacking lip sounds.

"Is that jealousy's ugly head I see, J. B.? Don't be concerned, I'll kiss you good-bye when I leave."

"Oh, thank you, sir," came the falsetto back.

Blonde and shapely at twenty-four years of age, Patty had worked for Hollister for about six months following the age retirement of the previous pool steno.

During that period of time she had come to like Hollister very much. More than she should, she thought. After all, he is happily married. Rumor, however, had it that he was "batching" it these days, but no one knew why.

Her eyes followed his athletic body admiringly, but her thoughts were interrupted by his voice.

"OK," he said, "grab your pad and pencil. I'd like to lay a few pages of dictation on you."

"Coming up," she said cheerily and slid a chair into position at the corner of his desk.

"This is to Chief Gerlich," he prefaced. "Usual copies and 'To-From-Subject' format. Remember, scream loudly if I get wound up and go too fast. That will get my attention."

"I'll remember to get your attention," she laughed.

Reading from his notes and occasionally looking off into space to picture the area in his mind, Hollister started his dictation:

"1. A survey of the housing site and dining facilities has been conducted by the writer. Twelve buildings at two separate locations and the grounds surrounding each of them have been inspected for this security plan.

"2. The northwest section of Hofstra University's campus is the largest area to be secured. As outlined in another report, the area north of Hempstead Turnpike, east of Oak Street, south of North Oak Street and west of the California Avenue entrance, contains ten buildings and two parking lots requiring security and the six-foot chain-link fence. Following are the names of the buildings and the nomenclature thereof:

a. Tower A, Alliance Dormitory (sixteen levels)
Basement
Main floor
Twelve floors of resident rooms (166 rooms)
Lounge
Roof with mechanics room

b. Tower B, Bill of Rights Dormitory (sixteen levels)
Same as Tower A

c. Tower C, Constitution Dormitory (seventeen levels)
Basement
Main floor

Thirteen floors of resident rooms (182 rooms)
Lounge
Roof with mechanics room

d. Tower D, Declaration of Independence Dormitory (seventeen levels)
Same as Tower C

e. Tower E, Enterprise Dormitory (seventeen levels)
Same as Tower C

f. Tower F, Freedom Dormitory (seventeen levels)
Same as Tower C

3. It is strongly recommended that the police units assigned to this detail be directed to refer to the tower-dormitories in just the fashion that this report does, that is, Towers A through F, inclusive. This will facilitate report-writing and make radio transmissions shorter and more readable, as opposed to using the lengthy esthetic names—Alliance Dormitory, Bill of Rights Dormitory, Constitution Dormitory, Declaration of Independence Dormitory, etc., all of which are alpha-related.

4. Towers A and B are connected to each other and to the central power station by separate underground tunnels and are the only towers connected to the power station in this fashion. Towers C and D are connected to each other by tunnel and Towers E and F are connected to each other by still another tunnel.

And the ankle bone is connected to the knee bone, he sang to himself before getting serious again.

5. A reception desk is located on the main floor of each tower. All are similarly equipped, to wit:

a. Each reception desk has a multiple extension telephone with a second telephone located on an adjacent wall. The telephones can be used to call any location on campus, utilizing the university's Centrex telephone system. These telephones can also be used to call a resident assistant's telephone located on each floor of the dormitory. The operating area of these telephones is also limited to the confines of the campus. A bank of three pay telephones is located in the lobby adjoining the reception desk and are used for calls outside the complex.

b. A fire alarm panel is located behind the reception desk and will identify the location of a suspected fire and at the same time activate a second alarm at Hofstra's security office. This fire alarm system does *not*, I repeat, does not notify the fire department, but is used only to initiate an on-campus investigation.

c. Each tower's elevators can be controlled by the reception desk and *do not* go to the top floor of the tower. The top floors can only be reached via the stairway. The hall leading to the elevators is within view of the reception desk as is the main entrance to the tower.

d. The two stairways opposite the elevators provide access to all floors. The basement entrance is normally locked. It is suggested that we have an electronic alarm installed on each of the tower's basement doors.

e. The stairways are narrow and could present an evacuation problem. Only the first two floors of Towers A and B are designed to be accessible to wheelchairs. Outside windows of these areas are designated and marked by stickers for emergency evacuation by the fire department.

f. Walkie-talkie communications have been tested in the towers and work well. Each and every police officer assigned to this detail must be assigned a personal walkie-talkie and an administrative channel must be designated for the housing site's exclusive use.

6. The student center is—"

At this point in his dictation Hollister was suddenly cut short by the sound of nylon sliding across nylon. A very distinctive sound.

It was Patty, uncrossing and then recrossing her legs into a more comfortable position. The steno pad was still held in readiness, pencil poised, but she was looking directly into his eyes.

"That did it," Hollister exclaimed. "That got my attention all right! Need a break?"

"Not really," she replied, trying unsuccessfully to keep a smile from spreading across her face. "Just wanted to see if you were paying attention. You're so intense. You need a break."

"Yeah," Hollister agreed, "I'm stretched a little thin these days."

"Suppose you relax a little while I get us some coffee, OK?" she proposed.

Hollister nodded. "Sounds good to me. I'll have mine . . ."

"I ought to know by now," she laughed, "black and sweet."

Hollister watched her with newly discovered curiosity as she got up from the chair and deliberately high-heeled her way across the office toward the coffee room.

Why wasn't I really aware until now, he thought, *of what good-looking legs she has. As a matter of fact, she looks good all over.*

As she reached the office doorway and just before going out of sight, Patty half-turned and looked over her shoulder, smiling.

"By the way, Loo," she giggled, "Do you know what the first thing is that a good secretary turns on when she arrives at work?"

"The coffee machine?" bit Hollister.

"Nope," she said. "The boss!"

With that remark she was gone, leaving Hollister with a laugh.

Damn, she knew I would be watching her! Caught me gaping! and that look . . . wow! Watch yourself, buster. You haven't even thought about cheating on Joy up to now, so watch it, he admonished himself.

Within a few minutes she was back, carrying two steaming coffee mugs. Her slow mincing steps showed her graceful lines to great advantage and gave him ample time to admire her undulating movements.

"Here you are, Loo. Be careful, it's fresh and very hot," she said as she put his cup down on a napkin at the corner of his desk.

"Thanks, love," he said, keenly aware of her presence.

"You're very welcome."

Patty reseated herself opposite Hollister's chair, just as she had been before, *or is she closer this time*.

"Oh boy," he exclaimed at the first sip. "It sure is hot. Someone must have cleaned the coffeemaker."

Then seeing that she was in some difficulty said, "Wait, don't try to juggle that cup, put it over here," and pushed the napkin closer to the desk edge.

He leaned forward, extending both hands to guide the hot cup onto the napkin. As he did that, she did exactly the same thing from her side of the desk. The result was that their faces came within two inches of each other and their hands touched lightly on the cup.

"Oops," Hollister said. "Sorry," and swiftly withdrew.

Still leaning forward and looking straight into his face, Patty said quietly, "That's all right. I don't mind if you don't."

At that precise moment Hollister's private telephone line rang—more shrill than usual, it seemed, startling both of them.

Hollister cleared his throat, swallowed hard and answered, "Hello," as nonchalantly as he could.

"Hi, boss," said the familiar voice of Pat Connors. "You wanted us to call you about something special today?"

"Yeah, but not at this very moment," Hollister mumbled.

"What? Waddaya' talkin' . . ."

"Never mind. Never mind," Hollister interrupted, glancing in Patty's direction.

Her lower lip protruded in a slight pout that slowly changed into a smile.

"Yes, I do have something special for you guys to handle."

Hollister leaned back in his chair and stretched mightily with his free right arm overhead in an attempt to relieve some of the tension building in his neck.

He thought, only fleetingly, about asking Patty to leave the office, considering the confidentiality of the upcoming conversation, but decided against it.

After all, she's been through many confidential reports before, he assured himself.

"Listen," he continued, addressing Connors, "remember the overbearing idiot I had some words with last night?"

"Yeah, I heard."

"Well he sets off an alarm in my head that warns, Jerk in Area. Joe Martin has confirmed through his contacts that Sal Tamarago is mobbed up pretty good."

Patty rose from her chair at this point and walked slowly behind Hollister, causing her sweet-smelling scent to surround him.

For the next few minutes she expertly massaged the heavy muscles across his shoulders and up the sides of his neck. They were as taut as bridge cables, but he could feel the relaxation start under her gentle touch. Her smooth, petite hands felt good on his body.

Flexing his neck, he continued to talk to Connors. "Well, I want you two guys to take some time from the things you're already working on and tail him for a few days.

"Start working when he does and keep track of everything his day encompasses. Be up with him in the morning and put him to bed at night. I have a hunch about him and I want to pursue it."

"What about Sergeant Wesson?" Connors inquired.

"Don't worry about that. I'll take care of my friend Tom at this end."

"What's up," asked Connors.

"Frankly, I'm not sure," returned Hollister. "I've been told he's connected and I want to see what he's up to. No big deal at the moment, but I'm more than a little curious about him, and besides he pissed me off last night. Do what you have to do for a few days to stay with him and I'll straighten out the time with you later."

"No problem, boss," said Connors. "But we'll have to keep off him a little bit. Egan made himself very visible last night."

"How well I know," exclaimed Hollister, "but I have a friend in the Major Frauds Squad who maintains that he could wear a tuxedo while tailing a suspect in the South Bronx and not be spotted! Institute a light Level Three Surveillance, and if it looks worthwhile, I'll throw a different team on him later. It may be nothing at all, but . . ." and he paused, deliberately leaving the sentence unfinished.

"OK, boss," said Pat Connors. "We'll give it our best shot and get back to you."

"Thanks, Pat. Incidentally, how did Animal make out at the barber this morning?"

"Fine. Just a dime-sized bald spot shows and if I know Tom he'll find some way to use it to his advantage."

"Uh-huh. It will probably turn out to be 'an old war injury' to the next bimbo he runs across," Hollister laughed.

"Yeah. I can see that you know my partner as well as I do."

"For sure. Be careful, Hammer," concluded Hollister and thoughtfully replaced the phone.

Patty returned to her chair and picked up her coffee cup.

Hollister silently shook his head and mulled over his decision. If his hunch was not substantiated by solid information of criminal activity on the part of Tamarago, he would not have pulled his men away from other activities with no more impetus than a hunch and would not have wasted important time and precious man-hours. On the other hand, if his hunch should bear fruit . . .

Hollister sat forward in his chair again and glanced self-consciously at Patty who was sitting there studying her shorthand notes, waiting.

Was her skirt a little higher this time?

To break the silence he said, "Thanks. That massage really felt fine."

"To me too," was her soft response.

Quickly flipping through several pages of notes, he said, "Er . . . where were we?"

"We were about to relax a moment and have coffee," she said very quietly. "I don't know how you can stand all this pressure. Almost every phone call we answer out there in the clerical office involves you in some form or other."

"The more pressure there is, the better I perform," Hollister replied. "I love it! That's also why I surround myself with the best staff—the guys in special enforcement, you, J. B. All top-notch people."

"Thanks," she said. "That's the way we all feel about you."

Chuckling, he said, "This is starting to sound like a meeting of the Mutual Admiration Society here."

"Hey Loo," came the voice of J. B. from the outer office. "We're all leaving now. We started early this morning, not at noon! Time for us to go home."

"Really?" said Hollister, glancing at his watch. "Boy, certainly didn't realize the time. OK guys, see you on the 'morrow,'" as they filed out of the offices.

To Patty he said, "Jeez, I'm sorry I worked you right past your time to go home. We'll continue the rest of this report tomorrow."

Chapter 7

Extra Work?

She didn't move to leave, but instead smiled and said, "I don't mind staying awhile to get more of the report done. I have nothing pressing to go to," and shrugged a tiny shrug.

"Well," he said hesitantly, "I do have several more pages to go. Would you like to make a call home to let your husband know you'll be about an hour late?"

He rose to leave to give her privacy and said, "You may use my private wire."

"No thanks," she said. "That won't be necessary. I have no one to report to. My husband and I are separated and contemplating divorce."

"Oh? I'm sorry to hear that," he said sincerely surprised. "I know from personal experience what a hassle divorce can be. It tears you up!"

"Sure does," she replied, then almost viciously, "but at least there's one consolation. I'll never again be struck by that drunk!"

"Oh no," said Hollister. "I can't believe that anyone could get angry enough at you to, to hit you. It's just unthinkable."

"Unthinkable to you, perhaps, but a stark reality to me on a regular basis. I blame it all on the fact that he's an alcoholic. He used to be so different . . ."

"I don't want to interfere," Hollister offered, "but only help. Have you tried all the channels available: marriage counseling? AA? The department has counselors available too, and it's all very confidential. Have you looked into that?"

She smiled a sad smile and said, "We've talked about most of those things. He just laughs at the suggestion of AA. But I didn't know about the department having help for people in this circumstance. What do I have to do?"

Reaching for his Bates rotary file of telephone numbers, Hollister said, "A phone call is all that it takes to start the ball rolling. I have the extension number right here for the sergeant who is the certified counselor. He's what they term a recovering alcoholic and as such has been through all the hell that an alcoholic experiences.

"He has lived the experience—didn't read about it in a book, but went painfully through it all.

"I know him very well and have even requested him to help a member of my own family. You can use my name, if you like, as an introduction.

"I could call on your behalf, but I'd like you to do it when you think both of you are ready."

"Thank you, Loo," she said, her eyes getting teary. "I'll think about it, but I don't have much faith in the possibility of turning him around."

"But you should try," was Hollister's advice. Then in an attempt to avoid a tearful scene said, "Now let's get back to work—no more self-pity for today."

"You're right, as usual," she said, composing herself again.

"OK," he smiled. "Where were we before you crossed your legs?"

Laughing, she said, "I thought you'd never notice."

Then she read, "6. The student center is . . ."

Hollister picked up the narrative,

> " . . . located immediately south of Towers A and B and contains the main cafeteria with several dining areas in a three level building.
>
> a. The athletes and trainers should have exclusive use of the main dining room.
>
> b. The east side wall carries fire exit doors which are alarmed to go off when opened.
>
> c. The west side houses student activities and general office space.

d. A security problem arises from the Rathskeller, the basement dining area, in that college authorities intend to use it to feed students attending Hofstra for the summer. This will require physical coverage by security personnel.

e. The central power station can be reached via an elevator and stairwell located in the basement of the center and from underground outside the center.

f. Note that radio communication in and out of the basement is limited because of its proximity to the central power station and the interference generated there.

7. The two separate prefab buildings without basements located north of Liberty Boulevard are called Liberty and Republic Dormitories.

a. These two dormitories share a single courtyard and all entrances to the buildings are off the courtyard.

b. One corner of the courtyard houses a security booth that has the alarm, telephone and vantage points contained at the reception desks of the six dormitory towers.

c. Due to their close proximity to Oak Street, the only feasible way to secure the outside of these buildings is by foot patrol.

d. The first floors of the buildings are more accessible for the handicapped, but have numerous ground floor windows that may cause a security problem.

e. It would seem that emergency evacuation from these buildings is easier than from any of the towers.

8. A prior report outlined the areas to be secured by chain-link fence. Many holes, particularly along Oak Street now exist in the fence already erected and must, repeat must be repaired."

Damn, I wish she didn't recross her legs every few minutes, Hollister thought. *That flash of nylon breaks my concentration!*

Then he continued,

"a. Access to the campus by vehicles may be gained by utilizing gates at North Oak Street, South Oak Street and California Avenue.

b. A walkway bridge across Hempstead Turnpike permits access by pedestrians to the student center.

c. An underground utility tunnel allowing access to the central power station and which does not show on any of the blueprints with which I have been supplied, has been discovered. This entrance is located on the south side of Hempstead Turnpike concealed in very heavy underbrush and closed off by a wire and timber grating.

The tunnel, although without bright lights and the bottom of which seems to be covered with approximately two inches of water, makes the central power station accessible from outside our security perimeter.

Granted it would take a persistent interloper to locate and transverse the tunnel, but the possibility does exist. It is therefore requested that this entrance be sealed in a more permanent manner.

9. North of Liberty Boulevard and approximately one hundred feet from Tower E is a building named "Hofstra USA" It houses a bar, restaurant, a large banquet hall and a stage which will be utilized for special events.

   a. One such special event has already been scheduled and advance tickets sold. The event, the production of *Cat on a Hot Tin Roof* will attract pedestrian and vehicular traffic round the perimeter and in dormitory areas. For that reason, among others, it is imperative that our security area be sealed off with the indicated fences.

A special gate will be utilized for access to 'Hofstra USA and is located north and east of the building.

b. It is anticipated that 'Hofstra USA' with its bar and entertainment facilities will be the focal point for a great deal of special activity during the Games and must be considered a priority in assigning security personnel.

10. The complex separated from the main campus by Oak Street is known as The Netherlands and is located at the northwest corner of Oak Street and Hempstead Turnpike. This complex, to be used for housing participants and staff is divided into three separate parts.

a. The center building of the complex is a cafeteria that will be utilized for athletes and support staff. It also contains a basement power plant and several meeting rooms.

b. On one side of the center building is a dormitory called North Court. North Court is really six separate buildings connected to each other by hallways.

c. South Court is five separate buildings connected to each other by hallways.

d. North Court and South Court are not directly connected to each other, but are instead connected to the central building, known as the Core Building. Each of the sections of the Netherlands complex has the capability of being separately secured.

e. The fire alarms, telephone and vantage points are as described for each of the towers on the main campus.

f. Fenced on all sides, legitimate access to these buildings can be controlled through one main gate.

g. A security problem arises when you examine the rear fence of the complex. Immediately to the rear thereof are the rear yards of a residential section of the Incorporated Village. The heavy underbrush coupled with darkness makes surveillance of this area very difficult if not impossible.

For that reason, nightscopes should be obtained for utilization during hours of darkness by security personnel."

At this point Hollister stood up and walked to the window, his back to the office. In the glass reflection he could see Patty as though he were looking through a piece of gauze as she shifted her body in the chair. The move caused her skirt to ride up on one side, revealing a scant area of white flesh at the top of her stocking.

Stockings? You don't see very many women wearing stockings anymore. Only those stupid pantyhose. Jeez, this separation is sure making me horny!

Hollister took a few moments to absorb the sight, then turned and continued:

11. As suggested in one of our many conversations, a command post for the housing site could be located in the faculty dining room of the student center. It seems to be a practical site, closest to handicap wheelchair area, the central power station and the student center.

a. Thus the command post can readily be divided into three rooms:

1. Communications and supervisory location.

2. Conference and briefing room.

3. Response team area and lunch and break areas.

b. South of the South Oak Street entrance and west of the student center is a small parking field providing ample parking space for private autos of the police personnel assigned.

12. In addition to the motorcycles requested in an earlier report, it is further requested that patrol vehicles be supplied for supervisory patrol and a department van be assigned to transport response teams to any emergency location. These vehicles should be assigned for the exclusive use of the command post as deemed necessary by the site commander.

13. More to follow."

Am I fantasizing or is her skirt a little higher each time I look, he mused. *There seems to be a lot more upper leg being shown now than was exposed when we started! Christ, you'd better get out of here your imagination is running wild!*

Hollister, now addressing Patty said, "Close this report out for now with my signature. There will definitely be 'more to follow'," he laughed.

"Getting to be going-home-time now for sure," he said looking out at all the empty chairs and covered typewriters in an area that had been buzzing with activity only a short time ago.

"Thanks a lot for staying," Hollister said, rising and stretching again. "I owe you one."

"For you, anytime, Loo," she said, also rising.

Suddenly, and without any warning to Hollister, she glided quickly forward and threw her arms around Hollister's waist, pulling their bodies together.

"Oh Loo! If you only knew how long I've waited for this moment to come," she gasped. "To be alone with you, at last."

She buried her face in his chest and emitted a series of deep sighs.

Completely startled, Hollister stood perfectly still, feeling her body pressed against his. The warmth of it was surprising and . . . *quite enjoyable*, he grudgingly admitted to himself.

He could clearly feel the contours of her young, firm body pressing against his from her breasts down to her thighs and beyond. His first impulse was to put his arms around her and pull her closer yet and permit the heat to weld their bodies together.

Instead, he began to inch backward little by little, fighting that initial impulse. For every inch he tried to put between them, she advanced two or more through steady simmering pressure.

The desire, fueled by the abstinence imposed by Joy, started to build within him and her voice, insistent now, was gasping, "I want you. Want you now!"

Gently, as gently as he could, he put his hands on her shoulders and exerted pressure on them, pushing her upper body away from his.

"Whoa! Just a . . ."

"I know," she said hoarsely. "We could get caught if we do anything here, but I want you . . . so . . . much!"

"Patty . . ." he said, struggling to control the emotion that threatened to break loose.

She continued to push forward, always maintaining body contact, but breathed, "All right. I'll stop, but now you know how much I want you. If not here and now, you tell me where and when."

He replied softly, "We're both married and have commitments already. This is something totally unexpected. I never thought you had these feelings for me. I just don't know what to say."

"Just say that there's a chance for some time for us. I've held these feelings for you secret for too long. You can't imagine what it's like to work so close to you day after day and not be able to tell you my innermost feelings."

Hollister, unaccustomed to being flustered by any situation said, "Let's slow down a bit here. I'm very surprised and flattered by this development, but I don't know how to react. You are a very pretty girl and desirable as hell. You've got a terrific body and you're intelligent and personable and . . ."

"What's stopping you then?" she said pointedly while renewing her pressure.

"I've never really looked at you that way before. At least not until today. Perhaps our circumstances are playing tricks with our heads—your separation and my temporary one—are raising hell with our emotions. Let's kinda slow down and look at what could happen."

"I've already thought about it . . . a lot," she replied, "and I decided to take the first opportunity that came along to tell you. Today was that time. I saw you watching me walk across the room, and I saw something different in your eyes. I think you want me too!"

Trying to keep from stammering, he said, "I won't deny admiring you just then, after all, you are very attractive. But once again, that could be because of our circumstances. I'm going through a short separation brought about by conditions apart from Joy and my relationship. It has nothing really to do with our feelings for each other. It seems that we're both trying to make a point, and both suffering because of it. I have no intention of making my separation permanent. It would be unfair to let you think that."

She leaned back, but still pressed her feverish lower torso against him and smiled, "I don't expect that you will just up and leave her. I'm looking for you to give me an opportunity to show you how much I care for you. I've been around you a lot for the past six months, and you are the most considerate person I know. You handle trying situations every day with an evenness of temperament and thoughtfulness that is unique in men. These feelings I have for you did not just happen today, but have been coming on during the months of close association with you."

"But that's not a good basis . . ."

"Please," she said, "let me finish."

Hollister took this opportunity to put a few inches between them, but her fragrance continued to cling to him.

The shuffling retreat by Hollister soon found him backing into the sanctuary of Deputy Chief Gerlich's office.

It was not a conscious move at the time, but once accomplished, seemed to be a great idea. The formal setting of Gerlich's office, as pretentious and unyielding as the man himself, may serve as a means to avoid the physical contact which was beginning to be overwhelming.

She now had his left hand in both of hers and continued to talk rapidly.

"I know your status is such that you can't afford any criticism. You are . . . 'way up here", she gestured by freeing one hand and holding it high over her head, palm down., "and I'm 'way down here in the chain", again gesturing with her hand down below her waist.

From that position she sensuously slid her hand up between his thighs and gently cradled his "family jewels", holding them in a gently pulsating grasp.

Surprised by that move, Hollister's mind said, *Hooboy!*

With a seductive smile she said, "Your words say 'No' . . . but your body is telling me 'Yes' . . . you are ready now!"

She continued in a whisper, "I won't cause you any embarrassment and it won't effect our relationship in the office. We can be very discreet and go somewhere away from here for dinner and . . . all the rest. I want to be with you, if only for a short time. I guarantee you won't be sorry"!

Hollister could feel her hand quivering slightly as she kneaded him a little more firmly. Her face was flushed and her eyes searched his face for a favorable response.

"Look", he said, "we're both operating under very . . . um . . . stressful situations. Er . . . let's not rush into something while these conditions exist. Let's both think about this for a few days and then we'll . . . talk about it again. O.K.?"

He found himself merely uttering the words without much conviction.

His mind and body were urging him, *Do it! Do it you fool!*

The pressure of her molten body was taking its' toll of his conscience.

At the same time, he found his strategic withdrawal stymied by the fact that he had backed into the corner of the chief's desk. He had no more room left in which to retreat!

Patty took full advantage of this and began feverishly exploring the waistband of his trousers, locating and opening his belt and zipper it seemed in one deft motion. Eager for what she groped for and found inside, she maneuvered to reverse their positions and eased Hollister, who was no longer resisting, between her thighs and lay back on the edge of the desk.

She never relinquished her massaging grip on him as she hurriedly hoisted her skirt with her free hand, clearly showing that she had prepared for him.

He caught a quick but erotic glimpse of her supple body. Except for a tiny garter belt and stockings she was naked below the waist . . . and not bikini trimmed!

Another plus for her, he observed to himself.

Then he thought, *Damn! No one in the world was meant to be strong enough to resist this*, and with one swift backward sweep of his forearm, Hollister sent almost everything on Gerlich's desk sailing into a corner!

The only item that remained was the chief's ornate heavy marble desk set containing miniatures of all the badges held by him during his career.

Hollister then surrendered to many, many minutes of uninhibited, unbridled, torrid sex with a woman who erupted almost continuously in the most passionate multiple orgasms he had ever witnessed!

Spectacular, spontaneous sex!

When the euphoria slowed and came to a conclusion, they were both fatigued and yet very gratified.

He had never, ever had such sensational sex in his entire life. It was astounding!

Her breathless gasping of the words, "Oh Loo. Yes! Do it! Oh God!" over and over in his ear led him to believe that it was the same for her.

For Hollister it was doubly pleasing when, in retrospect, he realized where it had taken place.

"If the chief's miniature badges could only talk," he laughingly said aloud.

No longer, he thought, *could this room be referred to as the 'rubber room' without provoking a big guilty grin.*

Patty, still enraptured, continued to cling tightly to him for a long while after they were disengaged and attempting to regain their composure.

Minutes later, looking down and observing his rampant state, she took him firmly in her tiny fist and softly giggled, "Again?"

Hollister hesitantly looked at his watch and said lamely, "Hey . . . ah . . . one of the enforcement teams should be here shortly," even though he wanted with all his might to take her up on her extremely tempting suggestion.

"Don't worry," she said, reluctantly releasing her grasp long enough to lean over quickly and kiss him impulsively on the glans. After one last squeeze she gathered her coat, handbag and other belongings to her chest and smiled, "I won't get in the way of your job. I've promised you that already. Don't think badly of me for saying and doing what I did. I had to take the chance when it arose," and she smiled more broadly. "No pun intended."

She obviously was extremely happy, almost giddy and still glowing.

Rhetorically she giggled, "Where'd you learn all those great moves? You responded as though you just got out of prison! Wow!"

He resisted saying, *At the same time I was taught the art of erotic toe manipulation in the Philippines*, as a joke. It didn't seem appropriate to make light of that moment.

Chapter 8

Another Team

Footsteps on the steel stair treads became audible as the Enforcement team made its way up from the 1st floor. Hollister quickly zipped up and Patty made some last minute adjustments.

From the tone of one of the voices, although words were unintelligible, one of the men was decidedly angry.

"Good night Loo," Patty said as she headed for the hallway. "Please talk to me more" and ran her hand lightly across his chest in one last gentle and pleasing touch.

"Good night," said Hollister, consciously leaving out the word "love" that he almost always used with female friends and acquaintances.

Patty, Rich Haise, and Tom Henderson passed each other in the hallway as Hollister watched from his office.

Patty and Rich exchanged "Good nights," but Henderson appeared not to notice the passing. It was he who was highly agitated.

Richie, on the other hand, turned and looked after Patty as she passed, mentally noting her slightly flushed face. Then he turned and looked at Hollister, curiosity in his expression.

Observing a few tiny dots of perspiration on Hollister's forehead, Rich thought, "*Well, the boss is human after all.*"

Grinning wickedly, he said aloud, "A little extra work, Lieutenant?"

"It's a tough job, Rich, but somebody's got to do it," Hollister rejoined and then, realizing that he was taking the encounter too lightly, quickly changed the subject.

"How's H and H Taxi doing?" (That was the legend on the side of the undercover car currently in use by Haise and Henderson).

"Running well, and we haven't been 'made' by the scuzzes yet."

Henderson broke into the banter with, "I'm going to kick his fuckin' head right off!"

"Cripes, what the hell bit you, Tom," Hollister demanded.

"That son of a bitch Joe Mazzio," Henderson blurted.

"Wait, wait. How about starting from the beginning?"

While Tom Henderson fumed and sputtered, Richie Haise attempted to make some sense out of the outburst.

"You know," he started, "about the petty jealousies some of the uniforms have over our assignment to the special enforcement teams, right?"

"Sure do—but that goes with the territory. Been going on for years between uniforms and plainclothes units. Just a bunch of bullshit," Hollister said, dismissing the statement.

"Tom doesn't look at it just that way," said Haise. "He takes all that shit personally. The old stuff was that we were kissing ass to stay in the 'lite unit. Joe Mazzio has a different wrinkle. With his sick humor he breaks balls by saying that we have to do a hum job on the lieutenant to stay in plainclothes!"

Hollister laughed out loud. "A what? A hum job?"

After a few seconds he partially recovered and said, "Hey, maybe that's not such a bad idea. Certainly might do the guys some good to get under my desk and hum a few bars of 'Moon River'! That's what I would call really sucking up to the boss!" and he proceeded to break up.

"Hum 'Moon River', eh," laughed Haise. "That's a great line. I think I'm gonna use it."

"How can you guys laugh about it? Dammit" demanded Henderson. "That guy is such a fuck-off that he wouldn't know a burglar if he jumped up and bit him on his big fat ass—and he's got the balls to knock the guys who make all the important arrests around here! Mazz just comes to work to get a break on his meals, the fat slob. He ain't worth shit otherwise."

"Easy, Tom, easy," soothed Hollister, still snickering.

Henderson, a longtime member of Hollister's special enforcement unit, had been an undercover man with the Narcotics Squad for over thirty months. Hollister believed it to be the toughest assignment in the department.

Most narcs, by the end of their assignments, were emotionally screwed up from the intense danger and pressure they experienced on a day-to-day basis.

Henderson's assignment to Narco was ended when, at the scene of a large drug buy gone sour, gunfire broke out. One of the dirtbags had leaped into a pickup truck and was attempting to flee the scene, meantime firing a handgun through the rear window of the truck.

Henderson, in a full-out sprint, ran along side of the driver's window and, placing himself at great personal risk, fired one shot from his .45-caliber automatic.

The shot struck the narcotics peddler in the back of the head, exploding his brain and killing him in the blink of an eye. The truck continued on and careened wildly into a bridge abutment over the Southern State Parkway, demolishing itself a split second after Henderson had leaped to safety.

All members endangered during this gunfight hailed Henderson's action as heroic. One top brass, however, who was not present at the scene, disputed the advisability of Henderson's action, stating that the perp could have been picked up later on a warrant since they knew his identity.

The dissenting top brass was none other than Deputy Chief Oscar Gerlich.

Fortunately for Henderson (and for the job) the Internal Affairs and Grand Jury investigations found Henderson free from any wrongdoing in the shooting.

Nevertheless, after a short period of time, Henderson's assignment to the Narcotics Posse was ended—again at the urging of Chief Gerlich.

It was after another short wait and some "string pulling" that Hollister acquired the services of Henderson for his own Enforcement unit since he considered Tom one of the street smart cops who were needed on the job.

His belief was that too many college boys had been accepted who had little or no knowledge of the seedy side of our environs. They could readily pass written tests, but were of little or no use "in the trenches."

Tom was always refreshingly frank and with his black belt could be of great service to the street crime enforcement people. Hollister considered Tom's combat experience in Vietnam to be a big plus as well.

Using his connections on the job, Hollister managed to circumvent Gerlich's objections and put Henderson to work in his plainclothes operation.

More fuel for the Gerlich-Hollister feud.

Hollister's judgment was again vindicated when Henderson and Haise, provided with information developed by Barclay and his computer, pursued and captured a serial rapist who had terrorized the area for several months. What made the foot pursuit and capture even more special was the fact that it was made during a raging snowstorm with little visibility and in knee-deep snow. Lesser motivated people could have surrendered to the elements and probably would not have been criticized for it.

Back in the conversation again, Hollister continued, "You have to realize who you're dealing with, Tom. Mazzio is one of those guys who comes to work determined to do as little as possible. His pride is in that area, while other guys have pride in accomplishment. I'm sure Joe doesn't like his reflection every morning when he shaves, but guys like you can look yourselves in the eye and be proud of the job you're doing."

Calmer now, Tom replied, "I know you're right Loo, but I get really pissed off when a worthless slug like Mazz makes wisecracks."

"Obviously that's why he does it. Gets you all worked up and takes the pressure off himself. Don't let him do it to you, Tom. Laugh it off."

Rich cut in with, "Hey, you know what you should do next time you see him? Casually tell him that you have to go see the lieutenant and that it's your turn to hum a few bars of 'Moon River' under his desk! Beat him to the punch."

"I'd still rather kick his fuckin' head off, but I guess you're right. I'll try it," said Henderson, grudgingly.

"Great," said Hollister. "I'd hate to see that slob running around without his 'fuckin' head' even though he doesn't use it that often!"

They chuckled over the imagined sight of a headless Joe Mazzio, huge stomach spilling over his uniform trousers, the cheeks of his elephant-like ass bobbing up and down, walking aimlessly around the room. But that's about the way his tour of duty went anyway. Aimless.

At this point Hollister chose to fill in Haise and Henderson on the assignment he had given Connors and Egan.

They, in turn, kicked around some of the information becoming available through a local "snitch" about a series of burglaries occurring along Hempstead Turnpike. They were instructed by Hollister to put together a "police information" sheet and give the sector car the benefit of whatever information they were able to get, along with the crime analyst's findings.

The team left to meet with their own contacts and Hollister sat down at a typewriter. He typed out an envelope addressed to "Detective Thomas Egan, special enforcement unit." In the upper left-hand corner, for the return address, he typed, OFFICE OF COMMISSIONER OF POLICE, setting up his ambush.

Inside the envelope he secreted a "mystery" item and a short note. Sealing the envelope he placed it in the interdepartmental mail slot with a joyful flourish, wishing 'he could be there when Animal received this official-looking envelope from the OFFICE OF COMMISSIONER OF POLICE."

Hollister headed for home, his mind occupied by Patty's unexpected overtures and how he was going to handle his moment of weakness without partaking of her very tantalizing offer again . . . without alienating a very fine secretary.

Guilt was setting in.

He was also concerned with the telephone call he was going to make to Joy, in Florida this evening.

What's the best approach, he thought to himself. *Let's see . . .*

"What kind of day did you have?" she would ask.

"*Oh fine. I jumped my secretary's bones tonight!*" he would reply.

Christ no, no. That wouldn't do at all!

He continued to mull this thing over in his mind throughout the ride home and through eating his makeshift microwave dinner.

Seated comfortably in his favorite chair, he leafed through the newspaper, not really reading, but merely glancing at the page and turning to the next one. Over and over.

Finally, he reached for the telephone, and using the piece of paper given to him by Elaine at her restaurant as a reference, dialed the numbers written there.

After two rings, the wonderfully husky and sexy voice of Joy answered, "Hello."

Making his voice sound gruff and deep, Hollister said, "Hiya, baby!"

"My God, it's finally you! Hello, sweetheart," she said with happiness evident in her voice. "I love when you play like that on the phone."

Resuming his normal voice Hollister said, "How're you doing?"

"Lousy," was her response. "I miss you like crazy."

"Me too."

"Still so busy with that assignment?" she blurted, and without waiting for an answer continued, "I've been trying to reach you for days."

Then came the stickler. "What kind of day did you have?"

Uh oh, does she know something?, but answered quickly with, "Generated a ton of paper work, so I guess progress is being made."

"Honey," she said with sadness in her voice, "I want you to know that I know now that I made a terrible mistake in judgment in not going back up north with you. I wanted you to retire so much that my brain wasn't working properly. It was a foolish, foolish thing to do and I've regretted my action every day since we've been apart. Please forgive me, babe, I need you very much. I hate being without you. We've never been away from each other like this, and I don't like it."

"Neither do I, love," he said.

"Are you behaving yourself?" she asked.

Dammit, she's on to me! but replied, "Oh yeah, I'm afraid so. Of course I'm behaving," he lied. "You're my girl!"

Then defensively he asked, "How about you? Bet there are a couple of rednecks lusting after your body."

"It all depends on how you conduct yourself," she laughed. "If you want the attention, it's there; but I have a sign on me that says 'I'm not interested.' That way no one bothers me. Besides, I have my man."

"Yes, but he's 1,200 miles away!"

"Not really," she said. "You're always in my heart and my thoughts are with you constantly. I love you."

"And I love you too," as the guilt gnawed big holes in him.

"When are you going to come down so we can get on with our lives?" she said with a definite sob.

"Honey," he said. "Please don't start crying. It won't be long now. Schooling starts in a few weeks and then it's only a short time until the athletes start arriving for the Games. Time will go quickly and we'll be together then forever. I promise."

"I can't stand being without you. Can't you come down even for a few days? I miss you so much."

Hollister started thinking in terms of a weekend flight and was silent for a few seconds.

"Honey? Are you there?" she asked.

"Yes, I'm here. I was just trying to think ahead to see if I can work that out. I'd like that very much too, but it probably would not be possible until after the terrorism schooling is completed."

"That's in a few more weeks, right?" she asked eagerly.

"Yes. As I said, I should be finished with that at the end of April or the first of May for sure."

Excited now she exclaimed, "Really, babe? Do you think that it would be possible? That would give me something to look forward to. It would make me so happy. Please try to work it out. I could meet you at Daytona Beach Airport and . . ."

"Whoa," he laughed. "Slow down a bit, sweetie. Don't get too far ahead with your plans."

"The only thing I'm planning on is being close to you for every second of every minute of every hour of every day that you're with me."

"Sounds mighty good to me," he answered. I really needed that reassurance," said Hollister. "I'll try to work out the details of a flight and let you know as soon as I can."

"Wonderful," she said happily. "Don't forget who loves you and misses you, babe. Don't forget. Call me as soon as you can."

"OK sweetheart. I'll let you go now. Keep your knees together," he laughed.

"Only until you get here," she sighed. "Goodnight, my love."

"Goodnight."

What followed was the best night's sleep Hollister had in the past couple of months. The phone call was just what he needed.

Chapter 9

Chopper

Hollister continued to burn the candle at both ends of his assignments as he juggled them to make sufficient room for constant contact with the Enforcement teams involved with the surveillance of Tamarago.

He also continued to spend days out in the field and only ventured into the station house during the evening hours to avoid contact with Patty. He was still at a complete loss as to how to handle that very delicate situation which seemed compelling at times. He just could not get the thought of amazing sex with Patty out of his mind.

The weeks began flying by as he immersed himself completely in his work, supplying Gerlich with volumes of reports, observation and suggestions, as ordered.

The deadline placed upon him by Gerlich was fast approaching and with only a very few days remaining before the schooling on terrorist tactics was to start, Hollister began to feel pressed for time.

He made contact, therefore, with the Air Bureau and arranged for an early morning helicopter flight in order to survey the area from that aspect.

The police helicopter shivered into the air from its landing pad at the Grumman Aircraft Plant in Bethpage precisely at 0730.

The April morning was crisp and clear and the cold was invigorating as Air ten approached the vicinity of the college. They flew noisily over the network of roadways and parkways that made their junctures nearby, casting an undulating shadow over the structures below.

Clearly visible were the wider roadways of Hempstead Turnpike, Meadowbrook Parkway and Southern State Parkway. Visible, but less defined at the chopper's altitude were Oak Street, Uniondale Avenue, California Avenue, Ovington Boulevard, Merrick Avenue and Jerusalem Avenue.

The residential streets with their single family homes (including Hollister's) crisscrossed around the complex. The still partially iced-over stumps could be seen glistening in the bright sunlight.

Hollister glanced around and could easily identify the New York football Jets' practice field; the Nassau County Veteran's Memorial Coliseum (home of the New York Islanders hockey team); the six tennis courts on university property; and the United States Army Reserve Center on Oak Street opposite Hofstra University's dorms.

The overflight, however beautiful, pointed up Hollister's apprehensions regarding the geographic appearance of the housing site.

In a scene mindful of H.G. Welles' The *War of the Worlds*, which panicked a good portion of the United States on Halloween Eve 1938, certain buildings rose to great heights over their neighboring buildings with glaring starkness, not unlike Welles' invading clanking mechanical monsters.

Just as the farm buildings in Grover's Mill, New Jersey were no match for the heat rays and poison gasses of the fictitious invading Martians then, the tall buildings of the college campus today appeared equally as vulnerable to the lasers and particle beams of modern weaponry.

Nassau County Medical Center, the European American Bank Complex (under construction) and the dormitories of Hofstra University towered above all other buildings in the area. The flat terrain of the hamlets of Hempstead, Uniondale, Merrick and Westbury made these tall structures most prominent, harshly delineated by their comparative height. There could be no mistaking the tall, sixteen and seventeen story dorms if one were trying to locate them. They stood out absolutely.

The high-rise structures of New York City were still almost thirty miles to the west.

The panic and hysteria of one million people created by Welles and his Martians as they mercilessly wiped out the civilian population and military forces could be repeated by a well-organized attack on the International Games.

An unstoppable cascade of chaos could result and spread quickly to surrounding communities. From these, who knows how far-reaching an incident there could be. Insurrection? Revolution? World war? It was all dependent upon how well organized a terrorist attack was and how strong our response would be.

At the very least, no matter what carefully planned security measures were undertaken at the site, the dormitories were extremely vulnerable from the air or from a distance on the ground.

Hollister knew he had to be prepared for every nutcase in the country to show up here with anything from a pipe bomb to a sophisticated explosive devise intending to draw attention to their cause.

Circling lazily back to Grumman's helipad in Air ten, Hollister listened to the rhythmical "*whop-whop-whop*" of the helicopter's blades and began thinking about his ultimate retirement and Florida.

He yanked up his coat collar against the Long Island chill in the cockpit.

Chapter 10

Sal Tamarago

The night before his chopper surveillance and while Hollister was nervously making his important call to Joy in Florida, Pat and Tom had been following their CO's specific orders.

Tom's "operating" at the bar the night of the infamous "chewing gum incident" had paid off with some early dividends. The pretty miss at the bar who had been showing a shapely thigh and who was not "trouble," was in fact an off duty waitress at the restaurant. Tom's contact with Sandra was renewed with mutual eagerness and information relative to Sal's attendance to business at the disco-restaurant was gleaned.

She stated that Sal's day did not start until late morning most times. He was in and out of the place frequently according to Thunder Thighs, as Egan had nicknamed her, but hardly ever arrived much before noon. Knowledge of Sal's "girlfriend" in Great Neck, and his visits to her two or three times a week, were common knowledge among the employees. He always left at 6:30 PM for these visits. Allowing for travel time at that time of the evening, the team calculated that Sal could not spend more than 1½ hours with his paramour.

Recently, the waitress reported, Sal had begun to spend lots of time on the telephone and made many quick trips out of the restaurant, leaving in his Cadillac and returning about an hour or so later. The maitre d' handled the operation during these absences, but Sal was always on hand to close out the night's receipts. The information made it easier for the surveillance teams to operate.

Thunder Thighs was no fan of Sal's and promised to impart any and all observations to Tom Egan and Pat Connors, including information about his rumored mob connections.

Reporting to Hollister regarding the information he had pried from Sandra Wertz, Animal was his usual angry self.

A very ugly picture had been painted by Thunder Thighs with confirmation supplied by the National Crime Information Computer. NCIC revealed the fact that Salvatore Tamarago had been arrested multiple times for charges ranging from assault to sexual abuse to false imprisonment with no convictions and no time being served by Slippery Sal.

"Can you imagine this shit?" growled Egan. "Sandra says that she went to the restaurant before it opened and applied for a waitressing job, the interview, if you care to call it that, consisted of Sal telling her to raise her skirt so that he could check out her legs. She says that he was apparently pleased and handed her a uniform that was going to be used for the Grand Opening. Grand Opening of what the sucker didn't say," continued Egan.

"She went into the ladies' room to put on the waitressing uniform and found that the costume consisted of one of those practically invisible push-up bras and a short skirt with a garter belt, black mesh stockings and high heels; you know, like the outfit that the gals in the 'Foxy Hutch' wore!"

"That whole scam was bullshit," said Tom Egan, "'cause the uniforms they actually wore opening night were nothing like that, the bastard!"

"Anyhow, she says that he gave her some decorations to hang on the wall and moved a step ladder to where he wanted the junk hung. When she got to the top of the ladder, the son of a bitch was standing at the bottom of the ladder, looking up. Can you imagine?!"

Connors, standing nearby laughed, "What the hell are you so mad about? Put in the same situation, you'd be there playing mailman and looking up her address too!"

"Not like this no-class schmuck, though! She says that she had left her own underwear on underneath and that at this point he got real pissed and started shouting at her, 'You're not supposed to have panties on. That's now how I want you to look!' as he kept ogling her from underneath."

"By now she's real scared at this behavior and said that she ran into the ladies' room again to change back to her street clothes. When she came out she said that Sal was composed and apologetic and tried to explain that he got 'turned on' by her beautiful body. He promised that it would not happen again—he was very sorry.

"Thunder Thighs," continued Egan, "knows several other girls who went through similar 'interviews' with Tamarago. One girl she knows got worse treatment than that when she applied for a job.

"This one was locked in Sal's office while he grabbed at her tits and tried to stick his fingers in her mouth!

"This time Sal almost paid a high price though, 'cause this broad's brother came back that night with a knife. The story is that the kid's brother was jukin' and jabbin' at Sal with the knife, screamin' and threatenin'. They say that Sal, in spite of his fat ass, demonstrated great agility by running around like a mad asshole, hiding behind every cover available to avoid the knife thrusts. A real fuckin' circus!"

This incident had been confirmed by John Barclay who had searched extensively through computer records for background on Sal. Both parties to the latter incident were arrested on "cross complaints," one against the other, but both charges were later dismissed when Sal and the brother reached some kind of compromise. The result was that both refused to prosecute.

As a matter of record, there were twenty similar incidents reported about Sal over the years at the several restaurants he managed. Strangely, none ever resulted in even one minute of jail time for the dirtbag. So far Sal had managed to somehow slip through the cracks in our legal system.

The more Hollister and his crew discovered about Tamarago, the more determined they became that he would not escape untouched this time, no matter what his involvement.

This crumb was long overdue for a stint in heartbreak hotel and these were the guys who could bring it to fruition.

Chapter 11

Revenge

It was inevitable that Tom would take this opportunity to rub into Pat the fact that this was his contact. He made a point of exclaiming that Pat's "altar boy" image had failed to produce a contact so far, whereas he, on the other hand, was now required to "give his body for the good of the job."

Days of boring surveillance came and went, with the only real diversion being the trips to Great Neck and one trip to Linden Service Station, apparently for the servicing of the Caddy.

On one such tiresome day, slouched in the car in the waning evening light watching the house on Steamboat Road into which Sal had disappeared, Tom was decidedly edgy.

"Damn," he said to Pat. "We sit out here ducking and hiding and that son of a bitch is in there getting laid. There ain't no justice!"

Pat's comment was, "I'm curious to see what she looks like. Sal is such an ugly schmuck, what could the bimbo who screws him look like . . . Gravel Gertie?"

At that very moment the front door opened and Pat dropped his burrito into the bag on the front seat, preparing to take up the tail again.

Out came Sal Tamarago, dressed conservatively, as usual, like a prosperous businessman—maybe even a banker. A fat, out of shape little banker, instead of what he truly was—a wise guy.

Behind him, framed in the doorway was a young, tall, slim, red-haired beauty. As she raised her manicured hand to wave bye-bye to Sal, her frilly housecoat sleeve slid up her arm, revealing the whitest skin either cop had ever seen.

She was as white and smooth appearing as a saucer of milk, and stunningly lovely besides.

"Holy shit," exclaimed Tom in a whisper. "What a doll."

Pat's retort was an incredulous "She's gorgeous."

And indeed she was, with straight white teeth and just enough make-up to bring out her dark eyes. Obvious class.

She closed the door as Sal tooled his Cadillac away, and the two open-mouthed cops followed after a cautious wait of a few seconds.

"Sal, you lucky bastard," Tom Egan said aloud as the tail continued out to traffic on Great Neck Road toward Northern Boulevard. "I don't know what you've got, but I sure wish you'd give me a couple of pounds of it!"

Sal headed west and after a few blocks pulled into a parking space, curbside.

The two surveillance cops, caught short, hurriedly looked around for hole to drop into from which they could watch Sal. Pat whipped the car into a gasoline station diagonally across from the white Caddy and popped the hood. He leaped out and buried his head and shoulders in the engine compartment.

Sal exited his car and headed into a store that proclaimed itself, "Little Neck Paper and Office Supply Co."

Egan scrambled into the rear seat of the tail car and trained his binoculars on the front of the building, straining to see inside. He had no luck as the traffic on Northern Boulevard continued to whiz by, obscuring his vision.

"What the hell is he doing in there?" mumbled Egan to no one in particular. "Can't see him, dammit!"

Meanwhile, Pat leaned over the open engine compartment but squinted in the direction of the store, waiting.

In a few minutes Sal came back out, carrying a white bundle held in both hands in front of his fat belly. He placed the package on the curb and proceeded to open the Caddy's trunk. As Sal picked up the package to put it in the trunk, Egan trained the binoculars on the bundle and could discern that it was made up of several smaller packages, stacked one on another.

He counted five packages, all labeled "Stuart Hall Bond Paper—One Ream" on the sides.

"Paper!" exclaimed a disgusted Tom Egan. "The asshole bought bond paper!" and dropped the glasses back into their case.

"Come on," said Connors. "He's leaving," and slammed down the hood.

"Boy, was Hollister ever wrong with this one," complained Tom as they continued westbound on Northern Boulevard. "Paper! Not grass or coke, but paper! What a fuckin' waste of time. This is a bunch of shit, tailing this boob!"

"Shut up and keep your eyes on him," said Pat quietly. "We're following the boss's orders, so calm down and pay attention to business."

A few blocks farther west on Northern Boulevard the scene was the same with Sal parking the Caddy and entering a storefront labeled "Modern Business Supplies." This time they were in a perfect position to observe Sal as he entered and then left the store.

It was a duplicate of the first scenario, with Sal leaving the building carrying and placing a similarly labeled package in the trunk of the Caddy.

The routine was repeated at "Industrial Outfitters, Inc." and again at "Eisenhower Office Supply Co." with the packages being carefully stacked in the trunk of the Caddy.

The tiny, two-car caravan then wended its way back to the Green Tree Restaurant.

The waiting game began anew.

Egan, agitated by the lack of obvious action turned to Connors and grumpily complained, "I'm going to call Hollister and tell him that we're wasting time on this turkey. All he does is get laid and go shopping. This is crazy putting us on this kind of shit!"

Thoughtfully Pat replied, "I don't know. The boss always seems to have the right slant on things. He's got to have something going for him to put us on to Sal. I'm a little leery of saying that he's wrong at this point. Maybe we ought to give it a little more time."

"Bullshit!" burst Tom. "I'm tired of sitting in this car with you and your stupid ulcer. At least when we're working another kind of caper I can escape from the car and you!"

"Hey, do you think its fun for me in here with you and that sewer you've got for a stomach?"

"Oh knock it off! It's those burritos you eat every night," was Tom's indignant reply.

Pat glared back at him and said, "I'd rather not know what you eat!"

"That settles it," Tom shouted. "Let's get a hold of Hollister and let him know how we feel about this bullshit!"

"How you feel, you mean! Don't include me if all you're going to do is bitch to him. If you can make a sensible argument against this I'll go along, but if you're only going to complain, I want no part in it."

"OK. Let's run into the stationhouse and talk to him," said Tom, still very annoyed. "Let him know that this guy is doing nothing except buying paper for his restaurant menus. The boss has always been reasonable, he'll see that we should go back to other assignments. The druggies are probably all back selling their 'nose candy' and 'whacky weed' along Linden Boulevard by now. Let's see if he's in the office and go talk to him."

A call to the desk officer confirmed Hollister's presence in his office, so they headed there confident that Sal would say put for a while at the restaurant.

They walked up the stairs to Hollister's sanctum and were greeted by a skeptical scowl.

"You mean you put Sal to bed already?" Hollister demanded.

"Well . . . no," said Tom uncertainly. "We wanted to talk to you about it. Right, Pat?"

Hollister dropped his pen on his desk and leaned back in his chair, looking from one face to the other. "Go ahead, talk. What have you got?" he prompted.

There was an uncomfortable silence for several seconds as Tom looked at Connors and Connors looked back.

"Well?" said Hollister, a little impatiently. "Come on. Since when do I have the Marx Brothers in the unit?"

It was Connors who finally had to pick up the conversation.

"We've been on Sal for quite a few days now and all he has done was to visit his girlfriend in Great Neck and do some shopping today. Seems as though the guy is in the clear; he's doing nothing that we can see. Meantime the drugs are probably starting up again in the dope holes that we had cleaned up once. Maybe we should go back to what we do best and drop Sal."

"Oh? Visiting his girlfriend and shopping? Tell me more about it."

Pat then embarked on the account of the previous several evenings' activities.

Hollister listened with patience until Pat finished his presentation with the observation, "Buying paper for the restaurant's menus is no crime."

"All right," said an interested Hollister. "Let me recap. If I understood you correctly, you said Sal bought five reams of Stuart Hall Bond Paper at each of four different locations, correct?"

"Yeah," Tom finally contributed.

"Why did he buy at four different locations? Why not buy it all at one stop?" asked Hollister pointedly.

Pat looked apprehensively at Tom and offered hesitantly, "Maybe the stores were low on stock?"

"Possible, but not likely at all four places," said Hollister slowly. "Do you know how much high quality paper that is?" he asked rhetorically. Without waiting for an answer he said, "10,000 sheets. That's a helluva lot of menus, wouldn't you say?"

"Uh-huh," they answered almost inaudibly, waiting for the bomb to drop.

Hollister emphasized his own statement, "I would say definitely that that's a whole lot of white bond paper!"

The next sentence was drawn out by Hollister with exaggerated deliberativeness. "Especially since the menus at the restaurant are printed on tan parchment and not . . . white . . . bond!"

Hollister again looked from one face to the other and detecting a slight flush rising on Pat's face under the beard, gave him a reprieve by saying, "It looks as though you guys may have hit on something. That amount of high quality paper could mean that Sal is mixed up in a counterfeiting operation.

"The fact that he spread his purchases out through four different locations leads me to believe that he was attempting to artfully conceal the large amount he was accumulating.

"Glad you spoke to me about it. Good work!"

He stood up and shook each man's hand firmly. Pat still looked sheepish, but Tom beamed broadly.

Hollister continued emphatically, "Now I want Sal covered around the clock. Everything he does has to be documented starting right now. Get in touch with Henderson and Haise and work with them on splitting up the hours. I want to know who Sal talks to or even sees. I want to know where he goes and what he does when he gets there! Is that clear? And keep me informed!"

"Yes, sir," said Tom. "We'll stay right on top of it!"

"I don't have to tell you," said a deadly serious Hollister, "that this is a strictly confidential caper. No one—and I mean no one—is to get any word about this except us in special enforcement. No one outside of us. Is that clear?"

"Don't worry," said Pat.

Hollister, musing aloud said, "Counterfeiting has been around since the years BC. Tyrants in those days used to mint lead coins and cover them with a thin layer of gold to increase buying power.

"Napoleon opened a counterfeiting plant in Paris to pay for his Russian campaign.

"Even the Pilgrims used counterfeiting to further their aims. They found that the Indians used strands of beads that looked like mother of pearl, wampum, as money. Our enterprising forefathers soon found a way to fashion imitations of bone and porcelain.

"The result was that they piously cheated the Indians right out of their jockey-shorts. Once we get a better line on Sal's activities and our suspicions are confirmed, we'll notify the Secret Service and see if we can get Sal to warble a tune for us.

"He's out there waiting for you to nail him, so get together on the hours with Tommy and Rich and get going!"

In the next instant, Hollister's blue eyes turned hard and flashed in a brief display of anger. The two men standing before him could not mistake the ice in his voice as he said, "One more thing. In the future you had best remember that I set the priorities on these assignments . . . and . . . not . . . you!"

Glancing warily at each other, both men had the feeling that they had been expertly reprimanded but yet encouraged to continue. As they left, their interest and vigor renewed, they were thankful that Hollister had let them off without losing his temper.

Once outside the office Pat turned to Tom and with a grimace said, "Now you know why he's the boss, you asshole. Don't ever get me involved in any more of your harebrained schemes. And by the way, I like the way you spoke up in there," Pat continued facetiously. "Really ballsy!"

"I can't help it," said a hapless Tom Egan. "He intimidates me one-on-one like that."

Disgusted, Pat shrugged, "You're a trench slug, Egan!"

On the way out of the building, they were admonished by the desk officer. "You guys better pick up your mail."

They went obediently to the folders bearing the alphabetically arranged names of every member of the command. In these folders were deposited copies of new orders and any personal mail left at the station house. Both men had a quantity of items.

Seated back in the car, Tom began leafing through the pile of mail, saying, "Bullshit, bullshit, bullshit" as he gave each item a perfunctory look and discarded it.

Suddenly he stopped and stared at a business-size white envelope addressed to him bearing the legend OFFICE OF COMMISSIONER OF POLICE in the upper left-hand corner.

"Holy shit, Pat!" he exclaimed. "From the commissioner," and crushed the envelope to his lips in a fervent kiss.

He tore feverishly at the envelope, gasping, "I've been waiting for this for a long time! Hot dog! It's probably my notice to appear for an interview for assignment to the Juvenile Aid Bureau. No more long nights, no more stupid stakeouts, no more—"

His delirium suddenly turned to shock as he unfolded a sheet of paper, and a flattened and hardened piece of hair-covered chewing gum fell out.

On the paper was typewritten in capital letters the legend GOTCHA and signed, "El General."

Connors pounded both fists on the steering wheel in hysterical laughter. "He did it to you again, asshole!"

Egan, unable to respond, just stared at the note, the envelope, and the dried contents now lying on his lap, and unconsciously touched the small bald spot just behind his left ear.

Hollister's vengeance was complete.

Chapter 12

Shock and Awe

Tom and Pat, chastened by their experience with Hollister in his office, applied themselves selflessly to the job at hand. Information developed, albeit slowly, was exchanged between the two teams now assigned.

Despite the fact that Tamarago's activities were routine for the next few days, the teams doggedly stayed with him at every movement. Their confidence in Hollister's hunches, which had born fruit many times in the past, added impetus to their renewed spirit of cooperation.

The second evening following their discussion with Hollister, Tamarago departed from his routine. Instead of heading for Great Neck, he just seemed to wander off into the vast parking area of Green Acres Shopping Center, on foot.

As he waddled toward the southwest portion of the parking field, an area well removed from the retail operation but reserved for employees' vehicles, Tom and Pat observed him through binoculars.

Well hidden by the hundreds of cars and trucks parked there, they moved a few aisles closer, scrutinizing his every movement. He frequently turned and looked in several directions, either looking for a tail or a meet with someone.

"What the hell is this guy up to this time?" said Pat, crouching with binoculars pressed to his eyes.

"I haven't the slightest," grumbled Tom, peering through the dim light of the evening. "Let's try to get closer." And he started to stand up.

Pat reached out and clamped Tom's arm in a steely grip. "Stay right here, ya boob. I can see him fairly well. Let's not blow this!"

Grimacing, Tom settled back and shook his arm to free himself from Pat's grip. "OK, OK, don't get so fuckin' physical, you ape!"

By staying low and between parked autos, the two were managing to avoid Tamarago's searching glances.

Waddling deeper and deeper into the recesses of the parking field, Tamarago made his way to the edge of Ring Road, a thoroughfare that completely circled the parking field.

Pat focused his vision on a 1984 grey Buick Skyhawk that came to a stop opposite Tamarago, and he whispered instructions to Tom, "Cut through this row of cars and get an angle on the rear of the Buick. Get the plate number. Do nothing else. Understand?"

"Yeah, yeah," said Tom peevishly as he prepared to move. Then he added, "What the hell are you whispering about? The guy's a fuckin' quarter of a mile away!"

"Shut up and move your ass," was the response he got before Pat slithered away.

In the meantime, Pat refocused his binoculars on the driver of the Buick but could not make out much more than what appeared to be a male outline.

Suddenly, Tamarago's lighter sparked, and the flame moved toward the tip of his ever-present cigar—illuminating the interior of the car momentarily.

Instantaneously the driver slapped at the lighter, sending it spinning and clattering across the macadamized roadway.

Enough light, however, had glowed into the driver's compartment of the Buick to afford Pat a fleeting peek at the operator. What he saw made him suck in his breath sharply, and he felt his pulse quicken noticeably.

"What the hell is going on here!" he said aloud to absolutely no one.

Despite the pounding in his chest, he continued to watch through the glasses, but the conversation between Tamarago and the driver of the Buick lasted only a minute longer and then broke up.

Tamarago began laboriously to bend over, searching for his lighter, which had skittered away from him. The Buick continued around Ring Road and out toward Sunrise Highway.

Animal was now making his way back to Pat's location, crouching as he ran.

Pat, eyes still glued to the binoculars observing Tamarago, said, "Did you get the plate number?"

"Sure did," replied Tom. "325 DEG, New York."

"Write it down now with a description of the car," urged Pat.

"I'll remember it until we get back to our car."

"Bullshit. Write it down, now," exploded Pat. "I don't want any fuckups over it later. Write it down!"

Puzzled by Pat's strong insistence, Tom reached into his pocket and wrote the plate number on the inside of a matchbook cover. "OK, I wrote it down. Happy now?" He pouted like a chastised child.

"I feel better, but I'm far from happy. Something very strange is going on here. I don't know what, but it sure looks like lots of deep shit ahead," said Pat, his voice very hoarse.

"Fill me in, partner. What the fuck are you so uptight about?"

As they started retreating, aisle by aisle, Pat whispered, "Wait 'til the Dago finishes looking for his lighter, and we can stop hiding like this."

Moving off between rows of cars, he said, "I don't believe it. No shit!"

"What? What?" exclaimed Tom. "Will you tell me what the fuck is goin' on here? Goddammit!? Did you see something?"

"Sure did, you hump. We've got to get to Hollister right away and fill him in," said Pat excitedly.

Exasperated now, Tom all but grabbed Pat by the throat. "Jeezuz, if you don't speak up, I'm going to kick you right in the nuts, you big ape. What the fuck is it?"

"What the fuck it is, is *Gerlich*," said Pat, eyes widening.

"Huh?"

"Gerlich!" Pat repeated. "Deputy—Chief—Gerlich!"

"What are you babbling about, you idiot? Gerlich what?"

"Gerlich was driving that car, asshole," said Pat, replacing the binoculars in their case. "Why would the chief be meeting with a slug like Tamarago in secret like this?"

"Are you sure?" said Tom skeptically.

"Yes, yes, I'm sure. Only had a quick look, but I'm sure," said Pat, checking on Tamarago, who was now retracing his steps toward the restaurant.

"Sure enough to get El General on the horn and let him know something real shitty is going down! Better yet, let's head for the station house, fast!"

Leaving Tamarago once again at the restaurant, Pat Connors and Tom Egan drove swiftly to the station house to find Hollister, luckily, still in his office.

They approached Hollister with a little more confidence this time and could withstand his hard look when he asked, "You guys got a problem, again?"

Pat answered immediately, "No, sir, but I do think we all have a problem."

"Oh? And what might that be?"

"Well," Pat started breathlessly, "we just witnessed a meeting between Tamarago and someone else in the parking field of Green Acres. The meeting was conducted in such a way that we have no doubt that it was supposed to be secret."

Continuing, Pat described in detail the tailing of Tamarago to the clandestine meeting in the far corner of the parking field—how he had dispatched Egan to get the plate number while he continued to keep the surveillance going and how he could not see the driver until Tamarago lighted his cigar.

Here he paused, whether it was for dramatic effect or just that he was out of breath, Hollister couldn't figure.

He found it necessary to prompt Pat with, "Well, would you care to tell me who it was, or would you rather that I start guessing!"

Breathing heavily, Pat blurted out, "It was Gerlich!" and then glanced warily around the office.

Hollister said evenly, "Gerlich? Our Gerlich? Chief Gerlich?"

This time, Tom replied, "Yep. One and the same!"

"You ID'd him too?" Hollister asked, looking in Tom's direction.

"Well, no," said Animal hesitantly. "I was getting the plate number when Pat saw the driver."

"Plate number? What kind of car, and what was the plate number?" asked Hollister as he slid a chair over in front of the computer terminal.

Glancing triumphantly at Pat, Tom read from the matchbook cover, "Registration 325 DEG on a 1984 Buick Skyhawk sedan, grey."

Hollister punched his access code word into the computer and, selecting the proper format, brought up on the screen, Limited Personnel Information.

After referring to a roster on his desk, he typed in Gerlich's name and department serial number.

In seconds, the monitor screen glowed with the information requested.

Under the heading Vehicles were two entries. The first showed a description of the vehicle supplied to Gerlich by the department. The second listed his Personal Auto—1984 Buick Skyhawk two-door sedan, color: grey, current registration: 325 DEG, New York.

"Looks as though your identification was good, guys. The computer confirms your sighting of the car as correct. The big thing we don't know is why. Why would the chief be meeting with a scuzzball like Tamarago? What would they have in common? What in the world could they have to talk about!"

Tom, musing aloud, offered, "Maybe the Guinea bastard spotted us one time or another, and he's meeting with the chief to blow the whistle on us."

"I tend to doubt that, Tom," said Hollister. "Knowing Gerlich as I do, I believe he would probably make a big deal out of a complaint like that and conduct an interview right here in this office just to embarrass the unit. No. I don't buy that complaint angle at all."

"What else could it be?" said Tom.

"I have no logical explanation right now," continued Hollister, "but whatever it is, we're going to dig it out. In the meantime, don't mention this to anyone. Just give the information to the other team so that they are aware of the development. I want to know immediately when and if this occurs again. Understand? I don't care what time of day or night, I . . . want . . . to . . . know!"

"Right, boss," said Tom.

Pat nodded thoughtfully.

Noting Pat's lack of response, Hollister looked at him for a few seconds in silence. Then he said, "You got a problem with that, Pat?"

"This could get hairy, couldn't it, Loo?" he replied. "I mean, I'm just wondering if you realize what you're going up against here. We all know you're fearless, but shit, the guy you are investigating after all is a deputy chief. This could be dangerous!"

"Yes, it damned well could be," said Hollister. Then anger starting to rise, demanded, "Does this mean that you wouldn't carry your weight if something does go down? Would you like to be replaced on this caper? No problem if you do!"

"No. No. That's not what I meant. I'm curious as to where we go from here. Do we report this to Chief Wildig, or what?" Pat inquired.

Hollister stared Pat in the eyes and said, "Look, I don't have to remind you that I'm the CO here and that anything that comes down, comes down on me! You guys are just following my orders if anyone questions you. There's nothing wrong, illegal, or improper in what we're doing. You report your findings to me, and what I do with them is my responsibility.

"My intention is to follow this up in whatever fashion is expedient. I intend to find out exactly what's going on, big or small, and reach some kind of conclusion, good or bad. Got that? Do you guys want out?"

Tom jumped in immediately, "No. Not me! I like getting involved in this shit. You can count me in, all the way!"

Pat answered with, "Me too. I didn't want to give you the wrong impression. I was just curious as to what was next. You know me, boss, I'll follow you're orders right down the line!"

"I'll tell you this much," Hollister continued. "I'm seriously considering talking to Willie—er, Chief Wildig about supplying us with some special equipment to make this surveillance easier. I have never gone off half-cocked, so we obviously need more surveillance input before any firm conclusions can be drawn. Stay with it, guys, you've done a fine job so far."

The team seemed to be on to something really big and was eager to get back into the hunt again.

Chapter 13

The "Hook"

The surveillance team left, and Hollister sat for some time by himself, mulling over the ramifications of his next move.

He knew he had to keep any suspicions he had out of the heads of the headquarters' smart guys.

Those pussies would sell out in the blink of an eye in exchange for a nod from Deputy Chief Gerlich or a little smile from the commish.

And what about the goddamn hired guns from *Today's News*? A leak to them would be fatal—not only to the investigation, but probably also to Hollister and his men for not going official.

He stared at the information being displayed on his monitor.

After a period of time, Hollister made his decision—follow the investigation to its bloody end. He was determined to do whatever it took.

He pounded his fist on his desk. "Shit!" he said aloud.

A troubled Hollister then placed a phone call to a very influential friend—one from whom he always got help and straight answers.

His "hook" was Chief Inspector William Wildig, straight shooter *par excellence.*

A very serious and insistent George Hollister made arrangements to meet Wildig "away from headquarters on an urgent matter."

It was not really a difficult job to convince the chief of a meeting place. They both enjoyed the food at the Blue Marlin Restaurant, and the owner was a mutual friend. The following evening was readily agreed upon for the meeting.

* * *

After Jimmy Volgars, the owner, had finished his usual very vocal fuss over them, Hollister and Wildig were escorted to a table in the dining room.

As the two friends finished the first of several cocktails, Hollister began to feel a little uneasy. It was not that he was uncomfortable with Wildig—they were very comfortable with each other, having been associates and, beyond that, close friends, for more than ten years. They had the respect for each other that only really close friends could hope for.

Hollister was uncomfortable, however, with the growing possibility that a fellow superior officer was dirty and that he would have to let Wildig in on his glimmering suspicion.

Hollister's quiet mood puzzled Wildig, and he said, "What the hell is botherin' you, George? You're too dam' reserved. Somethin's up, so why don't you get right down to bid'ness?"

"Yes," replied Hollister quietly, "something is up, but I don't know quite how to start."

"The beginnin' is usually a pretty good place." Grinned Wildig, white teeth flashing against his chocolate brown face. "Ah'm not accustomed to you being reticent!" Then he exclaimed, "Hey, get that word, 'reticent'? Ah'm startin' to sound like you."

Wildig was aware of what he believed was Hollister's only real shortcoming—his refusal to completely curb an explosive temper. Fortunately, Joy had softened Hollister's disposition and was credited with molding him into a more model citizen.

Notwithstanding this fact, Wildig was in the habit of warning people likely to bait Hollister that they stood the risk of being "cranked, but good" if they crossed a certain line distinctly drawn by Hollister.

It had been a few years since the last episode when some idiot last let his liquor speak for him and verbally trashed a cop known very well by Hollister. Unfortunately, the loud detractor was another lieutenant, but Hollister was never one to discriminate. The guy was cranked with a speedy right hand after failing to heed a very clear verbal warning.

On another occasion (there were several that came easily to mind), Hollister physically removed a deputy inspector from his office when the man became abusive and overly critical of the actions of Holly's Boys one night.

Then there was the sergeant—hell, Hollister was not one to swallow hard and slink away from some incompetent jerk whose elevator did not go all the way to the top floor. Hollister preferred to handle these head-on clashes on a one-on-one basis.

If you refused to heed his ample warnings and continued to attack and you deserved it, you got it—superior officer of not!

Wildig would, on occasion, step in and prevent his friend from being transferred "around the horn", a punishment designed by the department to bury the individual. In Wildig's view, Hollister possessed too much talent in organizing and administrating units to have that happen to him.

Despite the reformation that Joy had implemented, Wildig was certain that on this occasion, Hollister had obliged some asshole and clouted him after sufficient provocation, but after the poor soul had been carefully warned.

Thus the need for this meeting—or so he believed.

Serious again, he said, "Spill it. You slug some captain or something?"

"No," Hollister began, "it has to do with your deputy becoming involved in something that may be way over his head."

Wildig tossed his head back and chuckled. "Is that all that's botherin' ya? Gerlich has always had problems with handlin' personnel. He's an excellent report writer and can survey situation well, but he doesn't handle his authority or his people very well. His personality turns people off quick.

"Tell me what he's doin' to your people, George, and Ah'll have a little chat with him."

"Damn it, it's not that cut and dried," a tense Hollister shot back. "I believe that what he could be involved in is much more serious and damaging than a personnel problem. I believe that what he might be involved in can put him in prison and embarrass the department irreparably."

Wildig bit thoughtfully at the inside of his left cheek, a practice in which he indulged when confronted with pressure situations.

"Ah think you'd better get more specific, bud, this sounds pretty shitty."

Hollister raised his head, and his eyes searched out their waitress.

In a flash, she was standing by the side of the table. "Do you gentlemen wish to order now?" she inquired.

"Not just yet," Hollister replied. "I'd like another scotch sour, rocks, hold the fruit."

"How about you, Chief?" she asked.

"Shot an' a beer," was Wildig's response, forsaking the rye and club soda with which he had started the evening. "Got a feelin' Ah'm gonna need it!"

"We'll probably order after that," said Hollister with a small shrug.

She smiled. "Yes, sir," and disappeared.

Hollister surveyed the tables close to them and saw that they were all apparently deeply engaged in conversations of their own. He leaned forward, both forearms on the table, and lowered his voice to a confidential tone.

"This situation started innocently enough when, strictly on a hunch, I assigned one of my special enforcement teams to tail this guy Tamarago, the manager of the Green Tree Restaurant. I didn't have anything concrete, only a gut feeling that I thought was worth a little time spent on surveillance."

"Wait a second," Wildig interrupted, "you're 'posed to be totally involved in the assignment to the International Games 'cordin' ta . . . mah deputy."

Another set of drinks arrived at this moment, and the waitress said, "Let me know when you're ready to order," before departing.

Hollister looked into his glass, contemplating his next statement.

"Yeah, I know he thinks that I'm up to my ass with the Games assignment, but I'm still in contact with the enforcement units, and I know what's happening with them. You know that I find it difficult to completely separate myself from that gang. They're too important to me—they're my boys."

"I know that only too well," said Wildig before picking up his shot glass and downing the contents in one swallow.

Despite the fact that Hollister had seen him do that many times over the years, he could not help but think, *How the hell does he do that without his eyes getting watery or losing his voice*, and shook his head almost imperceptibly.

"Practice, frien,' jus' practice." Wildig smirked, reading Hollister's headshake. "Go 'head, continue."

"Over the past few weeks, this Tamarago his visited ten business supply houses and purchased reams and reams of high-quality bond paper."

"So 'cordin' to you, the guy does run a classy restaurant."

"The quantity amounts to over forty thousand sheets currently that the surveillance teams can document.

"Not incidentally, the restaurant's menus are printed on tan parchment paper, not bond paper."

Wildig poured the rest of the beer from the bottle into his glass while gnawing at the inside of his cheek and inquired, "Anythin' else that points to possible counterfeitin'?"

Then his voice became insistent, "And what the hell does this have to do with Gerlich? Is he tryin' ta stop the surveillance?"

"Nope," said Hollister. "He's not even aware that it's going on. I've sworn all my people to secrecy."

"That's not the way to handle it! What about the Treasury Department and our own Major Felony people?"

"I've told no one. I've been trying to preserve the integrity of this operation. I can't go around telling people about a confidential investigation and expect it to stay secret.

"Let me tell you more," said Hollister, again glancing at the surrounding tables.

"Up to now, the paper has been loaded into Tamarago's Cadillac and, in several trips, brought somewhere in Suffolk County."

Edgy now, his eyes narrowed to slits, Wildig demanded, "Somewhere? You bustin' ma balls? What's with 'somewhere'?"

"My guys have tailed the Caddy to West Islip but were forced to lie back when the car got to the beach area. The place is so wide open and deserted at this time of the year that they would stand out if they followed onto an empty beach road in daylight. We'll lick that problem with a phony jogger or a fisherman or something next time he heads out that way. The indication is that he has a house there in which the paper is at least being stored."

Wildig took a big swallow of his beer and shook his head slowly. "Ah know that this conversation is off the record, but if you had confided in the major felony squad, you would prob'ly know where the house is located now. Besides, you're infringin' on Suffolk County's territory and the Treasury Department's responsibility."

"Look, Bill," said Hollister hotly, but quickly lowered his voice again when Wildig raised his hand slightly in a calming gesture. "Look, you know damned well that either one of those actions require that everything be put in writing and submitted through official channels, right?"

"That's procedure."

Hollister hissed his next statement, "Well, I don't want him to be aware of this investigation just yet!"

Also impatient now, Wildig demanded, "An' why not? You haven' given me one goddamn indication that he's involved, have you? Our friendship is one thin', but makin' an accusation that my deputy is . . . !"

Hollister jumped in with, "Christ, give me a chance. Don't be so defensive until I've finished—you may not want to be by then!"

"But you haven't given me anythin' yet, have you?"

With that angry statement made, Wildig looked across the room at the waitress and jerked his forefinger down toward his empty glass. She knowingly moved into action.

Hollister now picked up the conversation quietly and deliberately.

"If you want to look at this like a Boy Scout—fine, be one—but the fact is that any cop can be dirty if the price gets to be big enough. That goes for ranking cops as well.

"A surveillance team has seen Gerlich under strange circumstances. Once, his private auto, not the department vehicle, mind you, was seen in West Islip in the vicinity where the tail of Tamarago was dropped.

"Last night, again in his private car, he was observed talking to Tamarago in the Green Acres parking field."

Hollister then described the incident in which the driver of the car attempted to avoid the light radiated by the cigarette lighter, but was unsuccessful and was identified by the surveillance team.

"This meeting was designed to be surreptitious and not intended to be witnessed by anyone," Hollister concluded.

He looked at Wildig, waiting for a sign of acknowledgement. Receiving none, he pursued.

"This meeting was not a chance, accidental meeting. Could not have been! My information through Green Acres Management and other sources is that Tamarago is a wise guy. He has fronted for the mob in a couple of disco-restaurant operations and has an arrest record a yard long!"

Still no outward reaction from Wildig, so Hollister said, "You don't buy this, do you! Bill, this guy's dirty as hell—a total sleazebag, and I intend to prove it. What would your deputy have in common with a scum like Tamarago, who has the intelligence of a lint-ball, anyway!"

This time, he paused longer, trying to force a response.

Wildig, again thoughtfully biting his cheek for a long moment, said, "Ah've never questioned your judgment before, but you and Gerlich haven't had the best of relationships in the world, have you? Are you sure that you're not readin' somethin' into this that's not there?"

His voice getting heavy with anger, Hollister ground out his reply slowly, "With all due respect for your rank and for our friendship, Chief—bullshit! I have carefully examined my heart and my thoughts in the event that I was permitting my personal feelings to cloud my police sense. My conclusion is that I have clearly eliminated all personal feelings from my determination that he is dirty.

"I'm sorry to have to say that, but you know that over the years, I've always said what I believe. There's a bad cop out there. I've been at this too long to be that wrong!

"One more thing. If this is going to turn out to be a lecture on what happens if this blows up in my face—"

Apologetically Wildig interrupted, "OK, OK, don't get your piss hot. It was somethin' Ah felt Ah had to say even though I don't believe it. Ah'm sorry, but don't threaten me!" His voice was rising at the end.

In control again, Wildig, musing aloud, said, "Maybe Ah oughta brief the commissioner on this possibility."

"Hold on, Bill," interrupted Hollister. "You know as well as I do that Paul is nothing more than a 'caretaker' here—a marshmallow—a lapdog to the politicians. Any hint of this to him would put the whole thing in the hands of the politicians, and it would definitely get all over us.

"Besides, if you really want something done, we all know you're better off approaching Sergeant John McCormick in the COP's office."

Wildig started to protest mildly, saying, "Well now, you jus' listen—"

But Hollister, warming to the task, continued rapidly, "I know that you have to play the old politics game, but you know in your heart that what I said is gospel. We, in the street, know that there's a particular sergeant in the commissioner's office who has more say-so over policy than anyone else, including the commissioner. Get real, Bill!"

The waitress unobtrusively delivered the round of drinks and hesitated for a moment, wordlessly. Her fortunate presence enabled both men to calm down.

Noting her hesitancy, Hollister turned to the waitress and inquired, "Need something else, love?"

"Not really," she replied quietly. "But excuse me. I was asked to serve you this the next time you stopped in."

Having said that, she brought her serving tray down from her shoulder.

A spotless gleaming metal plate covered by an equally shiny dome lid was ceremoniously deposited on the table close to Hollister by the young lady.

"Where did this come from?" asked Hollister, looking first at the presentation and then at the presenter. "I didn't order anything that would be served in this fashion."

Hesitantly the waitress confessed, "Some detective stopped by before and prepared this for you, instructing me to wait until you had finished at least two drinks before delivering it. Did I do wrong?"

"No," replied Hollister with a grin, "you did fine."

"What the hell is that? How come you get such special treatment?"

Slowly, still smiling, Hollister shook his head and slid the offering closer to his friend, saying, "You really want to know? Go ahead, uncover it!"

Suspiciously and very gingerly, Wildig grasped the domed lid by its top handle, raised one end, and peeked very carefully under the edge.

"What the frig is that!" he exclaimed, dropping the dome back down, once again covering the contents.

This time, the server reached over and, with deliberate ceremony, removed the polished dome from the plate with a flourish.

"Ta-da," she and Hollister sang in perfect chorus.

There on the plate were half a dozen washed and sparkling romaine lettuce leaves, carefully arranged in a perfect circle. Spaced around the lettuce were several bright red cherry tomatoes garnished with parsley.

Placed precisely in the center of this beautifully arranged gift was one crusty hard gum-encased hair ball!

"What the . . . !" exclaimed Wildig.

"Revenge," said Hollister calmly. "Isn't there a note?"

"Yeah," said Wildig apprehensively as he picked up a small envelope and removed a piece of paper.

"What it say?" snickered Hollister.

Wildig read aloud, "'The ball is in your court.' That's all it says."

Then turning to calm the waitress, who was now caught somewhere between tears and a nervous laugh, Hollister said, "Relax. It's an inside joke. As Jimmy always says, 'Don' vorry 'bout a ting.'"

He then recounted the occurrence in the restaurant in Green Acres, where this grotesque item was placed in his pocket, and his subsequent retaliation via the envelope sent to Animal ostensibly from the commissioner's office.

At the conclusion of the story, the waitress said, "I guess that's that. You're even now."

Hollister laughed. "Oh no! I'm not even until I'm ahead by one! This is not the end!" And he dropped the "item" back in the envelope, which he thrust into his pocket.

With a broad smile, Hollister said, "We're ready to order now, but take your time. Make it a leisurely dinner, OK?"

"Fine," she smiled back. "Appetizer?"

Hollister, without looking at the menu, ordered baked stuffed clams, a plain salad, New York sirloin steak (medium rare), baked potato, corn on the cob, and plenty of hot bread and butter.

Wildig, also from memory, ordered shrimp cocktail, Greek salad, rare Romanian steak, french fries, and string beans.

The waitress, a true professional, wrote nothing down, but listened intently to each man's order. "Perhaps a little wine with dinner? Jimmy sends his compliments and would like to buy you some wine."

Hollister looked across at Wildig and, getting a slight affirmative nod, replied, "Very fine. We'll have some Rose when the entree is served, please."

"Yes, sir." She smiled and left to place the order.

The brief respite gave Wildig an opportunity to recover from the shock of the allegation made by Hollister.

"Back to bid'ness. Where do ya wanna take this thin', George?"

"I'll tell you, Bill, I would like to continue the surveillance of Tamarago and also take a good look at Gerlich's activities with another team. That would probably mean putting two more teams to work on them. I think we should act quickly to take advantage of the momentum we have going."

Obviously playing devil's advocate, Wildig countered with, "How would you account for the decrease in felony-arrest numbers if your people are gonna be playin' hide-and-seek? You realize, of course, that Gerlich checks those figures on regular basis and will notice any drop in numbers?"

"I've got that covered. He's only interested in total numbers, not in the production of each team individually. The guys not assigned to the tail will take up most of the slack by increased productivity, and the decrease, if there is any at all, will not be an appreciable one."

"You've got an awful lot of confidence in those guys, haven' you?"

Hollister grinned at that statement. "You bet your ass. My job is on the line with this caper!"

"An' maybe mine too!"

"I'll not burn you with this, Bill, believe me. I could use a little assistance in one area though."

Skeptically Wildig said, "Yeah?"

Hollister was glad at this point that they had imbibed a few drinks before he had to broach this subject.

"You know that when I request special equipment, it has to be approved by Gerlich. Well, I need some stuff that you can order without anyone raising an eyebrow; after all, you are the top banana!"

"Stop blowin' smoke up ma ass and make your point, pal."

"I need," continued Hollister quickly, "a couple of nightscopes and a surveillance bug or two to be used in the tailing of the cars. I don't want to have to punch out any taillights to make them easier to spot. Both of these guys have been around enough to be aware of that old trick. Good equipment is the answer to this situation."

The unmistakable Greek accent of the owner, Jimmy, broke into their conversation.

"Hey, Unca' George, Chief Willie! How ya doin'? Ever'thin' hokay?"

"Fine."

"Fine, Jim."

Jimmy spoke broken English so rapidly and ran his words together most of the time that guesswork played a big part in carrying on a conversation with him.

"Unca' George don' like Grrrik salad, but Chief Willie do," he said loudly to the waitress across the room.

"I know, Jim, I know," she replied patiently. "It's all taken care of."

"Don' vorry 'bout a t'ing. I take good care of you boyz. You know, Chief, ever'body in the county know dis man. Unca' George the mos' pop'lar cop around." And he slapped Hollister on the back with a resounding whack.

"And by now, the most recognized one in the restaurant," said Hollister, pretending to be annoyed.

"Hoo, boy," sighed Jimmy. "Did it again, eh? Make too much noise, huh?"

"Yes, Jim." Hollister laughed. "You're a great cook and clever as hell when you bargain at the Fulton Market, but you sure can blow it for a couple of guys who want anonymity."

Softened by the several drinks, Wildig launched into a story—a trait with which all who knew him were familiar.

"Speakin' of which," Wildig began, "several years ago when ah was commandin' officer of the precinct and George was mah administrative assistant, ah wanted anonymity every once in a while, 'specially when a noisy and irate group of homeowners would come ta the station house ta vent their problems on the CO.

"They never expected a black man to be the commandin' officer, so before they came stormin' into the office, ah would take off mah jacket, pop open mah tie, and grab a push broom. Then ah'd put mah head down and casually sweep mah way past 'em and down the hall, right under their noses! They would automatically gravitate to mah main man here, who had ta take the brunt of the complaint until they calmed down.

"Worked several times, didn't it, George?" asked Wildig, tickled by the story despite the fact that he had told it dozens of times.

"Sure did, Bill, but I had my ways of getting even with you."

Laughing, Wildig assumed a darky accent and replied, "Oh, Lordy, yo' surely did."

Looking at Jimmy, Wildig chuckled. "Like the time Ah heard him yelling at someone over the telephone and walked over ta listen, 'cause it was so unusual. All of a sudden, he yells into the phone, 'Oh yeah, lady, well, screw you!' Then he listens for a second or two and says, 'Mah name, bitch? Mah name is Wildig, W-I-L-D-I-G.' He spells mah name and slams the phone down!

"I say, 'Holy shit, man, wa' cha' doin'?

"Then Ah look and see that the bum was talkin' on a dead line ta no one at all! Everyone in the office knew what he was doin'. Everyone 'cept me. Ah could see mah stars goin' down the drain.

"Then we had a great time and still got the job done!"

To the waitress, Jimmy laughed. "Give the boyz 'nother round. Don' vorry 'bout a t'ing. I'm goin' back in the kitchen now, an' make your steak jus' like you like 'em."

Hollister and Wildig smiled warmly at the hurriedly departing back of Jimmy, apron strings flying in his wake.

"He's really a fine guy," spoke Hollister, "but he sure needs a man with some polish, a maitre d' to meet and greet the customers."

Wildig agreed with a vigorous nod and then chuckled. "His food is fantastic, and the place is packed every night in spite of him and his dirty apron."

With the tension of the past few minutes broken, both men laughed easily. The meal was eaten with gusto, and the two close friends' conversation was light and frivolous, undoubtedly aided by the several adult beverages of choice they had consumed.

During the after-dinner, cordial and serious again, Wildig said, "Gimme tomorrow to get hold of the equipment you need, and you can pick it up at ma office. A couple of scopes and bugs is all that you need, right?"

"For the time being, anyway, Bill," and in response to a grimace by Wildig, added, "and I'll not ask for any more than I need to do the job."

"OK, Ah'll charge the stuff out to the Major Felony Squad, which will make the acquisition seem routine. Be careful, George, it's your call, just don' let this blow up in ah faces!"

"Don't worry, I'm going to be cautious. If my sketchy information is even close to correct, what we have here is fifty pounds. of garbage in a ten-pound. bag. All *Today's News* has to do is kick it, and the stink will be all over the police department for years. I intend to protect us all from that!"

Wildig's voice became almost apologetic as he said, "Ah've gotta put a little hook on your request though."

"Uh-oh. OK, shoot."

"If'n you don't come up with somethin' more concrete on Gerlich by the time the terrorism schooling is completed, ah want your word that you'll drop this investigation and toss what you have to the Treasury guys."

Hollister looked his friend deep in the eyes and said with a big grin, "You got it, man."

Wildig responded with a wry grin of his own and a wide slow shake of his head.

"When ah asked you to put this special squad together, ah never thought it would lead to this! Don' wanna piss on your parade, but ah sure hope you're wrong 'bout Oscar!"

Hollister's friendship with Wildig had paid off again, just as it had done on several other important occasions over the years. None of the previous occasions, however, were anywhere near as important or sensitive as this one, and they both knew it.

They parted with warm eye-to-eye contact and an extrafirm handshake, in contemplation of the difficult times that were ahead of them.

"You'll keep me fully informed?" was Wildig's closing remark.

"You betcha," said Hollister, whose spirits were sky-high.

Chapter 14

Bugs and Tails

With the approval for the special equipment he needed given by Chief Wildig and the items now in his possession, Hollister set about assigning another team to the surveillance.

Just as the teams had nicknames for Hollister, some not too flattering, he too had names for his personnel.

The third team assigned to the tail was comprised of Chris Beckert (nicknamed by Hollister, Chris Vicious) and Frank DePetri (nicknamed Fisherman Frank).

Chris was actually not a vicious person in the literal sense of the word, but was so tenacious that once involved in an investigation, he refused to let go, and thus Hollister's focus was on this tenacity—transposing it to Vicious—only because it seemed more colorful.

Chris Vicious was solidly built, something like a fire hydrant, as broad as he was tall. Very, very strong, he knew how to use that strength.

Fisherman Frank had his name derived from the indisputable fact that he spent all of his free time involved with water and boating activities. Single, he was he coach of a girl's rowing team sponsored by a local pub, an activity that used up a great deal of his off-duty time.

As the result of all the rowing, coaching, and whatever other physical activity was included in the club's function, Fisherman Frank had large overly developed forearms and biceps. Although the nickname Popeye was considered, Hollister decided that it was not appropriate.

He was the one most familiar with laws and procedures and had in fact at one time been the precinct's crime analyst, assigned there by Hollister.

Assignment to the special enforcement team was a reward for a job well done in that capacity, a practice that Hollister implemented frequently. He was a very successful motivator.

It was obvious that the men were unwavering in their loyalty to Hollister, but even so, there were nicknames, used from time to time, aimed at him that were not very flattering. Most of them were names that Hollister was not supposed to be aware of but was.

At various times, Hollister was referred to as the Boss, the General, that Dutch bastard, and even at one time was referred to by the Animal as Doctor Mengele!

Because of the extreme pressure and often danger under which the teams performed on a daily basis, familiarity was permitted and encouraged. Lots of jokes and clever banter were constantly passed back and forth.

However, a thin—almost invisible—line was maintained by Hollister beyond which his men knew they dare not venture. Nor did Hollister.

Assistance with personal problems . . . and policemen and their wives have many . . . was always forthcoming from Hollister. But they had to ask. Hollister never pried into personal lives and only took unilateral action when the job performance of an individual was affected.

Chris and Frank were filled in by Hollister regarding the purpose behind the assignment and its possible ramifications. They were as disappointed and upset as Hollister with the possibility of a dirty cop in their midst. And as he anticipated, his perceptions were accepted wholly and unquestioned.

The nuts and bolts of the surveillance were imparted to the other two teams involved at one of the many meetings.

The placement of the surveillance bugs was directed by Hollister and the course of the investigation set.

After her first visit to the A & P Store in Baldwin, Mrs. Gerlich returned to her home with an additional package.

Unknown to her, a portable electronic transmitter had been attached to the underside of the metal support bracket of the rear bumper of the chief's personal vehicle.

A tiny red dot and its beep were clearly discernable on the receiver unit placed on the passenger side floorboard of the current chase car—car 1242. The tone sounded once every two seconds, and the red dot appeared on a three-inch square grid screen on the monitor board. Over a short distance, the dot moved on the network as the transmitter changed its location in relationship to the receiver in the police vehicle—the two operating on the same frequency.

A similar device on a second frequency was attached to Sal Tamarago's Cadillac parked outside the Green Tree Restaurant one evening.

The electronic bugs could not be seen by the subjects of the surveillance unless one was to lie on his back and slide under the rear bumper of the vehicles.

Each working team had also been supplied with a nightscope to aid in the surveillance.

After only a few days, it became obvious that Gerlich used his personal vehicle infrequently. Invariably, when he did, however, it was when he planned to leave the county at nighttime or on weekends.

It also became evident that when he was operating the department vehicle assigned to him, it was his custom to do a radio check immediately upon leaving home.

Thus, "Car 32 to headquarters on a radio check, how do you read me?" And the Communications Bureau reply: "Loud and clear, Car 32" became the signal for the teams that Gerlich was on the road in the department vehicle and the surveillance teams need not be concerned with his personal vehicle and its tell-tale bug.

Near-disaster struck one of the teams involved in keeping Tamarago's vehicle under surveillance one evening.

The team watched the red dot on their screen as Sal labored his Caddy through Valley Stream traffic toward what the team believed was going to be a visit to Snow White in Great Neck.

Suddenly a second dot appeared on the monitor screen, signaling the approach of Gerlich's private auto to within the approximate three-mile range of transmission of the signal.

The additional two-second beep began to sound.

The detectives suddenly and surprisingly now had two lights on their grid screens.

Meanwhile, Tamarago had driven his Caddy again to Hendrickson Park and had stopped in the spacious parking field, which at this hour was practically empty.

Tom Henderson, his eyes widening in surprise, exclaimed, "Holy shit, Rich, we're right between the two of them!"

Rich, who was driving, stopped the surveillance vehicle and shouted, "Get the hell out! Get out! Watch them on foot while I get this car the fuck out of here!"

"OK! OK!" was Henderson's response, and he leaped out and sprinted for cover behind a stand of trees lining the perimeter of the parking field.

Stack quickly left the area and, undercover of the heavy traffic flow on Merrick Road, tried to keep track of the red blips on his monitor.

Henderson, meanwhile, was facedown in the grass behind the park's decorative trees, peeking at the tarmac parking field a scant hundred feet away.

Sure enough, Sal stopped the white Caddy in the center of the field and, with the engine running, waited, nervously puffing his cigar.

Stack, in the chase car, had his eyes glued to the monitor. He saw the first blip cease movement, but the second one kept approaching, closer and closer to his location. Suddenly he remembered that there was a second team in the undercover taxi following Gerlich's vehicle who could unwittingly follow the car right into the almost-deserted parking field.

That would put Gerlich's Buick, Tamarago's Caddy, and H and H Taxi staring at each other in the previously vacant lot!

He snatched at his radio transmitter and, through the car-to-car channel, practically shouted, "Break off, H and H, break off." Hoping that the other team, Frank and Chris, were monitoring the channel as agreed. He would know in a few moments as it looked on the monitor screen as though the two blips were about to collide.

After what seemed to be an interminable length of time, the blips merged into one red dot on the surveillance screen.

Rich's mind was whirring. "Shit . . . shit . . . shit! Did we just bust this whole caper?" he mumbled to himself through gritted teeth.

At the same time, Tom Henderson, lying in the grass, had a similar thought. He imagined himself lying there watching the whole process as the three vehicles entered Hendrickson Park and blew the whole bit as they converged on each other in the parking lot.

Tom maintained his vigilance as the Caddy's engine idled roughly, waiting. A few seconds later, the grey Skyhawk entered the park and, after a slow careful cruise around the perimeter, pulled up to the driver's side of the Caddy. Tom held his breath in anticipation of H and H taxi blundering unaware into the midst of the clandestine meeting, putting weeks of surveillance right down the shitter.

He continued to observe the two vehicles and the operators, wishing he could creep up and eavesdrop on their conversation. He knew that it was not practical, but earnestly wished it anyway. He was acutely aware that the operator of the Skyhawk was looking nervously into his rear-vision and side-vision mirrors, alternating these glances with quick looks from side to side.

Boy, he thought, *if that's not the look of a guilty man, I'll eat it!* and tried to dig himself into the turf for more concealment.

His chest began to burn, and he realized that he was still holding his breath. His temples were throbbing, and tiny flashes of light were darting about behind his eyeballs as he tried to release the pent-up breath in slow, easy stages. Any untoward sound now would certainly attract the attention of Gerlich and Tamarago, that's how close to them he was.

His lungs were screaming for more air, and he wanted to gasp out loud and suck in the precious commodity. He was about to be forced to do just that when the sound of the engines of the two vehicles picked up from idle and began to move away. He raised his head and blinked his eyes several times to clear his blurred vision.

The unanimated conversation was ended, and both vehicles left the parking field. The Caddy went north through the rest of the park and exited at Hendrickson Avenue from where it headed west.

The Buick left via the Merrick Road exit and, after some difficulty with heavy traffic, turned left and headed east. The full meeting, Tom estimated, lasted only about three minutes.

After the vehicles had left his field of swimming vision, Tom stood up from his bare concealment and gulped in air eagerly as Rich zipped up to him in the chase car.

"Get the fuck in," he said excitedly. "Got to get back on Sal's ass. Let's go, let's go!"

A choking Tom leaped into the front seat, and the car surged ahead as they tried to make visual contact with Sal's white Caddy again before it could be swallowed up in the heavy city-line traffic.

Tom, still uptight, said, "Man, that was some shit! I thought sure we blew the whole fuckin' thing right there. Boy, were we lucky!"

"Lucky your ass," exploded Rich. "Luck had nothing to do with it. I was the one who called Chris and Frank over the radio car-to-car and told them to break off. That's what saved our asses, not luck!"

Chapter 15

Row, Row, Row

Back in the "tail" mode, but still concerned, Tom picked up the radio microphone and, staying on the preselected car-to-car band, said, "H and H, what's your location?"

The lighthearted voice of Fisherman Frank came back over the radio, "Back in the race, man. We've got the grey. Pretty close though, eh?!"

"Thank Christ they picked the Buick again all right," sighed Tom. "Jeez, Hollister would have had a shit fit if we had blown this thing then."

"Relax," said Rich. "We didn't blow it, and there's no need for the boss to know how close we came. Just plain forget it!"

"Are you serious?" said Tom incredulously. "Keep something from "the General"? I don't think so! He'd know somehow, just like he knows about every other fuckin' thing we do wrong. I think we ought to level with him all the way."

"Yeah, I suppose you're right. You can't con a con man, and he's one of the best. I'll fill him in," replied Rich.

"I thought so," grinned Tom. "You won't pass up this opportunity to let him know how you saved the fuckin' day out here!"

"Points is points," retorted Rich, "and Lord knows I need 'em."

"Oh great! I crawl around in the goddamn grass holdin' my fuckin' breath, and you make the points." Tom laughed good-naturedly. "Don't seem right somehow."

Tom, carefully studying the surveillance monitor, said, "I've picked up the Caddy again. Seems like he's about a block away."

"You know," said Rich, glancing first in the rear and then in the side-vision mirrors, "I've got a funny feeling that *we're* being tailed."

"What the fuck are you talkin' about? You drink your lunch today?"

"No. I mean it. Just this evening, I've got this funny feeling. I think I've seen a dark blue Olds a couple of times tonight. Take a look out of your side mirror and see if you can spot it."

Then impatiently in response to Tom's attempt to swivel around to look over his shoulder, "Don't turn around! Just check the mirror, dummy!"

Tom studied the line of cars behind them for a minute.

"What is it with you? You getting paranoid or something? I don't see any Olds."

"I'm telling you I've seen one a couple of times," said Rich, highly annoyed. "I don't see the damned thing at this very moment, but I swear I've seen it a couple of times!"

"Uh-huh," returned Tom sarcastically.

"Oh, fuck you," said Rich. "Watch the Caddy."

This time, the Caddy did not head back to the restaurant, nor did it head for Great Neck. Instead, via a circuitous route, Sal crossed Linden Boulevard and then headed east on the Southern State Parkway, commuter traffic and all.

Falling into the second lane, four cars behind Sal, the two detectives were now more concerned than they had been in a while.

"This guy is doing something very different tonight," said Rich. "He's never done this since *we've* been on him!"

"Yeah, you're right there," agreed Tom. "And the other teams never said anything about him going on the Southern State before."

It was easy to stay with the Caddy at this point because of the heavy commuter traffic all around them. It was next to impossible to change lanes and the traffic was proceeding at a snail's pace, the usual rate of speed at this time of the evening.

After some fifteen minutes of slow-motion driving Rich said, "Hey, give Chris and Frank a yell. See what they're up to, we may need some more eyes."

Into the car-to-car mike Tom said, "H and H. What's your status?"

Back came the voice of Frank DePetri. "The 'grey' has gone back to the barn. We're free as the proverbial bird. What's up?"

"We're eastbound on the Southern State, approaching Nassau Road, can you assist us?"

"Be glad to handle your problem for you. Keep us posted on your location. Rest easy . . . the Navy's coming to the rescue," said Fisherman Frank.

Tom, slightly annoyed, toyed with the idea of saying "Up yours," but instead said, "10-4, Fish," into the radio.

Softly, to no one, he said, "Wiseass!"

Rich concentrating on his driving and trying to figure out what Sal was up to, did not reply.

The exits continued passing by slowly but in great numbers as the commuter procession continued.

Tom noted, "Nassau Road. We're near Hollister's house."

The Meadowbrook Parkway junction come and went next with the usual delay of merging traffic. Tom took this opportunity to say brusquely, "Eastbound, passing Meadowbrook Parkway interchange," into the radio.

He received a Fisherman Frank, "10-4," in response.

The exits continued to creep by: Merrick Avenue; Newbridge Road; Wantagh State Parkway; Seaford-Oyster Bay Expressway; all slipped by as did the minutes.

After a time they were coming upon Route 110, which seemed an appropriate time to announce their location, since they were crossing the county line into Suffolk County.

The same "10-4" was the only response from Frank and Chris.

Tom, seemingly uptight again and staring at Richie said, "What the fuck is this guy Sal up to. We're riding through Suffolk County now. Ain't we supposed to notify headquarters that we've crossed the line into another county?"

Rich compressed his lips tightly in a grimace and said hotly, "Yeah sure! That's a great way to let Gerlich know what we're up to! Don't be such a chicken-ass. We cross over the Queens line every day when we're tailing this guy or one of our 'druggies', so why should the Suffolk line be any big deal? Christ!"

"Yeah but . . . ," Tom said seriously and then broke into a laugh. "Just wanted to see what you'd say, partner. I don't give a rat's ass where Sal goes. Hollister said to stay with him and that's what we'll do. Maybe he'll go to Connecticut, or better yet for you, Fire Island."

"No such luck," said Rich with a chuckle, "the steamer to Connecticut and ferries to Fire Island only run during the height of the summer."

"I thought you'd know all about how to get to Fire Island," laughed Tom.

"Bend over and I'll tell a lot more, you hump," replied Rich without humor.

Grinning at his successful attempt to rile Rich, Tom picked up the transmitter again and said, "Still eastbound at the Sagtikos State Parkway Interchange."

"We gotcha'," was Frank's response.

Surprised, Tom spun and looked out the rear window saying, "Where the hell are you?"

"Look to your starboard, bub, about eight cars to your stern," said Frank, the humor evident in his voice.

"Never mind that shit," grumbled Tom. "Where the fuck are you?"

"OK you landlubbers. We're eight cars behind you in the right-hand lane."

At this point Sal steered his Caddy into the extreme right lane, slowed and appeared to be searching for an exit. Fifth Avenue and Commack Road exits passed by, but at Islip Avenue Sal's right directional started blinking and he exited at that point, southbound. Fortunately, traffic was still moderate to heavy and gave the two following vehicles sufficient cover.

That cover lasted all the way to Montauk Highway, where the Caddy made a right turn and then an abrupt left turn on Bayberry Lane, apparently heading for the beach area south of Montauk Highway.

Traffic volume was light at this intersection. Still fearful of being seen, however, Rich continued to the next left turn and made it, pulling to the side of the roadway as he did so.

Some thirty seconds behind him came H and H Taxi, which also pulled to a stop.

Chris sprinted out of the driver's side of the taxi and ran to Rich's side. He said quickly, "We've tailed him this far before. You guys take a walk down the street where Sal turned. Stay on the radio. We'll get back to you soon."

With that comment ended, he ran back to the taxi and drove past them on a course one street parallel to the one that Sal had taken.

Tom and Rich looked at each other in surprise for a few seconds, then shrugged and pushed their electronic receiver under the front seat out of sight. With darkness fast approaching, Rich grabbed the nightscope and Tom grabbed the portable radio unit.

They secured the vehicle and walked back to Bayberry Lane and headed south. It was a straight road leading directly toward water in the distance.

After a few hundred yards, the roadside took on a seaside look, with sand dunes becoming evident, covered by the environmentally helpful very tall grass—sea oats.

Eventually Bayberry Lane "T" intersected with Beach Front Drive. The two detectives on foot were on the horns of a dilemma now as to which way to walk, left or right?

Looking to the right they could see the dim lights of a marina or boatyard in the distance, but not much else except sand and water. Beach Front Drive was just that—a practically deserted roadway that ran directly through the sand facing an expanse of water known as the Great South Bay.

They decided to walk to the left of the intersection.

After a few steps, they were greeted by Chris's voice over the radio, "Good choice. Keep going."

Startled, their eyes were darting in every direction, searching for the place of concealment from which the voice emanated. They felt and looked foolish as they spun around on the sandy roadway, searching, searching.

"Why don't you look out on the water, you dickheads?" crackled the voice of Chris, not bothering to disguise his glee.

Both detectives, who strongly disliked walking, glared simultaneously out across the sand into the bay. There, big grins clearly visible in the fading light were Frank and Chris in an old paint-peeling rowboat, gliding smoothly and effortlessly along the shoreline.

"What took you so long? We've been waiting for you," said Chris in a hoarse stage whisper as Frank pulled his right oar and pushed with his left, causing the rowboat to perform a graceful 360-degree turn.

"What the hell are you assholes up to anyway?" growled Tom into the radio.

"Watch your language, please," teased Chris, "or we won't save your onions."

"C'mon, stop playin' your stupid games. We're supposed to be finding Sal, you boob," said the still-annoyed Tom, "not stealing rowboats."

"Our 'Cruise Director' has already found him. His car is parked in the driveway on the east side of a beach house down the block about one-fourth mile from you. We've rowed past there twice, so we don't want to go back. It's the next house you guys come to, all white with a boathouse on the left side and a wooden walkway along the water's edge. Just stroll close enough to get a house number and a layout and we'll meet you back at the car. *Bon voyage*. We're off to the Continent."

Frank spun the boat in another pirouette and took off back toward the marina, forearms and biceps bulging as he accelerated.

The two detectives headed for the beach house pointed out to them. Finally, they thought, they had a line on Sal's activities and the adrenaline started pumping.

The darkness, which was now upon them, gave good cover and they decided to take a good look at the house from behind the sand dunes that blanketed the entire area.

Noting that the house number was 538, Rich trained the nightscope on the house, looking for signs of occupancy.

The scope with its eerie greenish glow and black crosshairs tended to give the area under surveillance a phantom-like appearance. All things were in varying shades of green, from very pale to ominously dark. Making scientific use of whatever small amount of light was available, the unit made it possible to watch a subject's activity if he were in anything but total and complete darkness.

As night covered the house like a blanket, interior lights began to blink on in various parts of the house. Shades were drawn, but it was obvious that there were several people in the beach house, which stood ghostly by itself east of the sand dune line.

All at once, the front door was thrown open and Sal, along with three other men, exited and went to the rear of the Caddy. The two detectives flung themselves hurriedly onto the sand.

The car's trunk was unlocked by Sal and he leaned in and removed the reams of paper he had stored there. Each man stood by while Sal piled their arms with packages of paper. One by one they struggled through the beach sand with their burdens along the side of the house and then along the wooden walkway that led to a sort of boathouse in the rear.

After several trips, the trunk of the Caddy was apparently empty and the boathouse was secured with a padlock inserted through a hasp.

The two lawmen burrowed deeper in the sand dunes, scarcely breathing and listening to their own noisy heartbeats as they felt the nearness of Sal and company.

It was torturous not being able to scratch or swat the gnawing insects and both men began to have second thoughts about their career choice.

Sal's people stood near the Caddy's now closed trunk and conversed for a few minutes. It was apparent to the watching detectives that the men were having some difficulty communicating. It seemed as though Sal was giving instructions, or at least conversing with one man, who in turn seemed to convey Sal's words to the other two. Muffled voices but not words were all that the two Detectives could overhear, and try as he may, Rich could not lip-read any words through the use of the hazy scope.

Shortly, two of these men turned and reentered the beach house, leaving Sal and the "interpreter" deep in conversation.

"Damn," whispered Rich in Tom's ear, "wish we had an omnidirectional mike here to pick up that conversation."

Tom nodded vigorously, but silently, in agreement.

Abruptly, the remaining man with Sal turned and retraced his steps alongside the house, down the wooden walkway and after unlocking the door, disappeared inside the boathouse.

While the detectives breathed in a shallow, deliberate manner, Sal strolled idly around the parked Caddy, stopping to light yet another cigar.

Once again, the glow from the lighter bathed the immediate area more than the detectives expected and they both cringed, expecting Sal to look beyond the light patterns and discover them.

He didn't, this time.

In about ten minutes the "interpreter" returned, carrying a large brown folder tied shut across the center. A few more words were exchanged as Sal accepted the envelope and placed it inside the Caddy on the front seat.

The two men parted with a handshake, the unknown man returning to the house and Sal laboriously putting his fat body back into the Caddy.

As Sal backed his car out of the driveway and the red glow from his tail lights started back along Beachfront Drive, Rich whispered hoarsely into his portable radio, "The Caddy is leaving. Pick him up, guys. We'll join you ASAP."

"Right-o," was the reply from "Fisherman Frank" over the radio, volume down.

The ride westbound on the Parkway took only forty minutes since the bulk of the traffic was moving east. This permitted the surveillance teams to lay back a couple of miles, keeping tabs on Sal by use of the electronic bug and screen, guaranteeing that they would not be discovered.

Once back in the vicinity of the Valley Stream restaurant, the tail was turned over solely to Tom and Rich in car 1242.

Chris and Frank left to shake up the local druggies and keep the activity numbers high enough to avoid Gerlich's close scrutiny.

Tamarago returned to the regimen the surveillance teams knew so well. He went through his duties at the restaurant as though nothing different was happening in his life, until very late that same night.

Chapter 16

Heating Up

At that point, using a route heretofore never traveled by him and his following "blood hounds," he drove to the Village of Hempstead. His immediate destination turned out to be the bus terminal.

For many years, this terminal has been the meeting place for every kind of criminal imaginable—druggies, hookers, thieves and bad guys in general. All sorts of criminal activity flourished there, with very little interference from the locals.

Tom and Rich could only watch from a distance as Tamarago parked his Caddy and paid a local hoodlum to "watch" his vehicle.

Just inside the dim terminal entrance, Tamarago met with a flashily dressed young black man. It was impossible for the detectives to overhear any of the conversation and could only watch the actions of the two from a distance.

The conversation was fairly brief and apparently to the point, judging by the animation on the part of the black. As he talked, he was very demonstrative with his hands, waving them constantly, often dangerously close to Sal's face. It was his way of trying to intimidate Sal.

The action of his hands was easy enough for the detectives to follow, since every finger on both hands, except for his thumbs, were decorated with flashy, heavy gold rings. His neck was encircled by so many gold chains it was impossible to count them. Ironically, the biggest and heaviest was a gold cross handing halfway down his chest!

All the while he was engaged with Sal, he paced in a sort of stiff-legged combination of limp and swagger.

"Hey, man, ya got the 'queer' ya promised?"

"Well, almost," Sal replied.

"Almos'? Wha' da fuck ya sayin', man? We had a' 'greement that ya'd have it tonight!"

Tamarago opened the bow securing the large brown envelope that he carried tucked under his arm. The same one he had just picked up in Islip.

He pulled the sides apart to allow the black man to look inside.

"I have several thousand one hundred dollar bills right here. Take a look."

The black reached in and removed what appeared to the detectives to be a bundle of currency held together with a wide band.

He fanned through the bills several times and with an exaggerated movement, dropped the packet back in the envelope in a theatrical, larger-than-life movement.

At this point he tapped Tamarago on the chest with three fingers extended stiffly and placed his face within inches of Tamarago's.

"Hundreds?" he said with disdain. "Wha' da fuck ya tryin' ta do, take a'vantage of a poor dumb nigger? Hundreds don' go so fuckin' good in ma neighborhood. If ah wanted 'em, Ah could rip 'em out of yo' honky hands right now!"

Tamarago retreated step and said, "Hold on. The plate for the rear of the twenties has been delayed but we'll have them ready in a week or so. I'll be in touch as soon as they're ready, I promise!"

"How much dis gonna cost me?"

"No change from our original discussion. I and my partners have to get our ten points."

"Seems like a lot, with me takin' mos' a' da' risk, but OK."

Sal said, "I'll be in touch."

The black nodded briefly and sauntered away, using the same cocky stiff-legged gait he had used before.

Tamarago returned to his Caddy, which had remained undisturbed curbside and drove away—back to the restaurant, with the envelope still in his possession.

Tom and Rich followed along, fervently wishing that they had been privy to that conversation. They began to put a report together relative to the evening's startling developments.

It was extremely late by the time everything had been put into some sensible chronological order, and they mutually decided to wait until Hollister had had an opportunity to arrange his schedule for his upcoming terrorism schooling before submitting the report.

Things were certainly beginning to heat up.

Chapter 17

Complication

Another significant event began during the period while Hollister was exploring Hofstra University preparing for the Olympic Games assignment.

Thousands of miles away, an oil tanker was being loaded in Tirane, Albania. This tanker and portion of its contents were to play a massive roll in Hollister's life in the very near future.

The contents of the Greek-owned cargo ship were paid for in drachma and started on their long journey down the Balkan Peninsula through the Adriatic Sea. The ship, the size of three football fields, made its lumbering way on the Ionian Sea to the Mediterranean where it skirted Sicily and headed for the Straits of Gibraltar.

Once through the Straits of Gibraltar, its bow was pointed into the North Atlantic, battling the historically rough and stormy waters and plowing its way through the West Indies and the Caribbean, arriving at Santiago, Cuba, where most of its oil cargo was off-loaded, contrary to existing sanctions.

Within a few days, the huge ship passed between Cuba and Haiti via the Caribbean and steered clear of the Bahamas and Bermuda. Through the Sargasso Sea it made use of the currents of the Gulf Stream and made way for New York and the untamed southeast coastline of Long Island, where it would eventually affect Hollister.

The rambling journey covered some 14,000 kilometers.

The "oil" tanker had been especially constructed with a portion of its cargo area lead-lined to preclude the United States spy satellite from detecting the true cargo. It was also constructed to prevent the Coast Guard from becoming suspicious of the contents through radar contacts.

Once anchored off the eastern portion of the south shore of Long Island, the cargo belly belched the contents onto smaller, swift-moving boats. Quick work was made of removing the contraband weapons from the gut of the disguised tanker and depositing them ashore.

From there they were moved by light trucks and automobiles to a prearranged location in Islip, New York, a quiet beachfront community.

A shorefront bungalow was to be the weapons' place of concealment until the time was ripe for their terrifying use by criminal groups and eventually against Hollister and his Elite Corps.

Chapter 18

Training Begins

April 16, 1984—0900 hours

The enormity of the task confronting the police department was made vividly clear when Hollister arrived at the community college building designated for the antiterrorism schooling. Uniformed top brass seemed to be almost everywhere while three-piece suit types took up the remaining space.

In small groups, the early arrivals indulged in the morning ritual that was the lifeblood of law enforcement—coffee and—.

Two huge urns would be filled and refilled all day long for as long as the schooling was in session. Boxes and boxes containing a variety of donuts and small cakes (the "—" in "coffee and—") were to be purchased fresh every morning and delivered by the civilians in the Special Services Bureau.

Hot water and tea bags were provided for those who preferred tea and did not like the coffee, which was always strong. They were laughingly described as people who squat to pee.

A long table also held all the supplies required, and at the end was a small container where donations were deposited to guarantee the continued supply of "—."

The opening several hours of the training session were devoted to a general orientation of the supervisors.

Remarks by the Games director, Mike Milsett, painted a sterling description of past Games and the rapid growth in interest and participation in recent versions. The presentation, Hollister noted, strongly resembled

Gerlich's side of the conversation when he telephoned Hollister in January. Both probably came from early press releases promoting the upcoming Games.

Milsett stated that the cost of the Games had been estimated at three million dollars. In order to get the project rolling, seed money had been granted from the United Cerebral Palsy of New York City and from the United States Olympic Committee.

Hard cash was to be provided by the many cosponsoring organizations, according to Milsett. He then verbalized a long list of agencies and organizations involved in the project (i.e., Long Island Tourism Commission, National Association of Sports for Cerebral Palsy, and the United States Amputee Athletic Association).

The overview of the police department's responsibility was carefully outlined by the very articulate chief of detectives. He stated that the plans for security were already under way here, were better organized than those lain out for the Olympic Games in Los Angeles, California, but on a smaller scale.

He pointed out that hopefully, the Games for the Disabled would not have any of the jurisdictional problems plaguing the LA Games. The trouble there stemmed from the fact that there were more than a dozen jurisdictions involved, with none willing to give up jurisdiction to another.

In Nassau, all contiguous agencies had already agreed that this event was the baby of the County of Nassau and its 3,500 men plus police department. Interagency cooperation had been pledged by all.

The detective chief continued at length to remind the supervisors in attendance that the most obvious representative of the United States during the Games would be the police department. All foreign visitors would be observing the appearance and demeanor of the members of the department for the first time and comparing it to their own.

Gerlich's early admonition to Hollister, relative to "no beards, no boots, no nonsense" was brought to mind.

It was going to be difficult, he thought, *for the guys to play it straight after all the loosey-goosey capers in which they were involved on a day-to-day basis*.

The detective chief concluded with, "Positive or negative opinions will probably be formed about the United States as a whole based on their treatment and by the degree of professionalism displayed by this department."

With the pep talk portion consuming the first four hours, the distinguished group broke for lunch. The majority of the group had brown-bagged their lunch on this first day, not knowing what was in store for them. Many scurried round, making arrangements with acquaintances for lunch out on the town for subsequent days. Innumerable past friendships were renewed this day.

The final hours of the first day were taken up by discussions of preliminary plans for the breakdown of administrative responsibilities.

A very nervous headquarters captain described proposed plans for the communications network.

Two radio frequencies would be set up and monitored solely for the operation of the Games. He complained about the amount of radio equipment requested by the commanders of segments of the security detail and was greeted with a chorus of good-natured but derogatory boos from the group.

Portable charging units would be provided for the Games command post from which the Games site commander, transportation, traffic and crowd control units would operate.

The housing site, Hollister's command, being sealed off from most of the outside world by strict security measures and fences, would operate its own command post via the second of the two separate frequencies reserved.

The importance of the two command posts remaining in landline (telephone) contact as well as via radio was needlessly emphasized by the captain. He also overworked radio "courtesy," but made an excellent point by proposing that plain talk be utilized instead of the ten codes used in everyday radio communication.

This was, as one of Hollister's early reports had requested, to avoid any possible misunderstanding of intended meaning and possibly unnecessary repetition of voice communication to clarify statements.

The only code to be utilized was the phrase "code blue" in the event a possible defection was brought to anyone's attention. These two words would trigger a supervisor and response team being immediately assigned to the location and the alerting of the state department officials and FBI agents, who would be in reserve at the Games site command post. These latter officials would take charge of any defector transported to the command post.

Operation of the Games site command post was next to be outlined. Escort details to and from the various airports were to be handled from there, coordinated with the housing site command post. Hollister insisted that the housing site be appraised of any and all movement toward the dormitories or surrounding roadways in advance of their inception. There were no objections voiced.

These escorts would be handled by uniformed highway patrol police officers, both on motorcycle and in radio patrol cars. At least one uniformed officer would be assigned to ride on each bus used in transporting the athletes and support staff. This officer would remain in constant radio communication with the command post and have the capability of summoning immediate assistance should it become necessary. Radio patrol cars would be advising the command post of the location of each busload of athletes periodically as they made their way from the New York airports to the housing site.

Side trips to Roosevelt Field Shopping Center and Green Acres Mall, already requested by the representatives of several countries, would be handled in the same manner.

The Games site command post, housed in a former airplane hangar of the abandoned Mitchel Air Force Base, would be equipped to photograph and fingerprint every person authorized to carry the distinct coded security clearances. This monumental task was to be covered in greater detail later in the indoctrination segment.

Crown Control units would be held in readiness at the Games site command post to be dispatched wherever necessary. In conjunction with these operations, the hangar would house the capabilities of various other support organizations.

Deputy Chief Oscar Gerlich wound up the presentation for the day with a monologue regarding the housing site security.

With information garnered from Hollister's written reports and from their many personal meetings and telephone discussions, Gerlich made the housing site's importance very clear. All those present agreed that this would undoubtedly be the most vulnerable location for any untoward occurrences.

The possibility of noisy demonstrations by local radical groups against the foreigners housed at Hofstra University was pointed out. For that reason, along with the consideration of a terrorist incident, Hollister had requested other response teams be organized and held in readiness in the housing site command post. These units would be the second in the line of units that would respond to trouble areas.

Naturally, any investigation would be initiated by the first uniforms on the scene.

A small response team comprised of a combination of plainclothes detectives and uniformed police officers would then be assigned if the incident were perceived as more involved. Hollister proposed that the size of the response team, handled in this fashion, could be increased based upon the seriousness of the incident.

Eventually, specially-trained Bureau of Special Operations personnel, augmented by the FBI's Hostage Rescue Team, could be assigned if the incident escalated sufficiently to be termed a major incident.

Gerlich went deeply into justifying the necessity of assigning what on its face seemed like a lot of personnel to the dormitories and the surrounding grounds. There were no dissenting voices since all supervisors there believed the housing site to be most sensitive and vulnerable.

Gerlich's presentation with his businesslike demeanor and practiced voice impressed the attendees, most of whom were not aware that the signature at the bottom of the sheets from which Gerlich read was "G. Hollister."

April 17, 1984—0900 hours

On the second day, many hours were spent discussing the types of handicaps involved in the games.

The subject of sensitivity to the handicapped was presented by persons from the community of the handicapped. The lecturers, some handicapped themselves, pointed out in substance, that the members of the police department assigned should endeavor to develop positive attitudes.

Proper attitudes and knowledgeable awareness help nondisabled people in their contacts and relationships with people who have disabilities.

Attitudes which are insensitive and filled with prejudice will produce poor relationships. Careless use of terms and words in referring to the handicapped may reveal biases or negative attitudes and therefore a glossary of terms was discussed. Just as some well known four-letter words are offensive to the public, so are some words, phrases and actions used in relation to people with disabilities.

Hollister's notes included such no-no words and comments as:

afflicted: Is a negative term and suggests hopelessness

confined to a wheelchair: A person *uses* a wheelchair.

courageous: Disabled people do not usually consider themselves to be brave and do not want to be regarded as heroes

cripple: Creates a mental picture of a person who can't do anything; someone whom people would prefer to ignore

deaf and dumb, or deaf-mute: These out-of-date terms were used to describe a deaf person who also could not speak. Many deaf or hearing impaired individuals can speak, albeit their speech may be difficult to understand. Deafness does not make a person dumb or ignorant.

disease: Describes a contagious condition. Most disabled persons are as healthy as anyone else.

gimp: A word used to describe someone who walks with a limp. It's a definite put-down.

(Hollister could feel a slight blush to his cheeks as he wrote that comment, remembering his thoughts when Gerlich first approached him regarding the assignment.)

> poor: Describes a person who is without funds and one to be pitied
>
> retard: some disabled people are at times considered awkward, but this does not mean that they are retarded.
>
> spastic: Some disabled people lack coordination, but this is only a product of the physical disability and should not be ridiculed.
>
> suffering: To say that someone suffers from a disability means that he or she is in constant pain as a result of the disability. This is rarely the case.
>
> unfortunate: This implies unlucky, unsuccessful or socially outcast. Whether or not luck had anything to do with a person becoming disabled, he or she wants to be regarded as a real, likeable person.

Also included in Hollister's second day notes, were comments made by the New York State Advocate for the Disabled, who stated that when encountering a disabled person, feeling people should:

1. Offer help—but wait until it is accepted before giving it. An unexpected push could throw the wheelchair user off balance.
2. Accept the fact that a disability exists. Not acknowledging a disability is similar to ignoring someone's sex or height. To ask personal questions regarding the disability, however, would be inappropriate.
3. Talk directly to the disabled person, not to someone accompanying him.
4. Treat a disabled person as a healthy person. Because an individual has a functional disability does not mean the individual is sick. Some disabilities have no accompanying problems.
5. Keep in mind that the disabled have the same activities of daily living as you do.
6. If a disabled person asks for help and you want to help but do not know how, *ask* the disabled person the best way to give assistance.

Then in an obvious attempt to lighten a very burdensome topic, they added:

7. Never pat a wheelchair person on the head while standing next to them. Considered very tacky.
8. Never threaten to walk away after pushing a wheelchair out into the middle of Hempstead Turnpike, leaving the wheelchair in traffic, not matter what the provocation.

This discussion ended on a humorous note when a noticeably disabled cerebral palsy man interjected a one-liner. He recalled the time he ran away from home as a child. He said that he was found three weeks later at the end of his driveway.

Along that line, attendees were reminded that occasional difficulties in communication were to be expected, but that they should rely on their own natural sense of courtesy, consideration and common sense to get them past these incidents.

Many of the supervisors in attendance inwardly harbored some of the feelings that the representatives of the handicapped tried to dispel—that is, that the handicapped were lesser people to be pitied, feared or ignored. This attitude, it was presented, came from a fear of someone who is different, or more simply put, from a lack of knowledge about disabilities.

Educational programs have failed to eliminate negative stereotypes and unfeeling attitudes still prevail despite the fact that almost 15 percent of the population has a disability of some sort.

This whole lecture line brought into focus Hollister's personal contact with Jake Barrano, a headquarters maintenance man.

Barrano spoke with the coarse, throaty monotone peculiar to deaf persons who had learned or partially retained the faculty of speech. Often, because they can not hear and modulate their own voices, deaf speech is breathed airily out, making it difficult to understand. This was not the case with Jake, who although he squeezed his sounds out from his diaphragm, made his words fairly easy to understand.

He had amazed Hollister some years earlier when, after Hollister had raised his voice angrily at Jake, he rasped, "Don't yell at me, Lieutenant, it wasn't my fault."

Hollister stopped in mid-sentence and inquired, "How did you know I was yelling?"

Jake squeezed out, "By the way the cords in your throat stuck out!"

They had a good relationship and from time to time would tease each other.

On one occasion, Hollister started a sentence facing Jake's eyes, which was the way their conversations had to take place, face-to-face.

Almost through with his remarks and at a crucial point, Hollister began to very slowly and nonchalantly turn his head to the left. This, in turn, started Jake leaning to his right in order to keep Hollister's lips in sight. Farther and farther he leaned, until he was ultimately forced into a sidestepping sprint to keep up with Hollister's head movement. The game always ended the same way, with Jake exploding in a series of frustrated epithets and threats.

Other times, Hollister would merely mouth his words, not using his voice at all. Jake would read his lips easily until in mid-sentence, Hollister would insert a meaningless word, usually in Spanish or German.

This would immediately confuse Jake and he would wave his hands wildly and choke out, "Whoa, wait. What was that? What did you say?"

Jake Barrano had his ways of frustrating Hollister too. As conversation between them took place and Hollister was about to make a point or conclusion with which Barrano was not in agreement, Jake would simply turn on his heel and immediately face away from Hollister. There was absolutely nothing to be gained by talking to the back of Barrano's neck, while his shoulders shook in glee! Now it was Hollister's turn to be frustrated.

This game would end in the same manner—with threats and indignant behavior, but both men liked and respected each other and no bad feelings ever remained.

* * *

Members of the police department's Public Information office were next on the agenda, pointing out that a special office would be provided for the media in the Games command post.

When the subject of personal interviews of the foreign athletes was brought up, Hollister had a very strong opinion on the procedure.

He stated that because of the tight security around the housing site, he thought it best that no television or radio personalities be permitted clearance into the housing site. Anticipating that there would be many, many interviews requested, Hollister believed that TV and radio crews, which tend to be very large at times, should not be wandering around the housing complex with their large amount of remote and taping equipment, which could feasibly be used to conceal a public safety device. Permitting those wanderings would require that police personnel be assigned to search the equipment and further, to escort the group of working press.

He proposed, instead, that portion of the Games command post be designated for use by these crews. Handled in this fashion, the housing site need only be notified of who was to be interviewed, and this person or these persons would be escorted through the housing site security and deposited at the Games site interview area, thus not tying up his personnel for any protracted period.

Hollister believed firmly that the fewer people permitted to "wander around" in the housing complex, the safer all the athletes and staff would be. He always thought that the media were given too many concessions, and as a result, they usurped many more. He maintained through to the end of the media discussion that they should not be given Security Clearance One which would gain them access to the housing site unescorted.

The bottom line was that further meetings between the media people and Chief Gerlich should be held. Hollister felt somewhat betrayed by this turn of events since he felt that Gerlich would probably succumb to pressure and abandon Hollister's firm stand on the matter of interviews and he would be forced to assign police personnel to escort TV and radio crews all over the complex.

Hollister believed further that it was best to have the media on your side, but not at the expense of "giving away the store," as he thought Gerlich would do.

Anyone who has been witness to a live occurrence with attendant live press coverage knows that reporters, in their zeal to beat competitors behave like anything but normal, prudent human beings.

An often-quoted politician once equated media behavior in search of a hot story to that of sharks in a feeding frenzy.

As if to give more credence to Hollister's position, a *Today's News* reporter foolishly engaged Secret Service representatives in a test of strength.

During the preliminary discussion of the coverage, media and security of the president of the United States' impending visit to the Games, the Secret Service stated that the president would be coming into the site via helicopter. Herb Brown, representing *Today's News* at this conference, stated the newspaper's intention to cover the landing of the President from the air with their helicopter.

This statement was greeted negatively but politely, as was their attitude throughout the discussions, by the Secret Service members present. They informed Brown that it was procedure for them not to allow any other helicopters but theirs in the air around the President at any time.

Brown reiterated his statement with regard to the newspaper's air coverage and was *again* told that it would not be in the best interest of the Secret Service or the President to permit that to happen.

Brown continued on still another occasion to insist that *Today's News* would be on hand with their helicopter and was informed again, this time a little stronger by the Secret Service, that it is against their procedure to permit that.

Still, having already been denied permission for a "flyover," Brown continued to bring the topic up at every opportunity.

Finally, losing patience with the pushy Herb Brown, the Agent-in-Charge said, "Let's put it this way. If there is any other helicopter except ours in the air near the president's, *we will shoot it down!*"

That ended the discussion once and for all in a very definite manner, with Brown retreating from the meeting, only slightly embarrassed.

Public safety devices, (police radio jargon for "bombs") and threats were next to be discussed.

A sergeant from the Bomb Squad passed out preprinted schematics of rooms and buildings of varying shapes. The proper manner to be utilized in searching rooms and offices was carefully diagramed and would be utilized in searching and "sanitizing" the dormitories before the athletes and staff would be housed.

This search, therefore, would of necessity be the final step before admission of the foreign athletes since it would signal the start-up of the housing security detail as each building was searched and certified as bomb-free by the special squad. It was also decided that in view of the many complex buildings to be searched on the Hofstra campus, the recruit class currently in training in the police academy would be used to supplement the Bomb Squad personnel.

"Carefully supervised" was phrase often used in the discussion, but with a joking referral to the recruits as being expendable.

As a matter of fact, after lunch a well-drawn cartoon was being passed around among the esteemed group. The cartoon depicted a very young recruit "searching" for a bomb by tentatively tapping his foot ahead of him, face contorted in expectation, all the while holding his hands over his ears!

New York City and Nassau's bomb-sniffing dogs would be assigned throughout the Games. Hollister requested and received permission to have a bomb-sniffing dog and handler assigned to the housing unit on a twenty-four hour per day basis at the housing site command post.

The final speaker for day 2 was Deputy Inspector Ray Cramdon. Inspector Cramdon was the commanding officer of the Bureau of Special Operations, an unorthodox unit which operated very much like Hollister's special enforcement teams but on a very large scale. Cramdon was one of the young, new breed becoming more visible in the department.

He was a personable young man with more degrees that a thermometer, who seldom mishandled his wide knowledge. He was the loosey-goosey type that BSO needed to lead it. Hollister liked him and their relationship was very good—working in such a similar manner as they did.

Cramdon, comfortable at the microphone, detailed the special training his men had received from the FBI, especially for these Games.

Patterned after the FBI's Special Response Team, BSO had been outfitted with specially made black jumpsuits and boots similar to those worn by US Paratroopers. Multi-pocketed, the tight fitting jumpsuits enabled the personnel to carry extra ammunition, smoke grenades, tear gas and in some cases, antipersonnel grenades.

Topped off with riot helmets fitted with face shields and with POLICE painted in yellow in large letters across the backs of the jumpsuits, the unit of one hundred handpicked men was impressive indeed.

Their training included rappelling from the roofs of Hofstra's dormitories by rope in the event of a hostage situation, enabling them to enter through any of the windows decorating the dorms.

Coupled with that activity was training in the use of concussion grenades, in which the FBI had already become expert.

The purpose of these grenades, nicknamed "flash-bangs," was to produce a horrific, deafening explosion together with a huge amount of smoke to disorient and confuse the occupants of a room without inflicting personal injury.

At this point, the heavily equipped antiterrorist unit could burst into the area and quickly take custody of the incapacitated occupants.

Already proficient in the use of sawed-off shotguns, BSO had enhanced their sniper capability by adding what was dubbed a Precision Firearms Team.

Several members of BSO had been issued specially equipped high-powered rifles with scopes and had been thoroughly trained in their use. These men were on call to the scene of any hostage negotiations. Should negotiations fail, these men were prepared to make one very accurate "head shot" when and if circumstances permitted. Thus, the life of a hostage could conceivably be saved by this special unit and their sniper scopes.

The FBI's Hostage Rescue Team, who had trained Cramdon's BSO personnel, would remain on standby throughout the Games. Each member of the FBI's fifty man, fully mobile unit, was proficient in the handling of a .357 magnum revolver, the Armed Forces M16 rifle and the shotgun.

Unique, however, to this special unit was the MT-16, a twenty-six-inch long, five-and-a-half pound submachine gun which could spew out projectiles at the rate of eight hundred rounds per minute.

This weapon, obviously, was a vast improvement over the old .45-caliber Thompson submachine gun, which weighed ten pounds, twelve ounces, was thirty-three and a half inches long, and punched out six hundred rounds per minute. The Thompson, the weapon which had made the FBI famous and impressive in its day, was not modern enough for this elite unit of FBI agents.

Although they preferred low-key arrests, the FBI was prepared for any eventuality at the Games and pulled out all stops for that purpose.

Painfully aware that the loss of all hostages and all but three terrorists in the 1972 bloody battle at the Olympics in Germany was due mostly to one important factor, the FBI was determined to come up with solution to that problem.

The problem presented itself at Fuerstenfeldbruck, a military airport where Bavarian sharpshooters lay in waiting for the terrorists to arrive in their commandeered helicopters holding nine of the original eleven Israeli hostages.

The plan devised was to get each terrorist in a sniper's cross-hairs as they transferred from the helicopters to a fixed-wing aircraft and take them out simultaneously.

The plan was flawed, however.

First, the ever-present media people leaked information about the airport plan and roadways were clogged with rubberneckers trying to get there to witness the spectacle. This, in effect, produced a "blockade" preventing much needed manpower from reaching the scene of the ambush.

Second, the incomplete intelligence provided to the Germans did not account for *all* the terrorists and an insufficient number of snipers were on hand to take out the terrorists one-on-one.

Third, and possibly the most important detrimental fact was that the snipers did not have the capability of notifying each other when a terrorist was in their sights, precluding a coordinated shot—of primary importance to a successful "shoot" in this instance.

Since that disaster took place, the FBI has devised a system of lights controlled by individual snipers at each weapon.

Nicknamed STAMS (Sniper Target Acquisition Management System), the newly devised procedure would provide the snipers with the high degree of synchronization required.

After each FBI sniper activates a button lighting a signal on an electronic master display, which indicates that he has acquired his assigned target in his scope, a short countdown is initiated.

This guarantees a controlled shoot—all targets are hit simultaneously.

It is believed that the inability to obtain this coordinated shoot over a three-hour period at the airport was the cause of the loss of all hostages and most of the terrorists in 1972.

The three terrorists, it must be pointed out, were freed two months after committing this horrible deed, in exchange for passengers on an airliner hijacked by another "Black September" group.

After their release, they went to Tripoli where they were welcomed as *heroes!*

Chapter 19

Undercover Van

During a scheduled break in the lectures, Hollister, always on the alert for an edge, approached Inspector Ray Cramdon, commander of BSO, who was lolling about like everyone else, awaiting the next lecturer.

"Hi, Ray," Hollister began. "May I speak with you alone for a second?"

"Sure thing, George,"

Hollister steered Cramdon away from the bulk of the class and spoke in a confidential tone as they strolled along toward the outside of the hangar converted to a classroom.

"I have a very special investigation going with some of my guys on a difficult surveillance. We've been on it for a few weeks and have switched every vehicle at our disposal in and out. It's getting to be a bitch! I'd like to be able to throw something radically different at this guy for a change—something like your Lighting Company Van. What do you think of the possibility of doing that? Borrowing the van, I mean."

Cramdon hesitated thoughtfully for a moment and replied, "I'll have to get back to you on that one, George. I'm not sure of the availability at this moment. Since I've been assigned to this school, I've left everything in the BSO office up to Lieutenant Joe Van Kirk. How the hell do you find time to schedule surveillances and set up the housing site detail at the same time? You must be busier than an electric rabbit at a dog track! I'm certain that we can work something out, provided Joe has not assigned it somewhere. It's a fantastic piece of equipment for surveillance work and is in almost constant demand by my people. Incidentally, you know Lieutenant Van Kirk, don't you?"

"Hell yes," grinned Hollister. "Joe and I went through the police academy together as recruits. As a matter of fact, myself and a couple of other guys handcuffed Joe to a water pipe outside the classroom on a break one day as a gag. He got his ass chewed out for not reporting on time for the lecture when the class proctor had to leave the lecture room to unlock the cuffs and free him from the water pipe.

"We received our punishment a couple of days later when we had to run three extra laps around the outdoor pistol range, while the rest of the recruit class laughed at us!"

"Serves you right." Cramdon laughed. "Tell you what. I'll call Joe this afternoon and talk to him about scheduling and let you know—then you can talk directly to him about it. If we're not using it, I don't see any reason why you can't. Just bear in mind that it is *our* unit and our assignments that will have to take precedence over whatever you have going. If we need it, you'll have to give it up," he cautioned.

"I have absolutely no problem with that, Ray," said Hollister. "We won't hog it, and we'll take good care of it. Thanks for the cooperation."

"That's OK, George. I know that you wouldn't ask for it if it weren't needed. As I said, I'll get back to you soon."

Both men hurried back into the hangar-classroom, Cramdon searching for a telephone and Hollister for a cup of caffeine-loaded coffee.

Shortly after the class was called to order and the lecture again under way, Hollister glanced across the room in Cramdon's direction and found him looking back. Inspector Cramdon held his hand up briefly with his thumb and forefinger curled into the OK sign.

As Hollister nodded, the fingers switched into the shape of a telephone, with little finger and thumb extended and the other three fingers curled into his palm while he held his little finger to his mouth and his thumb to his ear.

Hollister grinned again and nodded acknowledgement, thinking, *I'll be on the phone as quickly as I can, that's for sure!*

His spirits were soaring at this point. *The van is just what the doctor ordered!*

The van he was maneuvering for was made up to closely resemble a Long Island Lighting Company repair vehicle, although it could not bear those words on its side. It was painted yellow with six-inch-wide red safety stripes painted in a diagonal pattern across the rear. It was equipped with a large amber revolving dome light on the roof of the cab and blinking amber caution lights on all four corners of the vehicle. The ladders in position on the roof carriers and the red traffic cones stuck carelessly on a projection on the front bumper completed the illusion.

It was showing all the signs of wear and tear accumulated over the years with numerous rusty dents showing here and there, including a rather seriously damaged right front fender.

The driver's compartment was closed off from the rear of the vehicle's interior by a large partition, and the seat upholstery was showing its age from high use. From all outward appearances, it was a well-used and abused Lighting Company van, just like dozens of others legitimately being used by LILCO.

Once one got past the outward cosmetic ugliness of the van and passed into the rear compartment, an astounding change took place!

All glass installed in the windows and doors on the sides and rear was one-way glass. The detectives on the inside could look out and observe or photograph subjects without any distortion or glare. On the other hand, persons looking casually at the glass from the outside could merely see what appeared to be lightly smoke-tinted glass.

The complete interior, however, was painstakingly designed for maximum efficiency—state-of-the-art surveillance equipment!

A well-organized shelf was suspended from the wall separating the rear compartment from the cab facing toward the front. It formed a desk that housed a base station for portable radio communication. A swivel chair and pedestal microphone stood in readiness in front of a reel-to-reel tape recorder. All conversations in or out of the van, once the recorder was voice-activated, were preserved on tape for review and critique later.

Each portable radio assigned to this vehicle was equipped with a coded crystal. Each one was serial numbered so that when the send button was depressed, the computer identified the sender and projected its number digitally on a lighted panel in front of the operator of the base station console. There could be no misidentification of voices in this fashion.

Storage compartments for the M16 assault rifles, sawed-off shotguns, and scope-equipped sniper rifles were built into the side of the van. Low jump seats strategically located at the glass windows completed that side of the van.

The other side was also equipped with a series of locked compartments. Some of these compartments held spare ammunition for the heavy firepower secured in other lockers. Another installation held additional walkie-talkies hooked up and constantly being recharged for immediate use. Window seats for observation purposes were also built into this side.

A clothing locker held blue jumpsuits as well as short jackets with POLICE emblazoned in yellow across the backs. A bulky full-body armored suit and helmet were also in readiness.

It was a thing of practical beauty for surveillance teams or for the Precision Firearms team because it was *so* prominent that it became invisible.

Another vehicle, smaller but similarly equipped and made to resemble the dull green New York Telephone Company trucks, was available for telephone tap and pole-climbing surveillance.

Hollister was positively euphoric as he made arrangements with his friend for the van. His next step was to contact the surveillance teams and instruct them to meet him in the parking lot of the station house, where the van would be secured and the teams brought up to speed as to its use.

The first five days of schooling proceeded as scheduled, with lecture following lecture, and training film following training film.

As the first week drew to a close, Hollister, strongly feeling the remorse and repentance of his lapse of self-control with Patty, vowed to make amends by flying to Florida and Joy for the weekend.

A quick telephone call, and he was on his way.

* * *

It was a little after 10:00 PM when Hollister disembarked from the aircraft and walked quickly across the tarmac toward the terminal building. Daytona Beach Regional Airport, tiny when compared to John F. Kennedy or LaGuardia in New York, had no portable lounges to meet the doors of the arriving aircraft. Instead, passengers walked down rollaway steps and into the terminal buildings to a luggage area inside.

Hollister had been coming to this little airport long enough to remember that at one time, the luggage recovery area had been located *outside* the terminal building, and he could recognize the progress the airport and the whole area was making.

He was reluctant to accept this growth because the city in which his retirement home was located was beginning to grow too rapidly. The governing body, a city council, seemed too eager to accept the population explosion without thought to the consequences in terms of needed public services.

The police department of Port Orange, numbering some twenty-six men in 1979 when the population was fifteen thousand souls, was now hard-pressed to handle the needs of forty-five thousand citizens. Other services suffered just as badly.

As he stepped through the doors from outside, his eyes began searching the faces of the people waiting there. Suddenly Joy broke through the front edge of the group that had formed a rough semicircle around the doors and ran toward him.

Her arms flew around his neck eagerly, and he, in turn, locked his arms around her. He grabbed his own hands behind her back about waist high and hoisted her off her feet. Their bodies touching everywhere, Hollister spun her in two graceful pirouettes and placed her gently back on her feet—still locked in the embrace.

He was suddenly very glad he had taken this weekend between terrorism classes to go to Florida.

"Oh God," she breathed into his ear. "It seems like an eternity since you've held me that close." And she kissed him on the neck.

"Easy, sweetheart," he said, looking around, embarrassed, "lots of people here."

She replied, "I don't care. I'm just so glad you're here with me again. How I've missed you!"

The crowd swirled around them, each small group of individuals engrossed in their own little drama.

Joy and Hollister were completely involved with each other as they walked arm in arm toward the parking field and their Astro Van waiting there. Joy clutched his arm tightly with her hand, and he could feel the warmth of her body against him even as they made their way toward the car. He was grinning like a schoolboy.

The twenty-minute ride to their home from the airport was punctuated by many terms of endearment spoken by each of them. Joy chattered on about her stay in Stuart and the well-being of her folks there. Those comments and a description of her job at the bank took most of the trip home to describe.

A feeling of serenity flowed over Hollister as they entered their newly constructed home again after all these months. The burden and anxiety of his assignment seemed to melt away merely by entering this gentle atmosphere.

Joy had aired out the house, and it was comfortably cool and fresh inside. He took his carry-on luggage into the master bedroom and placed it on the bed to unpack.

"Oh no!" Joy said as she picked it up and tossed it nonchalantly on the floor.

Fixing her gaze on Hollister's eyes, she gently guided him to a prone position on his back on the bed. She opened the top two buttons on his shirt and began kissing his chest as each opened button exposed more of his body. He lifted his head and watched the top of her head for a moment or two and then lay back with a deep sigh.

She breathed, "Too tired after your trip?" Her voice muffled by his body.

"Never happen!"

What followed then rivaled their first honeymoon night together, ten years earlier.

* * *

Chapter 20

Thunder Thighs

A few hours after Hollister had disembarked the aircraft in Daytona Beach, back in New York, Sandra Wertz walked wearily out of the restaurant in Green Acres. She entered the darkened parking field and headed for the employee's section of the lot, several hundred feet away. A few autos remained scattered in the customer lot even at 3:15 AM.

Cheaters, she thought to herself, except for the tractor trailer parked nearby.

Sleeping, was her thought on that one as she scrunched down inside the raised collar of her coat, covering her ears from the biting cold early morning air.

As she walked, shoulders hunched and head down, an automobile motor purred quietly into operation. With its lights extinguished and the engine barely humming, the vehicle was almost noiseless following a parallel path to Sandra's as it rolled ever so slowly just to the rear of her peripheral vision, one aisle to her left.

Her weary brain was rehashing the evening's happenings from being stiffed by one table of diners, to the more than generous gratuity extended by another. Her thoughts dwelled, however, on the recent sarcastic and pointed remarks being voiced by Sal Tamarago.

He had made remarks to her about her cop friend, referring to her developing relationship with Tom Egan. She worried also that Sal had discovered that she was feeding information to Egan regarding Sal's activities as clandestine as they were. From his surly attitude, Sandra believed that

Sal was close to letting her go, despite the fact that she was probably the most efficient and hard-working waitress in the whole operation.

She really needed this job which paid, tips and all, pretty well. Her feelings were that perhaps she should cool it with Tom and not risk her livelihood since Sal was openly displaying his displeasure toward her. But then, on the other hand, who was Sal to stop her from whatever she wanted to do with Tom!

It wasn't like she wanted Tom to divorce his wife or anything. He was fun to be around and he was paying attention to her of his own free will. If things were so great at home, he wouldn't be reaching out to her for companionship, would he? Hell, he comes across a lot of women in the course of his job. If not her, certainly someone else would be taking up his time, right? Right!

She smiled to herself, triumphantly, in winning this strange debate.

At this point she had reached her auto, walked around the rear and was approaching the driver's side. She fumbled for a moment in her handbag for her keys.

This slight miscalculation cost her valuable seconds in the darkness of the parking field.

The silent auto following her suddenly screeched into high speed, ripped into a tight right turn and cut across the white painted parking stalls. Skidding to a hard stop very close to her driver's door it gave her no room to escape and she jammed the key vainly toward the keyhole in panic.

A large hand knocked the key ring from her grasp and spun her roughly around. A rock-hard fist crashed into her face snapping her head backward into the edge of the roof of her own car, abruptly cutting off her scream. She remained just conscious enough to taste her own blood in her mouth and to feel another thunderous blow to her jaw.

Her legs gave way beneath her and she slumped downward, unconscious.

* * *

Meanwhile in Florida, morning came all too quickly for the lovers who had made the most of their night together after months of being apart.

Breakfast on the screened patio was in order and they sat in the warmth of the Florida sun, talking, hands touching frequently. Joy expressed her concern over not being able to contact Hollister on several occasions and how she, in near panic, had enlisted Elaine's help at the restaurant to contact him.

Joy said, "It's so nice to have you here with me again, babe. I feel so good when you're here and so empty when we're apart. You are everything to me and I am so sorry that I was so stubborn about not going to New York with you."

Hollister, relaxed in his chair, coffee in hand, said, "Except for missing you so much, it probably worked out for the better that way. The assignment takes a lot of my time and you would have been alone even more frequently than you have been in the past. I didn't realize that I would be this busy with the assignment when I accepted it."

"I'll be so glad when it's over," replied Joy, "and we can get on with our lives together."

"Me too, sweetheart. It won't be long now. We're in the homestretch with this assignment.

"How about thinking about a trip to Hawaii? That way we can get reacquainted with each other. Besides, you've always wanted to go there!"

"Really?" Joy said with her girlish enthusiasm. "I've always wanted to go to Hawaii—it's so beautiful there all the time!"

"Uh-huh. That's what I'm told. Let's get some brochures and put together a couple of weeks there, hitting a few islands. OK?"

"Oh that sounds just wonderful!"

"Besides," Hollister continued, "that will give you something to look forward to and the time will seem to go by faster. I'll leave the preliminary details up to you—prices, tours, whatever."

"Sounds great to me. Monday I'll call Port Orange Travel and . . ."

She was interrupted by the ringing of the telephone.

"Damn," she said firmly. "I hate the sound of that thing. After that last call from the chief, every phone call sounds like trouble. The tape is on—don't answer the phone, babe."

Hollister grinned and walked to the answering machine and looked down at it. "Makes you wish Don Ameche had never invented the telephone, doesn't it?"

The phone rang three times before the tape kicked in, repeating the prerecorded message in Hollister's voice:

"You have reached the home of George and Joy. We are currently in the heated spa being slowly turned into prunes. When we get out and get the wrinkles pressed out, we will return your call. Leave you name and number after the tone. See ya in a bit."

"Don't do it, please," Joy pleaded with both her eyes and her voice as Hollister reached for the receiver and then stopped, hand in midair.

Suddenly he reached out and lifted the phone to his ear in silence.

Heavy with urgency, the voice of Pat Connors rumbled through the earpiece. "Boss, Pat Connors. If you're there, pick up the phone. If not, it is very important that you call me as soon as possible at home!"

He studied the inanimate instrument for a few seconds and then Pat's voice continued.

"They've found a body!"

Hollister's hand shot out and punched the *stop* button, releasing the tape.

"Pat, it's me! What the hell are you talking about? What body? Whose body? What's going on?"

"Thank Christ I got a hold of you," said Pat. "I just got a call from Animal. He told me that a body was found in Green Acres parking lot early this morning, pretty well smashed up. ID in the clothing and handbag makes it Sandra Wertz."

"Who?"

"Sandra Wertz! Thunder Thighs! Egan's connection in the Tree's Restaurant. You know!"

"Oh yeah, now I know who she is," Hollister said while waving his hand in the air in a writing motion. Joy, after years of practice was already handing him a pencil and pad of paper.

She peeked over his shoulder quizzically as Hollister wrote: "Thunder Thighs" then "Sandra Wertz" and "Tree's."

Seeing her inquiring look, Hollister punched another button, putting the conversation on the amplified speaker.

Then he asked, "What happened? Do you have any details yet?"

"Nothing firm yet, boss. Animal's on his way to the scene to check it out now, but it looks like hit-and-run in the parking lot. From what Tom said, she's pretty well busted up. There goes our informant on Sal!"

"Dammit! How's Tom taking it? How involved was he with her on a personal basis. Is he going to handle this without falling apart on us?"

Thoughtfully Pat responded, "Yeah. I think he'll be OK. It seems that it was pretty casual for both of them. I'm going in right now, so I'll give him a hand."

"Fine. Stay with it and be of whatever assistance you can, but don't tip that she was an informant for us. Not just yet, anyway."

"Right, boss," said Pat. "I'll be back to you in a while with whatever I find out."

"You do that Pal. I'll be here until tonight. I'll be taking the red-eye back to New York then. So long."

Hollister placed he receiver back on the phone, adjusted the machine back to the "*Answer*" mode and stood looking at his notes.

"Thunder Thighs?" he heard Joy say.

"Thunder Thighs?" she repeated. "What's that all about! What's going on?"

"Just a nickname that Tom Egan hung on an informant of his. Worked as a waitress in a restaurant in Green Acres. Tom and she had a little 'thing' going and they found her body in the parking lost of the restaurant this morning. Apparently a hit-and-run victim during the night. There's an investigation going on. You heard him. No big deal," he fibbed.

"If it's no big deal, why the hurry-up call? People are run down every day, and they don't call you urgently every time that happens. Who is Sal and what was Thunder Thighs informing you about?" she demanded.

"Look, it's just a little caper we have going on. We always have several. Nothing to get uptight about. I'll tell you all about it another time," he shrugged.

"Sure!" she said, exasperation in her voice. "You'll tell me after it's all over so that you don't get me worried about you! I was under the impression that you were handling that detail about the Olympics. Now you're involved with the Enforcement teams again and people like Thunder Thighs, the poor kid. You're taking on too much work and responsibility. Now I know why I couldn't get in touch with you. Please, honey, slow down—you are too precious to me to have anything happen to you!"

"Hey, love," he said lightly. "I'm a big boy now. Besides, I've been doing this job for a long time. I'll be fine," he laughed. "I'll know more in a little while when I hear back from Pat."

"There goes our weekend, *again*," she sighed in resignation.

Chapter 21

Shots Fired

In an attempt to defuse a potentially explosive situation, Hollister went outside and strolled along the screened patio which ran the width of the house, looking out at the trees and underbrush between the house and stockade fence in the distance.

Joy busied herself with the breakfast dishes, immersed in her own thoughts about the situation before them.

Hollister ambled along casually listening with great pleasure to the sounds of the woods. The sound of the soft breeze rustling the fronds of the palm trees and gently swaying the towering pines was relaxing after the brisk tempo of the past few months, all of which was made worse by the terrible news he had just received.

As he reached the farthest corner of the patio, two sharp reports echoed from the thick foliage beyond the fence. A hole tore through the screen and Hollister was instinctively ducking and diving toward the rug by the time the second hole split the screening.

Birds, frightened from their nesting places in the trees by the explosions, beat the air feverishly with their wings and darted crazily in all directions raising a cacophony of shrieks. The sound of the gunshots and bird screams echoed and bounced off into the distance.

"Stay inside," he yelled to Joy. "Incoming fire! Don't come outside—stay away from the window," and he started to crawl toward the sliding door opening to the dining area.

"Dammit," he whispered. "I don't have my gun here!"

"Just a second," Joy shouted and ran for the door leading to the garage.

In a moment, she was back, thrusting a .38-caliber Colt revolver with a two-inch barrel into Hollister's hand. "It's fully loaded," she said.

Hollister grabbed the weapon and sprinted outside again, staying low and below the top of the stockade privacy fence he had erected.

He hunched tightly against one of the four by four fence posts and peeked through the cracks in the upright pickets. He could see nothing but bushes and trees and underbrush and could detect no movement other than the wild flutter of birds still panicked by the resonating noise of the gunshots. Dislodged leaves circled aimlessly toward the ground.

After a brief period of study through the fence, he yelled to Joy, "Call 911. Tell 'em MOF has been shot at and is in pursuit in civilian clothing!"

After another quick look over the top of the fence, Hollister labored over and dropped to a crouch on the other side. By now the sweat was running own from his forehead, burning his eyes and blurring his vision.

Expecting any second to hear another gunshot, Hollister fervently wished that he had his 9-mm in his hand instead of the short-barreled "pea shooter" Joy had handed him.

That pea shooter! Where the hell did she come up with that? She never had a gun before. Gotta look in to that!

Still bent over low and using trees for cover as he ran from place to place, he tried to approximate the area from which the shots came. Zigzagging through the underbrush he could neither see nor hear any human sounds, nor did he hear an automobile engine start up by the time he reached a dry dirt roadway about one-fourth of a mile behind his fenced property. There were many, many tire tracks, but since this was obviously a secluded lover's lane, it was impossible to determine which may have been left from the night before or more recently made.

He worked his way back toward his house slowly, painstakingly checking behind trees and logs for any sign of an assassin having been there. No signs were evident in the peaceful, beautiful woodland and the only indication that there was anything amiss besides the birds still nervously hovering was the wail of a police siren as it approached his home.

Getting back over the fence onto his property was more difficult the second time he found out, since there was no adrenalin surge and no two by four cross members for footing.

When he dropped to the homestead side, puffing slightly, nervous perspiration dripping from his face, he was greeted by two Port Orange police officers and Joy, looking expectantly in his direction.

"No luck," he said pointedly, shaking his head. "Whoever the son of a bitch was got away from here in a hurry. You guys see anyone leaving in a panic along the roadway?"

The two glanced at each other and said, "No, sir."

"No cars? Nothing?"

"No. Not a thing. What happened here, anyway?"

Hollister looked carefully at the two officers. *Babies*, he decided. One was tall, about meeting Hollister's six feet two inches, but the other was his antitheses, barely five feet. Mutt and Jeff.

Both were extremely young and looked unseasoned in their dark blue uniforms with light blue trim on the trouser legs.

Shirts were custom-fitted over bulletproof vests and each had a radio attached to his left side with a transmitter seemingly nailed to his left clavicle. A .357 magnum bulged from each man's right hip. Blue baseball caps topped them both off.

Short man stood with his right hand nervously on the butt of his firearm and his left poised above the red "panic button" of his radio.

Tall man looked over at Joy and said, "We got a radio assignment here for gunshots, MOF involved. What's that supposed to mean?"

Hollister at this point was bending over dusting off the knees and bottoms of his trousers.

He looked up sharply and answered impatiently, "It's something we use up north when a police officer is involved in an incident. MOF means 'Member of the Force,' so that responding officers don't make a mistake."

"Oh? You're a cop? What about the gunshots?"

"C'mon over here and we'll all take a look," said Hollister and pointed to the far end of the patio where he had been walking a few minutes earlier.

"Should find something 'long about here," he muttered and stopped walking.

He fixed his gaze along the soffit of the house where it joined the screened porch.

"There! There!" he exclaimed, pointing just a little higher than he is tall. "There's one!" and pointed with his forefinger at a clean hole in the wood trim below the soffit.

A few seconds later, he said triumphantly, "And here's the other!"

Sure enough he had found both bullet holes within a foot of each other. The two officers and Joy leaned forward squinting at the places pointed out by Hollister.

"This one," he said, pointing at an irregular elongated hole made by one of the bullets, "was deflected by something and hit the wood almost sideways!"

Dropping that observation on them, he turned quickly and looked toward the opposite side of the screened patio. "See there," he pointed, "one hole pretty clean and the other very jagged and much bigger."

He walked swiftly out of the side door of the patio and then approached the fence slowly, measuring with his eye the approximate distance he should cover, aligning the screen damage and the bullet holes in the wood trim.

Suddenly he stopped and peered closely at one of the pickets in the 6' high privacy fence along the back of his property line.

"Yep," he concluded. "One of the slugs ricocheted off the tips between these pickets and wobbled a little sideways the rest of the journey. Probably the second shot.

"See here, this fresh chunk taken out of the pickets?! The shooter most likely saw that his first shot was a little high because of the fence, adjusted and caused the second shot to plink the tips of the pickets and deflect slightly!"

By now Hollister's little audience was following his every gesture and word carefully and solemnly, although in reality he was only talking aloud to himself.

The magnitude of the occurrence had long since gripped Joy, but she could no longer project the matter-of-fact attitude displayed by Hollister.

She grabbed him around the waist, "Honey, what's happening? That was a very close call. You'd better tell me the truth, what is it you're involved in?!"

Hollister lifted her chin up with his hand. "It's over now, sweetheart and I'm not injured. Everything's under control, it was only a *little* close," he lied, putting the best face on the incident that he could.

Tall man said, "Maybe you'd better tell us all what's going on here."

Short man said, "We had been told that there was a cop from New York building a house here. You retired?"

Hollister, arm around Joy's shoulders, led the way back to the house. "How about a cup of coffee for us, love, and I'll tell these officers my story?"

Joy glanced suspiciously at Hollister, not believing for one second that he intended to tell these officers the straight story. Nevertheless she set out cups, creamer, sugar and spoons on the patio table and poured coffee from the pot she had just made for breakfast.

Tall man spoke into his radio, "We are 10-97 at the 'shots fired' assignment. No injuries."

Interrupting his own transmission he turned to Hollister and asked, "You want a detective to come here?"

Hollister shook his head, "No."

"Negative 10-93. We're 10-10," tall man said into his radio.

"10-4," came a female voice in reply.

"It's really pretty simple, guys," Hollister began. "I'm CO of a plainclothes street crime unit up north, called special enforcement teams.

"We handle the major street crimes of pusher level drugs, gang-related violence, local vice conditions, sleaze like that. Apparently one of our 'clients' has taken exception to our activities and decided to do something about it and take a potshot at the unit's boss. He missed and ran.

"There are two chances of pursuing this matter further; slim and none and that's that!"

Short man, eyes wide, said, "That's normal? That's nothing?"

"No, not exactly normal, but it's not that unusual for some kind of retaliation to take place."

"Christ!" said Short man.

Tall man asked, "You going to need some kind of protection here now?"

"No. I'm going back to New York early in the morning, and my wife is going to reside with her mom and dad in Stuart for a while. There will be no one here for a few months. Maybe you could put this address on a vacant-house list of some kind and just keep an eye on it, routinely?"

"Sure thing," said short man. "No trouble."

"How'm I going to close this assignment out?" said tall man.

"Easy," said Hollister. "Tell 'em a stray bullet came out of the wooded area, probably from a hunter, and cut the screen. No one was injured, and the hunter left the scene. I'll take care of digging out the bullets, and I'll patch all the holes. Case closed—no problems!"

"Sounds all right to me," said short man, relieved to get rid of this hot potato. "Let's go and report in. We'll take another spin through the woods again. Thanks for the coffee, missus."

With that, both officers left, their anxieties eased.

As soon as the officers walked out of the door, Joy turned to Hollister, furious, and said, "You're not going to get rid of *me* that easily. Something big is going on here, and I demand to know what this nightmare is all about!"

"OK. Take it easy, babe," he replied, trying not to exacerbate the touchy situation. "I'm not really sure myself what we are on to, but between the finding of our informant dead and shots fired at me, it appears that we are on to something involving some very important people!"

"Darling," she pleaded, "please don't keep me shut out of this. Tell me the truth about the whole thing. What are we involved in?"

"You're not involved in this, sweetheart, and you're not going to get involved in it. As soon as possible, you are going back to Stuart. I want you to stay there until I tell you it's safe to come back! Understand?"

"Yes," she said hesitantly. "I understand that I can't stay here alone, but I do want to know about this caper you're on. What is it that has cost at least one life so far and an attempt on your life?"

"Look, babe, all I can tell you for certain at this point is that there may be counterfeiting involved with the mob, and perhaps a dirty cop thrown in for good measure!

"Beyond that, it's all conjecture, but things are beginning to make more sense every day."

He continued, "I'd rather have you tell me something about this 'peashooter,' the .38 short revolver you handed me before. Since when have you had a gun? Where the hell did you get it?"

Looking at the Colt revolver now in Hollister's waistband, she said, "A few weeks ago, I was under the impression that a man was following me to work at the bank every day. I saw the car in the parking lot a few times and became concerned that someone was in fact following me.

"I called the Martin County sheriff's office, and a deputy came by to check it out. When he drove into the parking lot and left his car to come into the bank, the other car left.

"I've had some weird things happen while I was down there," she continued, "including the theft of my underwear from the wash line behind Mom's house. It's frightening to think that someone is following you and to have some pervert doing Lord-knows-what with your panties, so I told the deputy all about my fears, especially when I have to go to the bank at night when the automatic teller machine malfunctions."

The thought of some panty-sniffer skulking around his lady angered Hollister, and what he considered an imposition by the bank people to have her respond at night to the teller machine did not help the situation at all.

It was a struggle for him to maintain his composure and not lose his temper, perhaps saying something that would hurt his lady, who was already on the verge of tears.

"Do you mean that *you* have to go to the machine when something happens? Where the hell are the people who get paid to do those things—the manager or some other bank official?"

"Oh, come on, sweetheart! The bank is only a block away from Mom's, so it's very easy for me to walk over there and check it out. I call the sheriff's department before I go, and they usually send a deputy to stand by while I fix it. It's more convenient for me than anyone else.

"Anyway, this deputy thought it would be a good idea for me to have a gun for the nights when he can't follow me home or a deputy can't get to the teller machine at the same time that I do.

"He's been very considerate and went with me when I purchased the gun. It's small enough for me to carry in my purse and makes me feel better at night when I'm alone. As a matter of fact, the other night, he stopped at the house and left a little canister of Mace for me to keep in the car!"

Hollister grunted. "Yeah, it seems to me that he's taken a personal interest in you beyond his job. Also seems strange to me that he would do this much for a stranger—he couldn't possibly do all that for every woman complainant he has! What makes you his special case anyway?! Is he trying to get into your pants, or what?!"

She wasn't sure whether he was joking or not, but was annoyed.

"Don't be so crude. Of course, he's not. He hasn't said or done anything out of the way, and I haven't encouraged him. He's just being considerate. Besides, he's so young! What would a baby like that want with me!"

"Young guys get horny too, you know"—sarcasm evident in his voice—"and you don't exactly look like Mother Teresa!"

"Stop that, honey! You know better than to think that I would let anyone near me. You are my man and always will be."

"I just don't want anyone looking up your *a-d-d-r-e-s-s*," he said, drawing out the last word.

"Another thing that bothers me a lot is the fact that you haven't had any target practice since I took you to the police range years ago. The state of Florida lets anyone purchase and keep a gun regardless of whether they know anything about guns or not. Small wonder that they have so many shootings down here.

"Which reminds me—I have to get those slugs out of the wood outside. I'll keep 'em, but the gun that fired them is probably in the Halifax River or maybe the Atlantic by now."

They clung to each other for a long minute, wordlessly, both realizing how close that incident really was.

Hollister went about the task of retrieving the spent lead missiles. Although he showed outward calm to Joy and the two policemen, when it came time to dig the slugs out, Hollister found his hands shaking with the realization that he was obviously in big trouble.

The slugs had landed mere inches from his head. The second shot would have most certainly struck him had it not been slightly deflected by the fence pickets.

Although it was not a real professional hit, it was close enough to make Hollister acutely aware that he was making someone extremely uncomfortable with his burning curiosity.

He vowed to himself to *turn up the heat even more!*

Hours had passed since Connors' startling phone call and Hollister was getting anxious to grab a flight and get back in the game. Although his information had been preliminary in nature, Hollister knew that Connors was digging for more as he made his preparations to go back up north, while encouraging Joy to make preparations for her return to her parents' home.

As could be expected, Joy was resisting his return to New York one day earlier than had been planned, but Hollister was insistent.

Until such time as he could get to the bottom of this widening investigation, he knew that his presence was as threat to her safety. Being around him, she could be the subject of some unwanted attention as the bad guys searched for ways to impede or halt his ongoing investigation.

Just before nightfall, Connors was back on the phone.

"Don't put this on speaker, boss. It's not something you would want your wife to hear."

"OK, Pat. It's not on speaker. Go ahead with what you have."

"Well," he started, "it has been established that it is in fact Sandra Wertz' body that was found."

"Was it hit-and-run, or what?" demanded Hollister.

"The medical examiner says that some of the injuries are consistent with an auto-induced death, but there are many others that just don't fit into that generalization."

"Like what?"

"Like—she was apparently severely beaten before she died, according to the ME. The kinds of facial fractures do not conform to the usual pattern found in vehicle deaths."

"Tell me more about these anomalies," Hollister asked.

"The ME says that the jaw fracture and fractured cheek bones were suffered hours before the body was supposedly hit by a car and were definitely caused by deliberate and forceful blows to the face. She was, again according to the ME, run over by a vehicle, but was probably dead before that happened.

"She had a great many internal injuries but the things that have the guys in the autopsy room upset are the burns!"

"Burns?" asked Hollister. "What kind of burns?"

"Some were the kind of burns caused by an electric shock tool, like a stun gun or a cattle prod. The small burn holes were spaced the same distance apart at each place to properly support that theory.

"There were lots of them, but that's not all. She had several circular burns between her legs high on the inner thigh area!"

"Holy shit! Tortured!"

"Yeah. Besides the electric shock tool, the bastards burned her with something almost round and very hot!"

"Matches? Lighter? Cigarette? What's their guess?"

"ME says that it was larger than a cigarette. Possibly a cigarette lighter from a car or maybe a cigar. About half a dozen times."

"God, Tom and I would like to get our hands on the sons of bitches!"

"Hold on, Pat," said Hollister. "I know what you're thinking, but we can't jump the gun now that we are getting closer. Keep your partner under control and we'll even the score soon. What goes around comes around!"

"But burning her like that . . . !"

"And don't blow your cool, either, Pat. Just continue to do your job. I know what a shame it is because she really hadn't told us a whole lot, simply because she didn't *know* a whole lot.

"They obviously thought she knew a great deal more than she did and that's what makes it even more terrible. They could torture her for days and not learn anything, because she just didn't *know* anything to tell 'em.

"That's the real injustice—she died for absolutely no reason!"

"Yeah," Pat growled. "Nobody's got the right to do this, no matter what. We gotta get 'em, boss. Just gotta."

"I promise you that we will. We're getting real close, Pat, because they tried to 'cap' me today too!" Here Hollister related the incident of the two near misses.

"Jeez," Pat exclaimed. "What the hell are we into here? We're breathing down someone's neck and don't really know all the wrinkles of the scam yet. I hope you're coming back right away. That way we can keep an eye on you!"

With anger resounding in his voice, Hollister growled into the phone, "This has really got me pissed off! The sons of bitches had the balls to make an attempt on me in my own home.

"They just upped the ante. The gloves are off from now on, Pat. I want these bastards real bad and we are going to do whatever it requires to get these suckers!"

"What about Joy?" Pat inquired.

"We've kicked it around and decided that she's going to stay with her folks for awhile and I'm going to contact the local gendarmes and have them keep an eye on things down in Stuart.

"I don't believe that they want to hit her though. That could have been done anytime. Be much more effective to pop me.

"Anyway, I'll be back early in the AM. I have to go back to the antiterrorism school on Monday, so you guys will have to carry the load for a while longer. See you then, Pat. Keep your partner in check—we both know what a wild man he can be. We don't want to blow this thing now!"

"Right. Things are beginning to fall into place, and we want to see these guys burn and not get off on some technicality. We'll be careful. See you tomorrow, boss, and *you* be careful!"

"Don't worry, Pat, I'll be all right, 'cause I want Sal Tamarago so bad that I can taste it!"

"Sal?"

"Yep. I believe he's into this attempt on me and the hit on Sandra Wertz right up to his big fat ass, and I intend to get him and his people soon. See ya."

That final evening before his return to New York, Joy and Hollister made love in a special, tender, lingering way, knowing full well that it would be sometime before they could again.

* * *

Immediately upon arriving back in New York, Hollister arranged a visit to the Homicide Squad office. There he was given access to the report of the postmortem examination performed by the medical examiner on Sandra Wertz.

The unemotional words typewritten on the report coldly confirmed what every man in Hollister's squad firmly believed—that Sandra Wertz was tortured and murdered to gain whatever information the killer thought she possessed regarding their ongoing investigations.

The ME reported that despite efforts on the part of the killer or killers to conceal the true cause of her heath by faking automobile-related injuries, he was unequivocally convinced that the unfortunate girl was severely beaten and tortured before dying of strangulation.

The forensic pathologist stated flatly that many of her internal and some external injuries were inflicted and sustained following her demise.

His report listed, in the coldest of terms, injuries which she had suffered *ante mortem*.

Those viciously administered injuries were described by the ME as "a fracture of the left cheekbone accompanied by bruising and swelling of the left eye. The left mandible was also fractured and facial abrasions were noted on her upper cheek and eye."

The burns, which initially so angered Pat Connors and Hollister were also noted in the report as, "not life-threatening, but nonetheless painful."

Measuring approximately .025 cm were a series of tiny burns spaced at approximately 2.3 cm on Sandra's lower calves.

Larger areas of "degenerated tissue" were found on her inner thighs and measured approximately 1.05 cm in circumference. These larger burns were found to contain a residue of a grey ash, "consistent with the use of a lighted brand or cigar-type instrument."

The hypotheses outlining the use of a stun gun and a cigar seemed to be very plausible to Hollister who knew more of the background of Sandra than the ME.

The medical examiner also noted that her fingernails were fashionably long, painted and unbroken, suggesting that not much of a defensive struggle was presented by the victim.

At one point during the outrage, Sandra Wertz had been tightly restrained as evidenced by ligature burns on her wrists.

Her windpipe and larynx had been crushed by what the ME speculated was "a sort of commando stranglehold whereby a forearm is exerted with great force against the larynx by a powerful attacker from the rear."

The use of this type of stranglehold would probably forego any possibility that the victim emitted any sound at all, much less a scream.

Her tongue was gouged by her own teeth, suggesting to the ME that she was probably conscious at the time that she was finally strangled.

There was no sign of recent sexual contact.

The actual cause of death was officially listed as "asphyxia due to strangulation."

Chapter 22

Training Resumes

April 23, 1984—0900 hours

The Treasury Department's Secret Service segment was by far the most enlightening and entertaining.

Since theirs was the dubious honor of opening the morning session, the agents who were to lecture approached the podium sufficiently "sleepy" to catch everyone off guard.

The first man, the introducer, set the audience up admirably. He wearily stated that he and his partner had been established in their rooms at the Marriott Hotel adjacent to the community college and opposite the Nassau Veterans Memorial Coliseum since the previous afternoon. He continued by relating that as was inevitable, boredom had set in by evening and they decided to pay a visit to the cocktail lounge in the hotel.

In view of the fact that he is happily married, he pointed out, he decided to return to the room to look over his lecture. His partner, however, single and on the prowl, decided to "look over the chicks" in the bar. He made another point of stating that his partner did not return to the room until the wee hours of the morning and he, the partner, was not in any great shape this early in the morning.

Then he said, "Without further incriminating explanation, I would like you to welcome Special Agent Tom Wilson, fresh from his chicken-hunting expedition!"

Agent Wilson groggily mounted the stage and in a slow-motion stride, chin hanging down to his chest, approached the microphone. He struggled to suppress a cough a few times before reaching out to the mike stand with his left hand.

Once established in front of the mike, he took a deep breath and then sneezed heavily, covering his mouth with his right hand.

Immediately, a huge cloud of chicken feathers erupted in the air directly in front of him and hung momentarily in the air before fluttering down in all directions.

Caught by surprise, the attendees took a moment to react. But when they realized that the chicken feathers represented the results of Agent Wilson's "hunting expedition," they showed their appreciation by breaking into a spontaneous hearty laugh that lasted for several minutes.

Wilson and his partner had successfully broken the ice of the heretofore straight-laced audience by playing to their prurient side.

The remainder of their presentation was both informative and challenging as they continued through the morning session.

Extremely professional, they touched upon the myriad of tasks that the Secret Service had in preparing for a presidential visit. The Advance teams' manner of operating was talked about. Motorcades, sometimes consisting of up to twenty-three vehicles, were drawn on the blackboard with a careful explanation of each vehicle's part in the protection of the president. Area and lodging searches were discussed as were the eating arrangements handled by the presidential agents.

A huge overhead movie screen was pulled down and the agents readied a movie projector. While they did this, there was no period of quiet for them. They continued a running narrative of an incident that occurred while Gerald Ford was president.

Most of the people in the room, and as a matter of fact, most people in the nation were aware of the incident, but not in the detail to which they were about to be treated.

The story goes, that as the presidential motorcade approached a city in which Ford was to speak, the local police were to seal off certain intersections so that his motorcade could travel unimpeded by traffic tie-ups to his destination.

As is the case with most police departments, this one was shorthanded and as a result had their motorcycle patrolmen leapfrogging from one intersection to another. In other words, once the officer had stopped traffic at one intersection and the motorcade's passing was inevitable, he was to speed to the next intersection for which he was responsible and do the same thing—repeating this several times over the route of the motorcade.

As fate would have it, either the officer left the intersection too soon, or the more popular belief is that a young man, impatient with the wait at the intersection, cut around stopped traffic and drove into the intersection smashing headlong into the side of the Presidential limousine.

Complying with accepted procedure in the event of a problem involving the motorcade, a lead car of heavily armed agents pulled out of the line of the following cars, sped ahead and cleared the way for the Presidential limo to speed away from the scene, its armor plated body not badly damaged.

Meanwhile, other agents ran to the vehicle which had crashed into the president's limo and with firearms at the ready were prepared to face the possibility of an assassination attempt.

As the "weapons vehicle," running interference and the president's vehicle careened down the highway away from the scene of the crash and potential danger, the agent driving the president's car looked up into the rear vision mirror to satisfy his curiosity about the danger.

The result was that he drove smack into the rear of the weapons car, demolishing the trunk area!

Laughing, Agent Wilson said, "That driver has never been heard of since, and is now probably assigned to Alaska somewhere!"

They resumed the lecture portion of the presentation by stating that all operations of the Secret Service are painstakingly recorded on film as they take place and a critique is conducted afterward. This, they pointed out, was to find out if anything had been done in a manner not consistent with safety or procedure established by the Service.

One such film was about to be shown to the attendees to depict one of the more poorly handled of Secret Service assignments.

Before the film was started, the agents explained that it would be shown twice. The first time with very little comment and the second time with the severe critique it deserved.

The film was made in the Philippine Islands during a visit of some important members of Congress to a minor dedication in an obscure Philippine Province, one of the many special trip privileges afforded to congressmen.

The dedication was to be presided over by the First Lady of the Philippines, Mrs. Imelda Marcos, wife of the President, Ferdinand Marcos. The brief ceremony, which had been rehearsed earlier, involved Mrs. Marcos being presented with bouquets of flowers by several local officials. These officials, seven in all, were to form a line, mount the makeshift stage, present the flowers, show respect and leave by the opposite side.

The film was started and all seemed to be progressing according to the script.

Standing a few feet in front of Mrs. Marcos was a young Filipino girl of perhaps ten years of age. Her assignment was to relieve Imelda Marcos of a few bouquets when her arms became filled. One by one the line approached Mrs. Marcos, a brief handshake was accomplished and the flowers exchanged.

At this point the attendees of the class were giving each other side glances. "Pretty basic," seemed to be the consensus of opinion of the group.

Suddenly, they snapped to attention as the film showed a man bolt from the line of official flower bearers, pull a machete from beneath his coat sleeve and attack Imelda with it.

His first slash cut diagonally across her chest, inflicting a wound which later would require seventy-six stitches to close. The second slash was taken in the neck by a heroic Filipino security man who had leaped to her aid.

Immediately, others came into contact with the madman and fell to the ground in a boiling mass of humanity, screaming in both English and Tagalog. The attendees watching this real life drama were on the edges of their seats at this point and could hear a series of gunshots from inside the pile of writhing security people.

Others, meantime, had taken Mrs. Marcos out of harm's way and headed for the helicopters parked nearby, intent on getting her to a hospital for much-needed medical attention.

The film showed her being loaded into a helicopter and then showed her being taken out of that chopper and placed in another one. Hysteria gripped the Filipino onlookers.

The class was at a loss as to why so many precious minutes had been wasted moving from one chopper to another, but that explanation was to come shortly.

The film had run its course and was shut down by the agents. While the rewinding process was being instituted for the second showing, Agent Wilson again began his astute comments.

"This time through," he instructed, "take a look at the young girl standing in front of Imelda. I'll stop the film from time to time to make my point clear."

The film was restarted and ran to the point where the receiving line was moving one by one toward Mrs. Marcos.

Here Agent Wilson said, "Watch the little girl now. Notice that she is looking down the line of dignitaries and gets quite agitated in her demeanor. Notice also how she looks around for someone to speak to.

"She sees something of which no one else is aware at this point."

Freezing the film on a frame, Wilson said, "Now I'll show you what was missed by all the security people at the scene and what *you* all missed the first time around.

"Look down the line of flower bearers. How many were authorized to be there?"

"Seven," responded some of the group.

Wilson continued, "Count 'em. How many are *actually* there?"

"*Eight,*" came the incredulous reply from the attendees.

"Right," Wilson said. "That poor little girl knew there was something wrong and couldn't get her message to anyone in time. She knew that the rehearsal called for seven dignitaries to form the flower line. She, and no one else, noticed that the eighth man was one that did not belong there."

The film was restarted and ran through the attack on Mrs. Marcos again. At the point after she was struck and after the Filipino security man deliberately stepped into the second slash and the mass started fighting on the ground, the film was stopped again.

"This time," Wilson began, "I want you to use you *ears* and not so much your eyes. Listen carefully for the gunshots coming from the pile."

Again the film was restarted as the fight took place on the stage. Faces could not be seen, only backs and arms and legs as they piled on to one another in an attempt to subdue the attacker.

From out of that screaming, confused mess could be heard muffled gunshots.

Without comment, Wilson stopped the film rewound a few feet of it and showed it again.

Then he repeated the procedure.

Puzzled, the attendees were looking at each other for comments.

Wilson spoke again, "Doesn't the sequence of shots sound odd to you? Listen for the shots. *Bang, bang, bang . . . bang.*"

One more time he rewound and replayed the scene. Sure enough, there *was* about a five-second delay between the third and fourth shots! But what did that mean?

Wilson smiled a tight little smile and said, "The significance of that short delay did not come to our realization until later when the body of the would-be assassin was viewed after the fight."

Standing in the image of the picture being projected toward the screen, Wilson said, "He had three superficial wounds to the body. The fourth *and delayed one* was placed *precisely* between his eyes.

"Obviously," he said wryly, "one of the Filipino security people had decided not to waste court appearances on this madman and executed him summarily!"

A slimmer possibility was that there had been a conspiracy, and this participant would not now be in a position to name any others. Agent Wilson left all further speculation to the attendees.

He then launched into an explanation relative to the helicopter incident by saying, "The bizarre scene, as you have witnessed and can further imagine, was one of total chaos.

"Mrs. Marcos was hurriedly carried to a chopper for evacuation. The media, petty politicians, loyal supporters, security people and general 'helpers' all flocked to attend the injured lady. This resulted in a badly overcrowded and overweight chopper, so heavy as to prevent its takeoff, even if it could have revved its engine.

"The pilot found it impossible to start the loaded helicopter's engine, simply because when the two choppers were parked after their initial landing, they were pushed too closely together. The drooping blades of one chopper would have struck the blades of the second chopper!

"This made it absolutely necessary to move the unloaded helicopter several feet away by hand to provide room for liftoff, wasting precious minutes.

"Thus Mrs. Marcos' removal from one helicopter and placement in one not so overloaded finally put the rescue chopper in a position to liftoff without disabling damage and without the shoving, shouting, panicking gang of 'helpers' who had overrun the first chopper."

With a sheepish smile, Wilson said, "As you have just witnessed, not all tasks are completed flawlessly. It serves to point out, however, that full cooperation between all operating units is of the highest priority!"

Chapter 23

Mob Intervention

The training day had been particularly challenging and Hollister decided to eat lightly and leisurely at home and go to bed early for change. It was necessary to stop at the local Associated Food Store to pick up a few provisions.

He pulled the LeBaron into the rut-marred parking field of the food store on Uniondale Avenue, a few short blocks from his home. It was 1805 hours.

Finding a parking space at the far end of the second row, he secured his vehicle and started threading his way carefully back to the store, trying to avoid the deeper of the rain-filled holes in the poorly maintained lot.

As he walked, head down and aiming his steps, his peripheral vision caught the movement of a car door as it opened close to his left. As he hop scotched closer, a pair of shapely legs suddenly swung outward from the rear seat of the vehicle with skirt awry, exposing a considerable amount of thigh.

His eyes snapped spontaneously in that direction as a young red-haired woman slowly slid out, making no attempt to lower her skirt, all the while smiling in his direction.

Jeez, she's showing me her whole . . . !

Distracted, he stepped into an ankle-deep puddle of water and exclaimed disgustedly, "Oh for Christ . . . !"

At that very moment, he was struck at the base of his skull, hard, right where neck and head come together. His head filled with little white fireflies darting back and forth interfering with his vision.

Simultaneously, strong hands pushed him toward the yawning car door while other hands pulled him in. As he lurched into the blackness inside, his legs refused to function and he found himself powerless to resist. His brain decided that his body need not take this pain and mercifully rendered him unconscious.

He had no concept of time lapse, but through the buzzing in his ears, he heard a guttural voice say, "He's comin' out of it."

Still stunned, he could feel that he was being held upright in a sitting position, but his head wobbled loosely on his neck. He decided not to try to open his eyes just yet.

Suckered, he thought to himself, *by a pair of legs. Must be getting careless to be that vulnerable.*

Yeah, but was only a casual look and they were great legs, he thought back.

Jeez, I must be worse off than I thought. Here I am, not only talking to myself, but answering as well!

"How do you feel, Lieutenant?" asked a soothing male voice. "You are only a little disoriented, not cut. Ready for a little chat?"

Hollister, struggling to return to normal, shook his head slightly in an attempt to clear it, but stopped immediately because of the stiffness in the back of his neck. A rough hand worked the muscle there with what was not a very gentle massage.

Nothing like Patty had done a few weeks earlier!

"All right, cut it out!" he managed to blurt, annoyed by the lack of finesse.

"That's better," said the smooth Voice. "Now you are getting back to normal."

Hollister growled, "Who *are* you?!" as he strained to refocus his eyes. "What the hell's going on here?"

At that point, he made an instinctive right-handed grab toward his left armpit, which only proved to be a belated fumble created by his rocky condition.

"We already have your automatic, Lieutenant. You won't require it now, believe me," the Voice said.

As his eyes began to regain their focus, Hollister saw that he was in the rear of a spacious automobile, seated between two men. The one on his left was the masseur, a big, hairy masseur. The one on his right was the quiet Voice.

The Voice, a young, good-looking apparently Italian man, was dressed in the height of Brooks Brothers' fashion: cool and immaculate.

He barked out a few words in explosive Sicilian, but switching to smooth American English, spoke to Hollister almost apologetically as the car started to move slowly out of the parking field and headed north on Uniondale Avenue. The driver obeyed wordlessly.

"I'm terribly sorry we had to do it this way, Lieutenant, but I am sure that if we had asked you, you would have never consented to this conversation."

"You coulda' tried me," Hollister mumbled absently.

The Voice laughed lightly. "We know you well enough to know better. My employer is a reasonable man, Lieutenant, and wishes that you be made aware of certain facts."

"Your employer seems to be well off, and so do you, judging from the looks of the car and of your suit. Italian silk, isn't it?" Hollister said, his words still coming with difficulty.

"Very observant, Lieutenant, and correct. I was impressed with your reputation and thought that I would like you. Now that I've had a chance to talk to you in person, I'm sure of it. My name is David Frederico. Very pleased to meet you formally."

"You made a helluva impression on me too," said Hollister, rubbing the back of his neck. "What's up with your employer? Who is it?"

"Carlo Vernotico" was the terse response.

"Carlo Vernotico," Hollister repeated softly.

A name out of my past. The long, long, past.

"Handles most of the big-time gambling ventures in the country, as I recall. Have a vague recollection that he also handles money laundering for the mob. Right?"

"Correct again, Lieutenant," said the self-assured David Frederico, "except that we prefer to refer to it as the organization, not the mob. That term carries a very bad connotation."

"Call it whatever you want," said Hollister without malice, "but the fact remains that you guys skim 'juice' off almost every bet made nationwide.

"It also doesn't change the fact that you use muscle like this clown here to collect on bad debts."

"Without admitting that we do any of those things," replied Frederico in his suave lawyer's voice, "you must admit that people will always gamble and there is a need for bookmakers to handle their bets."

Hollister replied sarcastically, "Yep, and you people perform that service to the tune of billions of dollars every year!"

"At any rate," the fluid Frederico continued, "Mr. Vernotico remembers you from the last of the Frank Costello days when you got caught up in a power struggle going on within our organization."

"And I remember Don Carlo too," said Hollister as he picked up the narrative.

"Vito Genovese had taken out a 'contract' on Frank Costello when Frank announced that he was going to 'retire with honor,' apparently meaning that he intended to retain his seat on the ruling council even after retirement.

"In addition, Costello, who had acquired a bundle of money and power in organized crime, was one of those who were under intense investigation by the Estes Kefauver Senate Committee. Afraid that Costello might inform on the wise guys, Vito Genovese had the contract taken out on Costello before he had a chance to retire or turn State's evidence.

"Shall I continue?"

"Yes, please," said the Voice. "I find this very interesting."

"Vincent Gigante was hired to 'hit' Costello," continued Hollister.

"'The Chin,' as Vinnie was known in mob circles, messed up the shooting in the lobby of the Majestic Hotel in Manhattan and only wounded Frank.

"Vinnie's shout, reported to have been, 'This is for you, Frank,' caused Costello to whirl toward the sound and probably saved his life. The bullet tore a crease in Costello's scalp, just above his right ear.

"The shooter, seeing a lot of blood spurt from Frank's head, assumed that he was successful and quickly raced to the ever-present black Cadillac and sped off!"

Frederico interjected, "I'm told you were a rookie detective then."

"Yeah," Hollister continued, "but I remember the case very well. Gigante was a three hundred pound former prizefighter who disappeared for several months following the murder attempt. We found out later that he took refuge in Sicily.

"When he finally returned to New York, he had taken off so much weight that the only other witness, the hotel's doorman, could no longer identify him.

"Costello, true to mob code, *wouldn't* make an ID, so Gigante went free.

"Costello did a few months in a Country Club Federal Prison for income tax evasion and after more pressure from Vito Genovese, struck a deal with the family whereby he surrendered his council vote and retired with a great deal of accumulated wealth. How's that for a history lesson?" Hollister finished.

"You remember that portion of our history accurately," Frederico complimented, then continued. "Mr. Vernotico was regular visitor to Frank Costello's Sands Point summer home during the period when Frank was being guarded as a material witness in that case.

"As Costello's police-provided bodyguard, you spent a lot of time there too. Don Carlo liked the way you handled yourself under extreme pressure."

"Really?" said Hollister. "And I remember Carlo Vernotico as an up-and-coming 'Capo' in the late '50s and early '60s."

"That was quite an assignment for a rookie detective as I recall.

"But that doesn't help my head any. You'd best get to explaining real fast. I'm working on a severe dislike for Sal Tamarago and your throwback here."

At that remark, the hairy gorilla of gargantuan proportions sitting at Hollister's left side bristled and shifted threateningly, but was cut short again by a sharp word from Frederico.

Switching back to English easily and talking incisively, he said, "Mr. Vernotico is of the considered opinion that you are about to pick up Sal Tamarago. He knows that you've had your people following Sal for some time and are probably getting ready to move on him. He wants you to know that Sal's involvement with counterfeit currency was an independent venture on his part and had nothing to do with Mr. Vernotico's activities.

"Sal ran a few business places for us to give us a legitimate means by which we could introduce some gambling money back into the economy, thus laundering it. In some cases it was designed to give us a tax write-off . . . but you know how all that operates.

"The restaurant was never intended to be used by Salvatore to funnel his own counterfeit currency into the economy. Counterfeiting is not in Don Carlo's scheme of things. It is a matter of record that counterfeiting on a grandiose scale can destroy the integrity of a nation's currency. That would be counterproductive to our own goals.

"Besides, the penalty for the illicit manufacture of currency is far too severe for us to challenge."

"You said that Sal's operation 'was' an independent venture, and that he 'ran' a few places for you. Does the past tense mean that Sal no longer works for your 'Padrino'?" inquired Hollister.

The unflappable David Frederico answered, "By his actions, Sal Tamarago has said 'no' to Don Carlo Vernotico's leadership, which means that he can no longer be trusted to perform as directed. His detrimental actions contrary to Don Carlo's goals will not go without being 'rewarded.'. The bottom line is that he must be dealt with by us!

"He will be a dead man, *morte,* in about ten minutes from . . ." and studying his Gucci watch like a sprint starter, spat out "*Now*!"

Hollister sat bolt upright and tensed his body preparing to make a break out of the auto but was brought up short by a .45 automatic placed none too gently behind his ear by the gorilla.

"Relax, Lieutenant," came the smooth voice of David Frederico. "There's absolutely nothing you can do about it. I have more information for you, so why not sit back and absorb it?"

An angry Hollister gritted, "I have a team in loose surveillance of Sal. If anything . . ."

"Please, Lieutenant, we know what we are doing. We are experts in the field. Your team is in no danger whatsoever," was Frederico's calm response.

A few words in Sicilian and the car turned into the parking field of Hempstead General Hospital on Front Street and came to a smooth stop. Both the driver and gorilla exited and strolled a few steps away from the car but hovered there protectively.

"Would you like to go in and have the back of your head checked by a physician to put your mind at ease?" inquired Frederico.

"No way are you going to have me put on one of those hospital gowns and walk around with my ass hanging out, exclaimed Hollister. "I'm OK, just drop me off back at my car."

That remark provoked a smile from David Frederico. "Indulge me just a few minutes more, Lieutenant."

"Don Carlo," continued the smooth talker, "is a man of principle and as such, wants our organization to be free of any possible criticism with regard to the counterfeiting of US Currency.

"Sal had become a high-handed rebel gone into business for himself. That is never tolerated in an organization such as ours. We had supplied him with luxurious accommodations at the new restaurant in Green Acres and instructed him to lure customers legitimately with the finest food and best wines. Instead he used poor judgment and joined forces with someone whom you know well in setting up the counterfeiting operation.

"On top of that, we know that he independently had your informant killed.

"In addition, the amateurish attempt on your life was orchestrated by Sal Tamarago without the authorization and without the knowledge of Don Carlo.

"Christ," Hollister marveled, "you know an awful lot about my activities. Do you mean to say that your people had nothing to do with the attempted hit on me the other day? That it was Sal, on his own? What the hell is going on here?"

"A 'hit' on you, as you phrase it, would not be to our organization's advantage, but if it had been, it would have been professionally executed and not so badly botched!

"The demise of that poor girl was also not of our doing. That's not the way the Don operates. Sal, however, endangered our whole operation with his craving for fast money and by his lack of trustworthiness."

Bothered as he was by the use of the past tense in referring to Tamarago, the phrase 'with someone you know well,' bothered Hollister even more, since it sharpened considerably his perception that Gerlich was deeply involved. But who else?

Still having a little trouble with his thinking process, Hollister said, "Let's back up a bit here. Whaddaya' talking about—'someone' I know very well joined forces with Tamarago? If you're trying to scare me, let me tell you right now . . . *I don't scare!*"

Frederico countered with, "Actually we know you will not be frightened off and realize that it is only a matter of time 'til your well-known tenacity bears fruit. Your unquenchable curiosity will continue until you find the solution to that question, we know. Therefore, Mr. Vernotico has instructed that you take this address," holding out a piece of paper, "and investigate its ownership. That will give you a starting point."

Hollister unfolded the sheet of paper on which was typewritten, "538 Beachfront Drive, West Islip."

Puzzled by this unexpected development, Hollister was ready to begin firing questions at Frederico but was cut off when Frederico raised both palms in the air.

"I realize that you want many questions answered. However, we are a little reluctant to give you more direct evidence. I'm afraid the remainder of the investigation is in your capable hands, but we can offer a bit more assistance. Judge Marcus will look favorably on your request for a no-knock warrant to search that residence."

Hollister looked at Frederico for a moment.

"Are you sure your sphere of influence encompasses that judge? He's considered a real tough one!"

"I guarantee it!" Frederico said matter-of-factly.

Frederico continued, "You have one more excellent source of information at your disposal. Jimmy Volgars. He will be able to give you another direction in which to guide your investigation. He can help you in the area of arms shipments. Try him."

Arms shipments was something that didn't seem to fit into Hollister's preliminary perception of what was going on. He knew, however, that it would be useless to pursue the matter with Frederico, who was now pushing a button on his armrest.

"Drink?" he asked, as a compartment built into the rear of the front seat slid aside, revealing a well-stocked miniature bar. "Might help your headache."

"No thanks," Hollister said. "I'd much rather have that beautiful red-head massage my neck in place of a drink and instead of Mr. Gruesome there."

"I certainly agree with that statement, Lieutenant. That exquisite red-haired young lady is not only enchanting but brilliant as well. She deftly handles all of our computer programs involving spreadsheets, payrolls, business expenses and so on for our world-wide ventures. She is also my fiancé'."

"You're a lucky man, David," and deliberately expressing legitimate envy added, "no offense intended!"

"None taken," smiled Frederico.

Back to reality Hollister said, "OK, now all I want to do is get the hell out of here and consider what you've dropped on me!"

"It's much too late to do anything about Sal, Lieutenant," said Frederico, anticipating Hollister's actions. Tapping on the window lightly, he summoned the driver and the gorilla back to the vehicle.

The short drive back to Hollister's car in the associated parking field was quiet.

As Frederico prepared to push open the far door he said, "Lieutenant, no one but you and I have firsthand knowledge about this conversation. I will vehemently deny it, should I be asked about it. This conversation never took place!"

Hollister's Walther PPK .380 automatic, minus the ammo clip was thrust at him by the gorilla, who first scrubbed the weapon with his handkerchief.

Hollister replaced the weapon in his shoulder holster. Then he rubbed the back of his neck and in a rare display of real anger, looked directly into the gorilla's eyes.

Through clenched teeth he said, "You're ugly and you're dumb . . . and if you think I'm going to forget this lump on my head, you're fuckin' crazy too. I look forward to the time when I have the pleasure of meeting you again, without your boss there to protect you!"

The huge bodyguard grunted, "Yeah? Lissen-a-me, cop! Next time we meet you're gonna be the fuckin' 'catch of the day' in the Long Island Sound after I 'zotz' you!" and grinned his yellow-toothed grin at the prospect.

"And I thought we were going to be such good friends," said Hollister in a voice dripping with sarcasm.

Then turning to Frederico, Hollister hissed, "Your friend here looks and acts like a carry-over from the old days. You know . . . when Vindictatore like him used to stab guys thirty-six times with an ice pick and then shoot them in the head . . . just to make sure!"

David Frederico calmly smiled a tight-lipped smile, made no reply but stopped any further exchange from the gorilla with a hard look. His slight shrug to Hollister said a wordless, "Boys will be boys."

As Hollister shakily exited the car, out of nowhere, just as she had materialized earlier, the red-haired beauty was suddenly close at his side, still smiling invitingly.

"Excuse me," she whispered face-to-face, as she lightly brushed her body tantalizingly against his and disappeared into the car.

Left behind was a heady wisp of perfume and the memory of her milky white skin.

Through a scant two inch opening in the tinted side window, the dark shade of which prevented any further clear view into the car, the extremely smooth voice of Frederico came back.

"We'll be seeing more of you, Lieutenant."

As the Lincoln Town Car pulled slowly out of the parking field, Hollister read, "C V 2" on the New York license plate on the rear. It was an exact twin of the car he had seen outside the restaurant in Green Acres weeks previously . . . bulletproofing and all.

The whole incident had taken a scant twenty-five minutes.

Still feeling a little lightheaded, Hollister entered his LeBaron and picked up the radio transmitter.

"Car 1240 to headquarters," he said.

"Go ahead 1240," came the immediate response from a female communications dispatcher.

"Please contact car 1245 and have them signal 10 to Lieutenant 'H' at home, forthwith," he stated.

"Stand by."

In a few seconds the CB Operator was back on the air. "Headquarters to car 1240," she said.

"1240."

"Car 1240," she monotoned, "be advised car 1245 has been trying to raise you from the scene of a 'public safety device' in Green Acres, near the Tree's Restaurant."

"Responding," was his terse reply as he jammed the flashing "Kojak light" onto the roof of the unmarked LeBaron and headed, grill lights blinking and siren wailing, toward the scene of the assignment.

Chapter 24

First Explosion

While Hollister was going through that ordeal of being knocked unconscious and driven to the Hempstead General Hospital, the special enforcement team assigned to watch Sal Tamarago had been doing exactly as they had been ordered.

Sal had been inside the restaurant for a period of time, but as was his custom for the past several weeks, was due to leave at precisely 6:30 PM, 1830 hours, and drive to Great Neck. The information had been offered to the teams that Sal had a lady friend there and made visits two of three times each week. As a matter of fact, her impressive beauty had been passed along by Pat and Tom.

Tom Henderson and Rich Haise were seated in the camouflaged lighting company van, car 1245, waiting for Sal, having switched cars three times already this week as a precautionary measure.

Tom stretched and checked his watch.

"The freakin' 'wop' should be comin' out in about fifteen," he remarked.

"Oh yeah?" declared Rich. "Here comes the shithead now, well ahead of schedule. Get ready, Great Neck, here we come. Time for Sal to wet his end."

Sal Tamarago waddled out confidently and headed for his white Cadillac.

The team watched as he oozed into the driver's seat . . . They watched as Sal broke out a new cigar . . . They watched as he casually unwrapped and lighted it . . . They watched as Sal leaned forward slightly and turned the Caddy's ignition key . . . They watched as . . .

A thunderous roar and raging flame erupted from the front end as an explosive concussion blew the doors open and buckled the roof *inward*!

It seemed to them, in retrospect, more like an *im*plosion than an *ex*plosion!

All the energy was contained *inside* the Caddy and the only sign of escaping energy was the thick black smoke that gushed out of the shattered windows as human flesh, plastic and leather suddenly burned fiercely out of control.

They had watched . . . stunned, as the Caddy—seemingly in slow-motion—blew up before their eyes!

It was obviously a perfect bomb—manufactured and placed with expert care.

Anyone standing *outside* the car, even within a few feet of it, probably would not have been injured by the detonation.

It was just as obvious that anyone *inside* the car could not have survived. The energy was both deadly and controlled.

In spite of that, both detectives rushed toward the Caddy but were driven back by the intense 1500-degree heat. Even though Sal could not be seen because of the billowing smoke and crackling flames, Richie called via the radio for Hollister, assistance, fire apparatus and ambulance!

All were really unnecessary. In an instant, Sal had been all but vaporized and his white Cadillac left a hardly identifiable blackened shell. It was an event that no amount of assistance would be able to turn around.

The warning call that Hollister had been attempting to make might have been in time if Sal Tamarago had stuck to his regimen. His mistake of leaving a few minutes early had been a fatal one and one that was observed by the talented executioner who improvised to meet the challenge.

David Frederico was correct. They knew what they were doing!

All that remained for the surveillance team to do was to look on in awe at the fury with which Sal had been dispatched and await the arrival of Hollister.

* * *

As Hollister's LeBaron screamed into the huge shopping center parking field, he could see the chaos developing. Hundreds of shoppers, it was prime shopping time, were milling about trying to get ever closer to the wreckage.

A Minicam crew from a local TV station was already on hand and filming the scene.

Teenagers were jumping in front of the camera, waving their arms wildly and grinning foolishly into it, unimpressed by the fact that a man had just been brutally murdered.

Reporters were scurrying through the crowd, thrusting their recording mikes into faces of people, trying to ascertain if they had seen anything.

Morbid curiosity motivated the mob.

A frenzied desire for a news scoop motivated the media people.

Hollister could see by their faces that the press was almost out of control—pushing, shoving and swearing at each other. Their single-minded goal was to gain a closer look at the carnage in the burning auto and they fought for position in the buffalo herd.

Hollister, ID and shield in hand, shouldered his body through the crowd and searched for Haise and Henderson.

His men and the several uniformed patrolmen were hard-pressed to keep the growing crowd from overwhelming the scene. He triggered swift action in summoning the Crime Scene unit and immediately set up tight perimeter controls in an attempt to preserve whatever evidence might be left.

He abruptly interrogated Rich with, "Did you guys witness the explosion itself or did you react to the sound?"

Rich replied incredulously, "Boss, we saw the whole damned thing go up right before our eyes. Sal never had a clue or a chance. Never knew what the fuck hit him and there was no one else near the car, either!"

"OK," Hollister slurred, "Lissen-a-me. Your story has got to be that you were on routine patrol passing through this lot when this thing happened. Got it?"

"You mean . . ."

"I mean just what I said. You weren't here watching Sal's movements but were routinely passing through the parking field! When Gerlich gets here, and I'm almost sure he will, that's what you story is! Clear?" Hollister demanded.

"Yes, sir!" Rich and Tom replied, almost in one voice.

"And that's what you tell anyone else who may ask," Hollister continued.

"Boss, we've got to talk!" said Rich urgently. "We tailed Tamarago to a house in Suffolk County the other night. We were going to fill you in tonight at home when you finished that school, but he got toasted in the meantime!"

"Yeah," interjected Henderson. "Finally got a line on the house he was operating from. We watched him unload the paper and pick up an envelope from a house on Beachfront Drive in Islip!"

"House number 538?" Hollister asked.

Shocked, Tom said, "How the fu—how did you know that, boss?"

Rich, not so easily shocked, just shook his head in disbelief, a wry smile on his face."You're incredible, Loo," he said. "There's got to be a story behind that knowledge."

"Sure is," retorted Hollister, "and I'll tell you all about it after this mess is cleaned up. In the meantime, you guys maintain a crime scene log sheet until you're relieved by a uniform."

Spotting the arrival of a uniformed sergeant he called out, "Hey, Bob!"

After getting a response he continued, "Look, Sarge, two of my guys were passing when this thing went up. It was clearly an explosion and not simply a car fire. I'd like to have the Bomb Squad investigators respond immediately!"

Sergeant Whitson, startled, hesitated and said apologetically, "Loo, I can't authorize that kind of notification. That's got to come from my boss."

Hollister grimaced, "Swell! Where's Lieutenant Koller now?"

"He's 'on the air,' I'm sure," replied Whitson.

"Get him here," Hollister ordered, "and I'll talk to him."

"Gotcha'," said Whitson, who headed for the radio in the crime scene van, glad to pass the responsibility on up the line.

It was again only minutes until Lieutenant Koller arrived on the scene and was filled in by Hollister with the details as he wanted them to be perceived. He reiterated his request for the bomb specialists.

The lieutenant from crime scene looked quizzically at Hollister. "George, we don't usually do that without authorization from the division chief. Has Gerlich arrived? And what makes this so important to you?"

"No, Chief Gerlich has not responded that I know of, but to answer the rest of your question, this looks like the job of a 'pro.' C'mon Al, you owe me!"

"All right, all right, I'll gamble that you know what you're doing, George, but it's *your* ass if this thing gets sticky. I'll use the telephone to contact the Public Safety Squad Response Team. They should be here in short order. It's up to you to preserve the scene for them, though. I don't have the manpower right now."

"Don't worry, Al," was Hollister's reassuring reply. "By the time your guys get finished, I'll have sufficient uniforms here to safeguard the area."

"Done!" said Koller, shaking Hollister's hand as he left.

Hollister now requested and received assistance from the precinct in the form of a sufficient number of uniformed policemen to completely handle the preservation of the scene of Tamarago's "reward" by the "organization."

Even the Valley Stream Fire Department, upon their prompt arrival, cooperated by using spray nozzles to contain the few small fires on pieces of upholstery that were thrown out of the car by the force of the explosion. The heavy firefighting stream of water was unnecessary and would have blown debris throughout the area.

Their expertise in firefighting was evident.

The best scene possible was preserved for the explosives experts.

* * *

As soon as he left this grisly scene, the information regarding smuggled munitions sale; the activity at 538 Beachfront Drive; Tamarago's movements and subsequent demise; as well as the death of Thunder Thighs and the clumsy attempt on Hollister himself were all transmitted to the commander of the Special Operations unit, Ray Cramdon.

Chapter 25

Beach House

Based upon the surveillance information supplied by Hollister's special enforcement teams, a Bureau of Special Operations raid was organized against the isolated beach house bordering on the surf-washed south shore of Long Island's West Islip.

They had been provided with a no-knock search warrant in record time, just as David Frederico had "guaranteed."

Sitting by itself just east of the sand dune line, 538 Beachfront Drive was a difficult spot to approach. It was a command decision to take the place in daylight, with all inland personnel cloaked in white ponchos. The bright sun served to increase their cover but caused everyone to squint in the blinding glare from the white sandy beach that stretched for two hundred yards in every direction except seaward.

With the ground raiding party in place and lying prone in the sand dunes, Inspector Ray Cramdon, commanding this phase, took one last look to his left and right, satisfying himself that all was in readiness there.

He raised his walkie-talkie to his mouth and depressed the *send* switch, two quick pulsations. This caused two low-grade snaps to crackle over the radio frequency, alerting the men that a transmission followed.

After holding the switch down for three seconds, he said sharply with clarity into the microphone, "Go, one!"

Immediately seaward to the north and south, the roar of marine engines broke through the sound of the surf. Foamy water plumes rose in the air aft of the police armada as they quickly revved their engines to the limit, deliberately announcing their arrival.

The first segment of the raid was underway! Combined Marine Bureau units from Nassau and Suffolk counties darted across the water toward the rear of the house and its dock area.

After a delay of a few seconds, anticipated time for the surprised occupants of the house to react toward the noisy seaside and the advancing boats, Cramdon again raised the walkie-talkie.

"Go, two!" he ordered.

Now the white-cloaked raiders on the beach were up and sprinting toward their assigned sections of the house.

It seemed to them like minutes that they were running with great difficulty through the deep soft sand, exposed and vulnerable. Actually it was about forty-five seconds. To a man they also hoped that the decoy sound of engines worked and they would not be greeted by opposing gunfire as they approached the wood frame house in a full run.

Some headed for designated windows on each side, while others headed for the front and rear doors.

The Special Operations men lugging sledgehammers mounted the wooden steps in the front of the house and with two deft professional strokes applied simultaneously at the hinges, sent the door crashing inward.

Shouting "Police—Police" and bursting through almost at the same time as the broken door, were four BSO personnel, two armed with machine guns and two with sawed-off riot guns.

Windows were shattered on both sides of the building and police officers armed with handguns strained their eyes into the rooms, dark in contrast to the beach they had just left.

At the same time, other personnel had stationed themselves at either side of the rear door, weapons gripped nervously in sweaty hands. BSO began a sweep of the interior rooms.

The front room had been completely deserted by the bungalow's occupants, who had in fact responded to the noise in the rear. The sweep, therefore, moved rapidly toward the rear and side rooms as the raiding party fanned out, making use of available cover as they went.

Cranford was by now into the house himself and off to his right in a bedroom he heard a familiar voice shout, "Freeze, Police!"

He glanced into the room and saw two men in undershirts and trousers standing with their arms raised overhead, held at gunpoint by BSO personnel. They were wide-eyed in fear and were shouting what sounded like "*La, la*!" (Arabic for "No, no")

On the left, from a second bedroom, the phrase was repeated, "Freeze, Police!" but was followed shortly by the bark of a .38-caliber revolver.

A third occupant of the house had foolishly dived for a 9 mm automatic on the top of a chest of drawers instead of raising his hands. He was cut down by the police officer stationed at the north side window who fired his weapon as he had been taught on the firing range—twice in succession.

The first hit plowed into the culprit's left side, lacerating kidney and liver. The second entered his left upper back through the shoulder blade, deflected downward and severed the pulmonary vein.

He was dead when he bounced off the dresser and hit the floor.

Meanwhile, the combined Marine Bureau units had pulled into the dock and the beach. They assisted the personnel covering the rear of the house in approaching a boathouse joined to the house proper by a rickety wooden dock and walkway.

That door, broken in the same manner as the front door, crashed in easily and revealed a man standing over a set of lithographic stones, applying ink.

He screamed out in English, "Don't shoot, don't shoot! I'm only a printer!" and quickly threw his hands overhead.

The caper had taken only four minutes with no casualties on the part of the police units involved. These counterfeiters had suffered the only casualties of the operation—one dead, five others arrested.

Inside the boathouse, the police took inventory of several packing crates of twenty and one hundred dollar bills: US currency in the making.

On a workbench nearby were the small plates used to print the official Treasury Department Seal and several sheets of paper already bearing prints of the Treasury seal.

Nearby was a large capacity electric clothes dryer containing poker chips and talcum powder. A few minutes in this dryer softened the paper of freshly printed counterfeit currency, gave it a "used" look and sped up the ink-drying process.

All told there were 46,000 twenty dollar bills and 4,000 one hundred dollar bills, all printed on the back side only.

This raid had uncovered the plot to distribute $1,320,000 in counterfeit US currency. The printing plates for the front of the counterfeit bills, however, had not yet been found.

This was obviously only the beginning.

As Cramdon and his men continued to search through the house, they began to realize that there had been a potential for a hell of a gun battle had they not totally surprised the occupants.

They found a cache of weapons, including several foreign-made automatic and submachine guns.

An open crate was found containing an American-made "TOW" missile. The shipping crate was constructed to cradle two missiles securely.

The second compartment was empty. One TOW missile was gone.

The success of the strike was gleefully telephoned to Hollister.

The bad news relating to the missing missile was also given to Hollister.

The TOW (Tube-launched, Optically-tracked, Wire-guided) missile had a maximum range of about 2.3 miles. Weighing about forty-five pounds it was easily launched from the shoulder. Achieving a speed of over six hundred miles per hour, its high explosive warhead was devastating.

Not very comforting news for a man who had the safety of many thousands of people on his shoulders.

Chapter 26

Start-Up

As Hollister strode into the now operational housing site command post, he felt a little self-conscious in uniform. After all those years in "soft clothes," it seemed as though all eyes were turned in his direction.

His smiles, handshakes and greetings notwithstanding, he was slightly disappointed by some of the supervisors assigned to him by Oscar Gerlich. The deputy chief had placed several of "his" men in key positions, contrary to the promise he had made relative to Hollister choosing his own men.

One man in particular, Sergeant Richard Bernsen, assigned as desk officer, had been interviewed by Hollister some twenty-two years earlier while Hollister was an investigator for the Applicant Investigation Bureau. Even as early as that time, Hollister had reservations about then Applicant Bernsen as the result of an intensive interview and background investigation which delayed Bernsen's appointment as a probationary patrolman.

Hollister's recommendation to remove Bernsen from the list of eligible's based upon his erratic past, was supported by the commanding officer of the bureau and by a special review board.

Richard Bernsen was appointed, however, by order of the court after appeal and a long delay.

Bernsen's performance over the years had been less than satisfactory and scrape after scrape, he had gained a reputation as a flake. After his probation period had been served and almost powerless to remove him, it was the department's policy to overlook his mistakes in judgment and even to chuckle over them.

Why he was selected by Gerlich for this assignment confounded Hollister and he immediately made a decision to keep a very close eye on all things that took place near "Ritchie" inside the command post.

Sergeants Robert Handy and John McCaw were assigned as patrol supervisors to oversee the activities of the men assigned to posts within the housing compound.

Sergeant Handy, in the opinion of the site commander, was not what he would consider a strong supervisor but tended rather to be a lax disciplinarian. He tried very hard to be "one of the boys" and was strong on ideas but weak in performance.

He had annoyed Hollister early on in the planning stages of the detail when he made a rather unconventional proposal.

He put into writing, in all sincerity it must be noted, a suggestion that life guard's high observation chairs be obtained from the various parks and beaches throughout the county. He suggested that the tall chairs be placed around the perimeter of the housing compound and be manned by police officers!

What an impression for athletes and coaches from sixty-two countries around the world to take back home with them. Stalag 17 reborn!

In addition, placing these chairs as he suggested would require the assignment of an additional one hundred men to the housing site detail staff, which had already grown to 216.

Sergeant McCaw, the other supervisor, had been requested by Hollister and was known by him to be a steady, heady type; not one to become rattled and one who would unquestionably contribute to the operation of the command post. Hollister knew he could trust and rely on John McCaw.

A third supervisor, a last minute addition assigned from the police academy with no apparent value, was Sergeant Peter Taylor. His first comment to Hollister was to the effect that he did not know what he was doing there and that he had no idea why he was assigned. He seemed to Hollister to be a "write off."

Why would Gerlich deliberately try to sabotage the command post operation?

With personnel such as Handy, Bernsen and Taylor assigned by Gerlich, Hollister would have to spend a lot more time inside the command post and not be able to supervise the important security perimeter outside. He much preferred being a hands-on administrator in the midst of things and not hearing about them after the fact while stuck inside an office.

The actual performance of functions in connection with the command post desk were to be performed by two police officers hand-picked by Hollister for their special abilities.

Police Officer Jerry Klick was a sort of computer whiz in his own right—knowledgeable, loyal, and hardworking. He was assigned to record all appropriate information and activities concerning the housing security personnel. The blotter and computer were his primary responsibilities, but he also assisted Police Officer Stan Sinsky in radio and telephone communications.

Jerry, in his regular assignment in the precinct, was charged with handling telephone emergencies from civilians and taking reports from police officers via the phone while they were at the scene of a crime.

He then promptly entered the information into a computer and made proper notifications to investigators.

Very often he lightened the tension involved by answering the phone with a mumbled, "Officer 'Clit'," instead of his straight name, Klick.

If the person at the other end turned out to be a civilian, he quickly became Officer Klick again in response to a startled "Who?"

If, however, it turned out to be a police officer at the other end, the response usually was a chuckle accompanied by an off-color remark relative to that most intriguing portion of the female anatomy.

Sinsky, who had a fantastic Polish sense of humor, was charged with the responsibility of radio and telephone communications and also served as a backup to Klick.

Both were men in whom Hollister placed a great deal of confidence and were, he thought, the backbone of the command post.

Another segment of the command post on hand was the response team, comprised of nine men—four detectives and four police officers, supervised directly by a detective sergeant.

The detective sergeant was assigned from the relatively quiet north shore area as were two of the detectives and two of the police officers.

The remaining two detectives and two police officers were assigned from the busier area on the south shore. As a matter of fact, the two detectives, Surfer and Swede, were from Hollister's own special enforcement teams. They were there, naturally, because Hollister had demanded them. They too had his full confidence.

Placed strategically and frequently throughout the whole compound were the security guards who worked for Bob McCauley on the college payroll.

During the many weeks preceding startup, it was obvious that Hofstra University was cooperating fully. Their security chief, McCauley, was friendly and helpful, while Deputy Chief Gerlich preferred to be uncooperative and even belligerent to them at times.

At one point during early negotiations with Hofstra University officials, the president of the college requested that he be assigned Security Clearance One. Security Clearance One, normally reserved for police personnel, indicated that they were armed and gave them free and complete access to the Olympic area, including the housing site.

Hollister could see no problem in granting this request. After all, it *was* his college grounds the police department were using.

Gerlich overrode Hollister's decision and turned down the president's request as being unnecessary!

Can you imagine telling your friends and acquaintances that your ability to walk around your own college campus had been vastly curtailed by the visitors from the police department!?

The next several days were a blur of media attention.

The blitz continued day and night and soon Gerlich had abandoned the stand that he and Hollister had agreed upon. "No media interviews *inside* the housing site," one of the basic premises agreed upon went by the boards like so many other security agreements.

Ill feelings had developed here and were to get worse as Gerlich ultimately violated almost every earlier agreement forged during endless meetings regarding campus security.

They give us the keys to all the buildings and we give them abuse!

Hollister was well aware of the fact that terrorists look for publicity to turn into propaganda for their "cause." Their aim is to disrupt normal living manner and style—revenge for imagined injustice.

He also recognized that the best deterrent to terrorism is a high state of alertness on the part of security forces. He was, therefore, moving his security force into a full state of readiness. No easy task.

Chapter 27

Masaad

As the days and nights wore on, Hollister was becoming convinced that the whole detail was falling into a trap that had been predicted as a possibility . . . complacency.

The lack of incidents for a few days began almost imperceptibly to change the attitude of the men assigned from one of "watchfulness" to one of "party-time." Little things began to pop up indicating that the detail was become more and more lax. The security people began to be observed in situations that pointed up their waning alertness.

Hollister's awareness was brought to a head by a visit from "Mordicaii" of the Israeli delegation.

As the Israeli team's personal and specially trained security man, Mordicaii was the only armed nonpolice person on the whole campus outside of the campus cops. He had been given permission by the State Department to carry a 9 mm automatic when accompanying the Israelis outside of the housing compound while they were on one of the many shopping expeditions.

He had admitted to Hollister privately, that he was with "Masaad" and was in effect, a "trained killer." His assignment was to wreak vengeance upon anyone causing death or injury to any of the Israeli complement. They would never again permit 1972 to be repeated. The terrorists would forfeit their lives this time!

As a member of the Israeli Secret Police, he was critical of the security measures undertaken throughout the Games as a whole. In short, he thought that the detail should be concentrating their efforts on outside perimeter security as opposed to what he described as "checking athletes and handlers every fifty feet or so inside the compound."

He stated flatly that the members assigned to the night tours were becoming careless and challenged Hollister to take a walk with him one night—late.

Hollister immediately agreed and that very night the self-proclaimed "killer" and he went on a brief tour.

Hollister, mind you, at this stage of the assignment was in full uniform and easily recognizable by anyone interested in doing so.

The Masaad member immediately guided Hollister to Tower C, which housed the Israeli contingent. Their approach from the outside walkway was open and straight forward. The police officer assigned to guard the outside perimeter of Tower C was so engrossed in conversation with aides and coaches that he never took notice of the two men approaching and they entered the building unnoticed.

Once inside they observed a detective with his back to the entrance door, assisting a foreign athlete in trying to make a change-making machine operate properly.

A second detective was stooped over helping to adjust the restraining straps on the wheelchair of an autistic man.

Once again, neither of these guards observed the entry of the duo. They went unchallenged.

Afterward, prompted by Mordicaii's complaints and his own observations, Hollister instituted a series of impromptu patrols intended to give him a more complete picture of how the detail was being supervised and handled.

At one point Hollister passed by Hofstra, USA, the wild nightspot of the campus, a real swinging location where drinking, dancing and generally madcap behavior were the order of the evening. It was the only spot at the Games where students and foreigners met and interacted freely.

One of the police officers assigned to this prime area was taking full advantage of his assignment. Obviously, he had brought a shopping bag full of tradeable items from his home. It included buttons from his uniform shirts, some shoulder patches and even an eight-point uniform cap. Everything was open to barter if one could hold a conversation above the din and this officer was doing a land-office business.

Hollister immediately ordered this man relieved from this much-desired assignment at the most swinging of all locations and reassigned him to guard the door of the boiler room in the basement of the Student Center . . . a dark, dreary place where he probably would not see a human being for days on end.

Word of "the Act" (as Hollister had planned) soon was spread throughout the detail and became known as being "banished to bogey-land" by the rest of the personnel. It served as a warning to all!

These late night tours pointed up to Hollister that both the athletes and the security detail were "carrying on."

One of his own handpicked men became involved in an incident, which except for its serious consequence could be termed laughable.

The one and only Animal, assigned to work a late session patrolling on a golf cart, began to race the cart around in the rear of a building, the basement of which housed a large loading platform.

The underground loading platform was designed to accept all food and beverage deliveries for the huge campus. Access to the platform was gained by the many trucks being required to back down a steeply sloping incline to the underground area, where they were unloaded and the items dispersed from there.

The bottom also housed two very large dumpsters that contained the tons of "wet" garbage generated by the kitchen and restaurant areas.

The dumpsters were removed by the trucks mechanically lifting these giants and emptying the nasty, messy contents into the truck bodies for removal to the local incinerator.

In showing off to other police officers assigned in the area, witnesses said, Animal made a squealing turn on his golf cart and began racing down the incline at the highest speed attainable, all the while exuberantly shouting, "Yippee! Yahoo!"

However, as he reached the bottom of the incline, the golf cart refused to slow down and his "Yippee! Yahoo!" suddenly turned to "Oooooh shit!" as he crashed head-on into the huge garbage dumpster waiting with yawning open cover at the bottom.

The force of the collision unseated Animal and catapulted him over the front end of the golf cart . . . over the edge of the fully loaded garbage dumpster and . . . into the stinking, sloppy mess inside.

Convulsed witnesses say that he did a complete heels-over-head spin in the air before splashing down! YUK!

Unfortunately, however, he sustained a severe gash in his knee, requiring stitches at the medical center close by.

On the other hand, the athletes, predictably, took full advantage of the prevalent atmosphere and one wheelchair bound Australian athlete made this fact abundantly clear.

In the wee hours of a morning, 3:00 AM to be more exact, he was discovered on Hempstead Turnpike in front of the university. The fact that the Turnpike, a six-lane road, was heavy with fast moving traffic even at that time did not seem to matter to the Aussie.

He was very intoxicated and was cranking his chair eastbound in the westbound lanes.

"Searching for Sheilas," he laughingly explained.

Fortunately he was removed from the express roadway before meeting up with a tractor trailer instead of a loose female.

Athletes and aides frequently attempted to smuggle newly found acquaintances and intimates into their rooms late at night. It was necessary to constantly check the security clearances of everyone at the checkpoints prior to admission to the housing site to prevent some clever infiltration plan.

Hollister was embarrassed to think that he was reacting like a Mother Superior.

It seemed odd that the participants would attempt to circumvent the very procedures that were designed for their protection. But as the old saying goes . . . a rigid digit has no conscience.

Another happening involved the fact that daylight hours found the rooftop levels of Towers C and D (both seventeen floors up) crowded to overflowing with police, athletes and handlers, most of whom were carrying binoculars.

The attraction proved to be the strange sunbathing habits of a couple of Swedish ladies . . . completely nude on the roof level of Tower B—sixteen floors up!

Careful scrutiny through the binoculars led to the unmistakable conclusion that they were real blondes!

These incidents and others prompted a simultaneously amused and annoyed Hollister to call a meeting with all patrol supervisors. Needless to say, the meeting was a heavy one and served to warn the supervisors of impending doom—theirs—if they did not do their jobs!

Chapter 28

Second Explosion

With startling suddenness, a distant explosion shook the windows of the housing site command post. All hands, momentarily startled, looked to Hollister.

Hollister, anticipating radio communication requests from patrol personnel eager to respond to the scene, yelled to Sinsky, "Have everyone hold their posts until told otherwise!"

Then, "Tom! Rich! Follow me. Let's see what the hell that was!" and the trio bolted out the door toward Hollister's car. Billowing smoke could be seen in the night sky south of the turnpike and east of Hofstra University.

Hollister and the response team sped toward the smoke and the sound of the explosion—the European American Bank Plaza on Hempstead Turnpike. They were among the first to reach the scene, and among the first to observe the horror.

Millions of dollars had been poured into this newly constructed and almost completed engineering marvel which had been unrivalled in its beauty by anything in the county. It had stood there majestically, pleasing all who came to admire it from distant points.

It was apparent though, that in a matter of seconds this distinctive structure had been completely devastated by an explosion of colossal magnitude.

Instead of the luxurious light blue reflective glass windows and doors, installed with unusual imagination, the structure stared back at the shocked team through blackened, burned out eyeholes like an ancient skull uncovered in a horror movie. Charred debris and scorched rubble covered with a muddy soot were everywhere.

Choking smoke continued to pour from within, in silent testimony of the frightening occurrence that had just seconds ago broken the tranquility of a sleeping neighborhood.

Like thieves in the night, Hollister suspected that the terrorists they had been preparing for had broken the peaceful surroundings of the bedroom community and transformed it into bedlam.

Distant sirens screamed closer and the close ones died out gradually as the skidding emergency vehicles round to a halt nearby. Flashing blue and red lights were everywhere and personnel were being mixed with the startled and curious residents tentatively approaching the scene.

Squinting through the smoke and debris, Hollister could see that the first floor was almost completely skeletonized, with bare steel girders twisted into frightening contours clinging precariously to each other.

Like the tentacles of an enormous octopus, the steel reinforcement bars, which had only moments before had been embedded in concrete, were now flailing haphazardly in space, supporting absolutely nothing. The remainder of the building, three floors, was in immediate danger of complete collapse making entry for investigation impossible.

The whole building had been compromised.

The demolitions personnel from the US Navy and FBI on standby for the Games, could not perform their expertise until the building was made more safe, but were already conferring.

It appeared, preliminarily, that the structure, as unstable as it was, would have to be completely leveled.

Even the grounds surrounding the unique complex had been decimated by the dreadful conflagration. Trees, bushes and flowers, carefully and artistically placed and nurtured for months, were nothing more than incinerated, wilted stalks, flattened as though by some gigantic foot.

As manpower continued to pour into the area, Hollister and his team prepared to return to the housing site command post, leaving the investigation to the Games command and the specialists assigned for this purpose.

Just before entering Hollister's vehicle for the return, they were approached by a disheveled and terrified elderly woman in nightclothes.

She grasped Hollister's arm with trembling hands. "What in God's name has happened here?" she gasped, breathing heavily.

"It's over now," soothed Hollister, patting her hand gently. "Nothing more to frighten you. Whoever did this is long gone from here. Are you OK?"

"Yes, I think so," she panted.

"Sit here a second," offered Hollister, indicating the passenger side of his car. "Take it easy. Do you live close by?"

In a voice still quivering she said, "Yes. Right there," and indicated with the wave of a wrinkled hand, a neat little home immediately to the rear of the European Bank parking field. Just one of the hundred or so similar homes that had been in this area for many, many years.

"Are you sure you're not hurt? How about your home—any damage?"

"I don't think so," she replied, glancing back at her home. "A few pictures fell off the wall—that's about all, I think. But what about the man who was hurt in the parking field?"

"What man, mom?" Hollister urged.

She continued, "As soon as I heard the noise, I got up and looked out my back window. There were two men dragging another man toward a car in the parking lot. He looked to be badly hurt and couldn't help himself, the way they were dragging him. He was covered with blood." She shuddered noticeably at that last statement

Hollister turned to Rich and said, "Get the command post people and FBI people here right away!"

Rich sprinted back toward the ruins in search of the expert bomb investigators.

Hollister, meanwhile, continued to speak in a soothing voice to the elderly lady.

"The FBI will want to speak to you about what you saw. Feel up to it?"

"I'm still shaking. This is horrible. What's going on? Who would do this? I don't understand," she blurted out.

"Easy now, easy," said Hollister, putting his arm around her shoulder. It was imperative that she articulate what she had seen before a complete breakdown set in.

"Can you remember anything more about these men? What they looked like, what kind of car, color, things like that?"

Hugging her a little tighter he continued, "Just relax for a minute and think back to the time of the explosion and what happened right after."

She sat here shivering in the damp air and Hollister feared that shock was beginning to set in. He decided that she might feel more at ease if she were interviewed in her own home, warmer and in her familiar surroundings.

"Tom," he said, "take this fine lady back to her house. Check it out with her and try to locate a family member to stay with her. I'll send the bureau to check with her there."

With a gentleness that Hollister never suspected he had, Tom Henderson took the lady by the arm and walked slowly off while she leaned her tiny body heavily against him.

In a few moments, Rich returned with an agent whose face was red from trying to enter the still-hot first floor of the bank.

"What's up, Lieutenant? Why the rush call?" he asked.

Hollister pointed to the lady's house and said, "We may have a witness to the bombing. The elderly lady in hat house said that she saw three men and a car in the parking lot right after the explosion. One appeared to be badly hurt and was carried or dragged to the vehicle by the other two. One of my men is with her right now.

"She's very shaken and may be going into shock. You may need a medical technician for her before you can interview her."

"Thanks a lot, Lieutenant," the agent said and scurried off toward the house, speaking into his wrist as he went.

Hollister waited for Tom to return, and the three left the scene of the explosion to the people whose responsibility it was to investigate.

Hollister knew that in short order, teams of agents from the Federal Bureau of Alcohol, Tax, and Firearms would be pouring over the scene. He knew their procedures.

There would be a chemist and a bomb specialist gathering evidence. They would be supported by others videotaping and photographing the site along with an artist sketching and charting the scene.

Still others, trained to package physical evidence in vapor-tight containers for transportation to the forensic laboratory, would be sifting through the debris.

Upon reaching the lab, the items would be analyzed by equipment too sensitive to be shipped, searching for minute traces of accelerants or bomb fragments.

This scientific and sophisticated work would undoubtedly play a crucial role in determining the cause of this cowardly act and hopefully pinpoint those who committed it. The expert claimed that each bomb-maker had a signature that was traceable.

The first terrorist act had obviously taken place with a casualty having been suffered by their side, perhaps by one who was caught in a premature explosion. Fortunately, the unfinished bank complex was void of occupants, avoiding casualties by the good guys.

The second terrorist move followed almost immediately.

* * *

Out of the darkness came the unmistakable sound of gunfire, emanating from Hofstra's campus.

"Let's go, you guys," shouted Hollister, already sprinting toward his car. "This is a decoy for something else!"

He drove the car at breakneck speed toward the ominous gunfire, and upon closing in on the buildings, he could see students and cops sprinting in all directions.

Grabbing one student by the arm, he shouted, "What do you know?"

The reply came in short spurts, "Someone . . . is . . . shooting . . . inside . . . and . . . they've . . . taken . . . over . . . the . . . whole . . . student center."

With that almost-breathless statement, he ran off, not really knowing where to go.

"We've got to get inside before they take any hostages," Hollister yelled. "Follow me—I think I can get us inside!"

Chapter 29

Tunnel Rats

Hollister, Tom Henderson, and Rich Haise began pushing and stomping aside bushes and low weeds in a frenzied attempt to locate the abandoned utility tunnel entrance that Hollister had discovered during his preliminary examination of Hofstra's grounds months ago.

"Here it is, Loo," yelled Tom, uncovering a large pipelike opening that had been boarded over in crisscross fashion with some timbers and a wire grate.

Six hands clawed feverishly at the old wood and finally dislodged it. A probing search with flashlights failed to reveal much beyond a few feet inside the foreboding tunnel.

"Not very inviting," offered Hollister apprehensively.

"I'll go first," said Tom quietly. "I was a 'tunnel rat' for a while. Stay close, here we go!"

They scrambled into the darkness and found they had stepped into a foul-smelling hellhole.

Their lights poked random holes in all directions, cautiously. Pipes dripped fluid overhead. Wet mushy material squished underfoot, and webs of all sizes clung to their faces.

"Man, this place really stinks," said Rich. "Like something died in here," and produced a simulated retching sound. "Aaaaggghhh!"

The mumbled reply from Tom was, "Not as bad as some I've been in 'in country,' man. The VC used to live for weeks at a time in underground places like this. This one smells like 'Chanel #5' compared to 'Charlie's living quarters."

It was necessary for the three men to move about in a semi-crouch to avoid banging their heads on the exposed piping above them. The pipes lining the sides of the walls did not afford much shoulder-room and before long the three were smeared with mud and filth.

The farther they crept into the tunnel, the deeper the water and the darkness became. Little and some not-so-little scurrying sounds were heard on the pipes, but none of the three wanted to know what caused the sounds.

Every twenty-five feet or so on alternating sides, they came across a metal sign bolted to the wall. *Danger—High Voltage*, it shouted at them in large red lettering. That warning made the water in which they splashed feel even more uncomfortable.

As they crept cautiously ahead, the men began to feel the effect of an unbearable heat building up and stifling their breathing attempts. By now their uniforms were soaked in perspiration and weighed them down like wet Turkish towels wrapped tightly around their bodies. Sweat dripped into their eyes, burning and making it difficult to see.

After what seemed an interminable time, Hollister called a halt to their slow advancement.

They had reached a parting in the tunnel.

Whispering, he said, "The outlet to the right leads off to the power station. The one straight ahead comes out near the student center, which is where our command post is located. Let's head for the command post first and get the lay of the land."

Accompanying these comments, he shown his light onto the chest of each man, allowing the beam to spread out and extend upward, bathing each man's face in a spooky soft light.

He found Rich to be staring back, eyes open wide.

Tom, on the other hand, had a strange, wild look in his eyes, and his face was taut with strain. This wild, almost deranged look in Tom's eyes worried Hollister.

"You OK, Tom?" he said, soothingly.

In a hard, hoarse whisper, Tom replied, "I'm all right, Loo. I'll get us through this tunnel, no problem. Those bastards are not going to get me, man. No way!"

Hollister flicked the light back to Rich's face momentarily, who answered with a slight grimace and shoulder shrug.

"Let's keep moving," growled Tom. Then almost inaudibly, he mumbled to himself, "The stink . . . can't get over how familiar the fuckin' stink is gettin'."

They moved off again slowly in the branch of the tunnel leading to the command post. The water, getting deeper, now showed over two inches on their feet. The sound of rushing water and steam was audible, surging inside the water pipes all around them. Electrical conduits were everywhere overhead.

Not a very comforting combination—all this water and high voltage.

Gradually, Hollister became aware of a strange bass register reverberation. Puzzled, he began a concentrated effort to locate it.

After listening intently for several minutes during their advance, he found the source of the odd sound.

It was coming from Tom Henderson! He was humming! Softly, but he *was* humming!

The son of a bitch is actually enjoying this!

As they passed by another of the *Warning* signs with its red bulb close by, Hollister stole another peek at Henderson. The reddish glow glanced off Tom's face, causing the sweat and grit to give off a phosphorescence that hid his eyes and made them appear to be nothing but black sockets.

Hollister made a warning statement that had to be said. "Be careful when we get closer to the command post. Try not to fire your weapons while we are down here, most of the steam pipes are under extreme pressure and do not react well to bullets!"

"I'll take 'em without a sound, Loo," Tom hissed back.

Tom Henderson's demeanor had changed, and his whole body appeared to be on alert as he led through the maze of darkness, stopping occasionally to flick the cobwebs away from his eyes.

Once, as they approached the end of the tunnel, he stopped and thrust his clenched fist into the air shoulder high at the sound of a loud thump overhead.

"Grenade," he said without emotion and, unperturbed, started his forward movement again. His low, disturbing humming continued.

At this point, it was clear that a firefight was going on above them, and each shockwave from the explosions caused dirt and God-knows-what to rain on the men from the slime of the ceiling.

After a period of time, how long it was impossible to judge—claustrophobic darkness will cause that to happen to you—Tom suddenly came to a stop.

"This the ladder you were looking for?" he mumbled.

Hollister looked up the length of the ladder, and about one story higher was a platform and the doorway he knew they would eventually find.

"Yep," he said, sotto voce, "and beyond that door is the entrance to the command post located in the faculty dining area of the student center."

Inwardly he was thankful that he had spent so much time searching around the little-known areas of the university's acreage. It had just paid off handsomely.

Hollister motioned the two response team members aside and labored up the steel ladder leading to the fire door and whatever waited on the other side.

At the top he grasped the doorknob with both hands, praying that it would somehow be unlocked and further than that, unattended. Ever so slowly, he applied turning pressure to the knob and encountered no resistance.

Grenade concussions were now very close by, and the sounds of men in battle were almost overwhelming. Again, automatic fire erupted just outside the door, and Hollister's body flinched in response to the frightening sound, but he kept applying pressure.

Slowly the door began to give way. Taking full advantage of the crack that appeared by placing his eye against it, he permitted his eye to become reaccustomed to the light.

He could make out the back of a man standing there, astride the body of a prone uniformed policeman. The man wore a shawl-like cover over his head and shoulders and was motioning wildly to another person out of Hollister's line of sight.

Hollister permitted the door to close silently again and just as slowly released the doorknob.

By now, his two men had also scaled the ladder and were at his side on the landing.

Talking as quietly as he could under very noisy conditions, he said, "There's a terrorist right outside the door here. This door is normally locked from outside, but it's unlocked now. I believe this guy is coming in here to see where this leads! Watch your gunfire, remember what's all around you!"

Tom, in that peculiar husky whisper, said, "Hope the son of a bitch does come in. I'll take care of him, Loo. Watch out!"

With that declaration, he produced a knife from his jack pocket and snapped a spring-loaded six-inch blade out of the handle and at the same time nudging Hollister away from the door.

"Tom," mouthed Hollister, "are you *sure* you're all right?"

The intense look was back on his face, and Tom's eyes were unblinking.

"I'll get ol' Charlie when he comes through that door. Without a sound too," he said with a tight smile. "This fuck is mine!"

There was no time left to discuss the merits of the move. The doorknob was turning from the other side, so Hollister gave his tacit approval.

He and Rich, weapons drawn, flattened themselves against the wall as the door was slowly eased open.

Entering from the brighter outside to the tar-blackness of the tunnel, the terrorist's eyes took a few brief seconds to make the adjustment as he tentatively poked his head and shoulders through the doorway. He tugged at his hood to center the eyeholes.

That was more than enough time for Tom, with obvious skill, to jam his left forearm under the terrorist's chin from behind and against his voice box. He yanked back sharply, eliminating all but a muted gasp. This slight sound was lost in the din of battle outside and was further muffled by the effect of the tunnel inside.

As he dragged the man past the doorway, Tom jammed his knee into the terrorist's lower back, lifting his feet off the ground and bending him backward at a severe angle.

The blade of Tom's knife flashed forward in a sweeping uppercut and slammed into the upper left side of the man's back. Three times Tom thrust the knife in this movement without removing the blade, forcefully burying the blade deeper with each lunge. Twice the terrorist moaned softly. After the third thrust, there was absolutely no sound and only limpness from the body as it dropped to the platform floor.

Tom deliberately leaned over and wiped his bloody knife blade and hand on the terrorist's checkered head covering, probably his most prized kaffiyeh.

"Another good VC," croaked Tom through clenched teeth. "That's the good ol' American way!"

Then in a studied, callous move, Tom rolled the body off the landing with his foot. It tumbled over and landed in the dankness below with a *squish* as it was cushioned somewhat by the foul mud.

"Next!" he whispered.

Hollister had overheard some of the wild stories about Tom's past activities in Vietnam as a tunnel rat, but somehow they were much more believable now!

Rich reached out and tentatively touched his partner's arm. "Tom," he said gently, "everything is OK. Calm down. You're here in the tunnel at

Hofstra, not 'in country.' You got yourself a terrorist, but there's lots more to be done! Snap out of it!"

"Flashback."

"Come on, Tom," Hollister directed. "We've got lots more to do. Get with the program. This is no time to revisit Vietnam. That firefight out there is at Hofstra University, not 'Nam!"

Tom spun sharply and looked at Hollister, the knife still in his hand at his side. His eyes were unblinking and wide. Slowly he raised the knife until it was between his own face and Hollister's.

The sweat streaming down Henderson's face through the dirt and filth formed eerie designs that glistened even in the near darkness.

Hollister cautiously drew and raised his .38 just as slowly and cocked the hammer, shaking his head gingerly while watching the knife carefully. He could feel the pulse in his temples begin to race, and his mouth went completely dry.

The dankness of the tunnel was almost unbearable as George Hollister stood motionless, staring at the knife blade, his own revolver a scant inch from Tom Henderson's chin.

Suppose one of those grenade explosions goes off just outside that door. Could it startle one or both of us and cause a terrible calamity when one or the other spasms?

"Tom!" he croaked almost inaudibly.

"My little friend here . . ." Henderson said threateningly. Then apparently realizing what was about to happen, changed his demeanor 180 degrees. "My little friend here got him for you, boss! What's next?"

The crazed look was gone from his eyes, and he casually snapped the blade closed.

Both Rich and Hollister forcefully expelled the air they had been holding in their lungs.

"Whew! Had me going there, Tom," breathed Hollister.

"Hey! I'm with *you*, boss," returned Tom blandly, as though nothing had transpired.

"Holy shit," murmured Hollister in an unusual use of street talk while disarming and holstering his weapon. "You really get off on this shit, don't you?"

"I don't think much about it. Just part of my training," was Tom's response.

"OK," Hollister managed to say. "Here's the plan. I'm going to go through that door and see what the situation is at the command post. You guys double back to the fork in the tunnel that leads to the power station. There is a setup there with the ladder and fire door just like this one. I want you guys to barricade that door and hold the power station against any attempt by the terrorists to take it. This is extremely important, so be careful."

"But that leaves you alone out there, boss," said Rich.

"Don't worry about that, I'll be OK. Hopefully there are others still defending the command post. It's imperative that we hold the power plant, so get your asses in gear!"

A silent three-way handshake concluded the brief meeting, and Hollister said, "See ya later, guys."

The two detectives stepped over the body of the fallen terrorist and padded back along the muck-filled tunnel.

"Good luck, boss!"

Hollister turned and slowly reopened the door to the outside. He poked his head momentarily into the slight opening. He quickly withdrew after a fleeting exploratory glance outside. Twice more he did this from different positions behind the protection of the steel fire door.

Then his eyes accustomed to the light. He stepped tentatively through the doorway and back into the open, leaving the blackness of the tunnel behind. The comparative safety of the black tunnel was also left behind.

The first person he saw as he emerged was the disabled blue-uniformed policeman he had seen briefly during his peek through the crack a minute earlier before Henderson had dispatched the first terrorist.

Just around to my left should be what remains of the housing site command post.

Shouts, screams, and moans coming from that direction could be heard now, mingling with the automatic weapons fire and an occasional grenade explosion.

The man in blue at his feet was bleeding from wounds in the lower body only. Apparently he had worn his body armor as Hollister had suggested to all hands assigned to the detail and had shielded his chest and stomach from serious injury.

That was a move that in hindsight he would regret he had not made himself!

Hollister reached down with his left arm and cradled the wounded man under his armpit, hoisting him first to a sitting position and then to a position draped over Hollister's back. With the wounded man's hands locked around his neck, Hollister started in a semicrouch toward the command post, his revolver now clamped in his right hand.

Suddenly, bullets began scything through the air around him, ricocheting off the brick wall behind him. Pieces of brick and powdered mortar sprayed his face.

Hollister dropped to his knees and half-turned to see a black-and-white checkered kaffiyeh before he saw anything else. He snapped two quick shots from his weapon at this man.

Crack! Crack!

The incoming fire abruptly ended as the man spun and fell, throwing his AK-47 in the air with a scream.

Hollister knelt there, stunned for a moment. He had taken out the terrorist with two bullets.

He got to his feet and continued his struggle with the wounded man half-hanging from his back. He was forced to bypass two other men in blue, also injured.

"Be back!" he yelled.

He placed the first wounded man on the floor in the CP, and it was only then that he recognized the man as the one he had banished to bogey-land days earlier. The man had obviously abandoned his post at the boiler room door, complicating Tom and Rich's assignment.

Hollister returned to the injured men again and again, darting for cover as the deafening concussions exploded around him, hefting the men in blue one after the other onto his back and into the command post. Most were bleeding heavily, and soon Hollister's back was soaked.

A few men were still in fighting condition, and after setting up a sort of skirmish line facing the blown-out windows, Hollister began to pass out extra ammunition to the defenders, imploring them to "make sure you have a clear target for every shot."

The statement was made just in time.

A probing yelling move by the terrorists to gain control of the command post was repulsed as they tried to claw their way over broken windows and frames. The accurate return fire by the policemen had at least postponed the overrun while inflicting losses on the terrorists.

After two quick probing attacks in which they lost more manpower, the terrorist's attack suddenly took a different turn.

With startling suddenness, a wire-guided rocket *smashed* into the remaining front wall.

Shortly thereafter, another burst went through and destroyed the office to the rear in which Hollister had been housed during the saner portion of the Olympics.

Still a third squealed through and hit the rear wall, raining rock, insulation, and ceiling tile down on the beleaguered men.

Tangled wire strewn about by the TOW missiles made any movement extremely difficult as the men took cover behind any available debris.

Unless you've been through it, it is impossible to imagine how terrifying this kind of close contact fighting can be.

Right there in front of you—and you can look into his eyes—is another human being whose sole purpose in being there at that moment is to kill you!

The deafening roar of explosions, the whine of projectiles close by, screamed curses, and the pleading of some wounded are all taxing, even on the toughest of individuals.

Beyond that, it is a horrifying experience to hear and see your friends dying only a few feet away and to be powerless to help them!

Chapter 30

Fight for Life

Hollister crouched behind his desk, contemplating his next option.

Emanating unexpectedly from the rear of Hollister's small island of refuge came the urgent voice of Deputy Chief Oscar Gerlich.

"Hold it! Hold your fire, George!" he screamed. "I'm coming in!"

Immediately following that foolhardy declaration, several concussion grenades, flash bangs, were hurled past the besieged policemen and into the gaping holes through which they expected terrorists to pour any second.

Boom! Boom!

With the bursts of blinding flashes and harmless but deafening explosions aiding him, Gerlich sprinted through the dense smoke and flung himself on the floor next to Hollister at the corner of the upended desk.

"Listen up, George," he gasped. "I've got some people momentarily controlling that piece of the student center to the rear of your position. If you act quickly, you can get your people out of here now!"

Jumping at this last chance, Hollister issued brusque but clear directions to his men. He had his fit men and slightly injured men aid the more seriously wounded prepare to retrace Gerlich's path and escape out through the rear of the command post.

"Go ahead, take 'em out, and I'll keep the invaders occupied while you and your people escape!" Gerlich ordered.

"Bullshit, Chief" was Hollister's retort. "It's going to take both of us to delay the next attack, so let's not argue for a change."

Turning to his men, now awaiting escape, Hollister said, "Ready? Go! Go!"

The able-bodied men aided their less fortunate comrades in moving as quickly as they could through the rear exit of the command post, now being lightly defended by other forces.

Side by side, Gerlich and Hollister faced the gaps in the front wall, awaiting the inevitable assault.

"We only have a few minutes at most, so I'll have to talk quickly, George," gasped Gerlich.

While Gerlich spoke hurriedly, Hollister searched with his eyes for more ammunition. Theirs was almost depleted by now.

Gerlich continued, breathing heavily with emotion, "I know how close you and your guys are to closing in on me and the counterfeit operation. I know now that I have no legitimate excuse, but I must be given an opportunity to explain."

Hollister became very impatient and coldly interrupted, "I don't know how you can explain away the fact that you violated every portion of the oath we all took when we were sworn in.

"The fight against the dirtbags is the one we fight daily to keep from being overrun by the criminal element. The fact the one of 'us' has violated every rule of the code of ethics and behavior is unforgivable.

"The public places their trust in us to maintain that wall between the good guys and the bad guys. We risk our lives on a daily basis for that because we believe in it. Then suddenly someone like you comes along and puts personal gain ahead of his sworn duty. There can be no excuse for that kind of betrayal."

"George, please listen to me. My youngest boy had gotten into the cocaine habit big-time. At first the easy way out because I love him and couldn't bear seeing him in so much pain, was to help him obtain the coke for his habit.

"I got into a very serious financial hole when the addiction, as it always does, got out of hand. Then I met Sal Tamarago after he was called in for a license hearing regarding the restaurant. His reputation as a wise guy was known to me, and I knew he could be enlisted to help obtain more coke for my boy's growing habit. From time to time, he even provided 'credit' for the heavy drug purchases.

"Then I tried, as a solution, sending my boy to a private care center in Nevada.

"The expense was huge, and Sal again provided the help necessary to get the treatment. Before I could come to my senses, Sal had me hooked but good!"

Hollister interjected, "Why didn't you look for local help? You know that we have programs available to kids who are in trouble."

Gerlich continued, "Yes, but my career would have been placed in jeopardy. You know how this job is, the slightest hint of impropriety in your personal life finishes you! I would have been relegated to innocuous obscurity, buried in some menial assignment from which I could never escape.

"I've already been passed up for deserved promotions too many times. This would have finished me completely and forever if it ever got out.

"Sal used that knowledge to involve me in his get-rich scheme. The counterfeit operation seemed to be a victimless crime and a harmless way to provide the ready cash to protect both my son and my career.

"In the original agreement, all I had to do was remove you and your special enforcement people from Green Acres, the primary focus of the operation, and keep you from getting too close to Sal and his operation.

"When you were assigned to the Olympics, it seemed a perfect time to expand the operation. So I thought . . . but I didn't believe that you'd have enough time to do both jobs simultaneously."

Hollister started, "I'm this close—"

"Hold on, please," said Gerlich. "We only have seconds now. Give me a chance to clear my conscience. I must finish now.

"At first it was the money that I thought I needed badly to help my son. After a period of time though, it got to be money that I wanted and did not necessarily need. Sal had cunningly snared me into his trap. His money was like quicksand, pulling me down with it.

"Let me clear this situation up. I had nothing whatever to do with the decision to kill the girl, nor did I know anything beforehand about the attempt on your life. I swear to God, I didn't know," and his voice disintegrated into sobs.

"But you *did* take the money!" Hollister said bitterly.

"Yes, yes! I took the money. What was I supposed to do, let the boy suffer?!

"My family is gone, my career is gone, and I face certain shame and imprisonment. Let me take this honorable way out. You take off safely, and I'll take my chances and remain here to delay these people!" insisted Gerlich.

Hollister continued to press for information which would enable him to close the investigation. *If we ever get out of this situation,* he thought.

"Answer this question and don't lie to me—just don't fuckin' lie to me! Where is the missing front plate of the $20 counterfeit bill?"

"Concealed in the metal footrest of a wheelchair which came in from Syria at JFK! Sergeant Bernsen was assigned by me to pick up the chair separately and bring it back to me personally, not to the command post.

"It's in my car. The fedayeen want the money to finance their worldwide terrorism. That was not part of the bargain with Sal either. He really turned this thing around to include political as well as monetary gain.

"One more thing, my mother-in-law's summer home in Islip is being used as a place to print the bogus money and store some weapons for their overall terrorism plan."

"Yeah, Chief, we're aware of that building, and measures have already been formulated to close that operation down."

Gerlich's confession was scarcely finished when there was definite movement starting up the front wall which had been all but destroyed by the wire-guided missile a few minutes earlier.

The terrorists were foolish at first by sending in one or two fedayeen to feel out the resistance. Hollister and Gerlich made optimum use of their limited ammunition as they fired at targets of opportunity presented when terrorists attempted to enter through the blown-out wall. Each group of two was expertly picked off by Hollister and Gerlich, who were still crouched down using the overturned desk as cover.

Nevertheless, they knew their .38s were a poor defense against the sophisticated assault weapons of the terrorists.

Even though they were stingy in expending rounds, it was an inevitable outcome that they would run out before long.

Almost as though he knew of their predicament, a single terrorist in a dark jumpsuit and kaffiyeh soon stood in the giant hole brandishing an AK-47.

Without warning, a bullet tore through the desk and into Hollister's left leg—*wham!*—sending him to the floor like a wet rag, spurting blood. He grasped the edge of the desk and tried to right himself, but all he succeeded in doing was to send himself tumbling over the desk and toward the gunman when the leg collapsed, landing him in front of the desk on his back.

He scrambled around in great pain to face the invader, raised and pointed his .38 at him.

Who the fuck am I kidding? This thing's empty! But he aimed it anyway.

He had enough time to look at the gunman and his Kalashnikov assault rifle—the feared AK-47.

* * *

Everything slowed down and seemed to be happening in super-slow motion.

At that slackened speed, he had time to remember that, from the lectures at the anti-terrorism schooling, the weapon was the favorite of terrorists throughout the world

Every detail of the deadly firearm became abundantly clear. Looking at the barrel, he could see that it was, as described, simple yet rugged. The ammunition magazine projected downward in a gentle, graceful forward curve, concealing its thirty rounds of 7.62 mm cartridges. This terrorist had added a wrinkle by reversing a second ammo magazine and taping it to the first. In this fashion, he would have an additional source of ammo in a split second.

Eyes wide, he recalled the voice of the FBI agent relating that set on automatic, the weapon can spew out at the rate of six hundred rounds per minute.

Focusing on a perfect-sight picture along the barrel of his .38, Hollister squeezed the trigger, but all he heard was a sharp *click* as the hammer came down on an already expended cartridge in the chamber.

He was tempted to say, "Bang! You're dead!" but somehow knew that wouldn't work.

It was not an unexpected sound; he knew his weapon was empty.

Still in that strange slow-motion mode, Hollister watched as the terrorist tensed noticeably in preparation of firing his AK-47 into Hollister's prone body. Hollister was absolutely defenseless in this ghastly scene, having tumbled out from behind the only cover available, with his shot-up leg preventing any further movement!

The low-pitch explosion of rounds from the assault weapon began as the shooter, grinning, started a slow right-to-left pan with his weapon.

Chuk-chuk-chuk. Large chunks were being bitten out of the desk against which Hollister had propped himself and wood fragments flew everywhere.

Hollister winced and involuntarily yelled out, "No! No!" as the projectiles dug angled troughs in the desk, coming closer and closer to his chest. He could feel his stomach muscles cramp up. His arms and palms were extended as if they could somehow fend off the deadly rounds of ammunition about to reach his body.

Suddenly, Hollister became aware of another projectile—this one blue and gold—that twisted in the air between him and the muzzle of the gun. The sickening *thump* of bullets pounding flesh assailed Hollister's ears, along with the pain and heat of a round hitting him in the chest.

He realized in a flash that the blue and gold projectile was the uniform of Oscar Gerlich, who had hurled himself deliberately across Hollister's body as a shield, absorbing several of the high-speed bullets intended for him.

The horrendous pain in his leg and chest from the bullets became overwhelming. Teeth tightly clinched, Hollister lost consciousness.

* * *

Several minutes before this incident and before the terrorist had taken up his position in the entrance blasted to the command post for his final assault, a tank had been sitting like a museum piece in the National Guard Armory on Oak Street adjacent to Hofstra's campus.

Now its powerful engines roared to life, and it jolted across the street toward the command post, operated by an unseen specter.

It careened through the chain-link fence and shortcutted across the beautifully manicured expanse of lawn, its tracks throwing sod wildly to the rear. Billowing black smoke hid everything behind it.

Sounding much like a freight train, it whipped around the corner of the core building approaching the command post and rocked and bounced to a gut-wrenching stop. At the sound of the automatic weapon held by the terrorist, the hatch was thrown open roughly, and the driver popped up from inside in time to see the gunman hurry over to the prone policemen and kick at their bodies.

He could see that the fool who had leaped out from cover and into the path of the AK-47's fire was bleeding heavily from innumerable slugs and was lying across the legs of the other infidel. This one was also bleeding heavily from bullet wounds to the chest and leg.

The terrorist received no response to rough poking probes into the bloody bodies with his gun barrel and so turned and triumphantly strutted back to the holes blasted by the rockets.

Brandishing his assault rifle in the air with bravado, he howled loudly to no one in particular, "The dogs are all dead!" and started that odd-looking raised knee dance that residents of the Middle East use in celebration that strongly resembles the "running in place" used by exercising Westerners.

"Allahu akbar (God is great)!"

His exultation was abruptly destroyed as the tank operator, from his vantage point atop the tank, fired his 9 mm continuously at the celebrating gunman. A successive hail of eight slugs from a 9 mm automatic convulsed his body and threw him limp and dead across the threshold of the command post.

* * *

The rashness of the man in the tank was demonstrated even more when he vaulted down from the turret and ran to the two fallen officers. Checking for signs of life, he quickly determined that one was dead and the other almost dead.

As he hoisted the barely alive one into his arms and strode quickly to the tank, he heard a soft moan from the catch of the day!

"Compliments of Don Carlo, cop," he said in his coarse guttural voice and grinned a familiar yellow-toothed grin before placing Hollister on the rear platform of the "borrowed" tank.

He then proceeded to expertly guide the tank over, through, or around the many obstacles between Hofstra and the medical center half a mile away. He ground the machine to a halt at the emergency entrance and, despite his hugeness, gently carried Hollister like a baby into the emergency room.

He deposited Hollister on a trundle and, ignoring the stares and questions directed at him, merely walked away in a sort of primate shuffle.

The medical staff immediately sprang into action, giving hurried attention to the seriously wounded man.

* * *

In the time that followed his being wounded, Hollister passed in and out of consciousness several times, and his recollection of the chronology of events was uneven and erratic.

He did, however, recall that he was afraid that he was going to burn to death at one point when an electrical fire threatened to burst out and destroy what was left of the command post.

He recalled hearing the recorded voice of the phone company's trouble operator.

He recalled blood . . . blood everywhere. *Whose? Mine?*

He recalled the weird sound of a freight train. *A train? No, can't be!*

He recalled something else . . . *Don Carlo?* A strangely familiar voice saying, "*Compliments of Don Carlo.*"

What did these disjointed flashbacks really mean?

Chapter 31

We're Losing Him

Out of the monstrous pain of the bleeding chest wound, a feeling of weightlessness slowly overwhelmed Hollister. Awareness of his surroundings returned, but he was bewildered and confused as to exactly how he had arrived at the hospital and away from the savage slaughter.

He was no longer cramped and bleeding on the floor of the command post, staring down the barrel of an AK-47, nor was he fearing the outbreak of fire. The sounds of the firefight were gone, and the depressing darkness had turned into the painfully bright lights of a hospital emergency room.

The terrifying sounds and sights of the battle were gone, and instead he watched, confounded, from a position hovering just above the emergency room. He felt almost like a spectator in an operating room amphitheater. Three doctors and five nurses were feverishly each doing their own tasks in relation to a man lying on the table surrounded by highly sophisticated apparatus.

Boy, they're working like hell over that guy!

Then he recalled his own mom's warning from years ago when he was a rookie cop. *Sure hope he has clean underwear and socks on.* He smiled.

The well-coordinated swift movements by the medical personnel continued and Hollister remained floating effortlessly overhead, moving slowly upward, defying gravity. Soon he was high enough that thin, white fleecy clouds began to obscure his witnessing the emergency procedures below.

As the figures began to get smaller with each added foot of space as he rose, he heard a nurse say loudly, "No pulse!" Urgency in her voice.

A doctor looked up at her sharply and lamented, "We're losing him! We're losing the lieutenant!"

Hollister narrowed his eyes in an attempt to get a closer look at the figure on the table.

Lieutenant?

He squinted even harder.

Dear God, that guy is ME*!*

He continued to look on in shock as the medical people seemed to redouble their efforts.

Slowly he became engulfed in an ethereal mist as he ascended. The figures began to fade from his view, and he soon lost sight of the continuing drama below. It was like looking through the wrong end of a pair of binoculars, with intermittent vapor obscuring his line of sight.

What the Christ is happening to me?

The feeling of gently soaring through fluffy down continued until he felt his feet and legs take command as he stood, transfixed, the edge of a grotto-like recess in the cloudy haze that surrounded him. He was bathed in a soft, warm white light and was inexorably drawn to step inside to be enveloped in this place that seemed vaguely holy.

White silkiness swirled gently around his body, conjuring up a feeling of tranquility and peace. The glowing mist changed from white to pastel shades of blue and pink and eddied around his legs. All apprehensions were left behind as he slowly melted into the shadowy passage.

Pain, pressures, and tensions had left him, and he was more relaxed that he could ever remember. The feeling of well-being was like something he had never felt before. It was a wondrous experience.

As he was gravitated along, buoyed up by these gossamer clouds, he became acutely aware of a spectral presence, although he saw no one.

He searched, penetrating the haze with curiosity, finally locating a brighter spot farther along inside the chamber. Somehow, he knew that it was his goal and was compelled to slowly continue onward.

He must reach that light!

Hollister turned halfway and took a lingering look over his shoulder. The glaring harsh lights of the emergency room were barely discernable and were mere specks disappearing from sight and memory. It suddenly didn't matter to him though. The tranquil place through which he was meandering was much more inviting, and he looked forward to reaching the appealing brightness awaiting him ahead.

"George!" a quiet yet sonorous voice said.

Hollister's forward progress slowed, and it seemed as if he were a sailing vessel becalmed on a motionless sea.

"George!" the comforting voice repeated.

"Yes?" Hollister responded in the stillness, wonder in his voice.

His eyes frantically searched the cavern for the owner of the reassuring voice.

Through the swirling clouds ahead of him, he could barely discern a tenuous figure draped in white cloth from shoulders to feet. It was a vision of a tall bearded man who stood with arms outstretched toward him in a welcoming posture, but which, at the same time, was delaying Hollister's progress.

"Your journey must be interrupted."

"But why?" Hollister inquired. "I'm very comfortable in making this journey. I feel I must continue forward to reach that beautiful compelling light."

"No, your trek is premature. You must return immediately from whence you came. The preparations are not completed for you. You have several unfinished tasks ahead of you back there, and I have decided that you are to remain as you are.

"You must return, now!" the voice urged.

Reaching out with long slender fingers, the nebulous figure pressed an object into the palm of Hollister's right hand. Hollister could see the glint of highly polished metal before the figure folded Hollister's fingers over it.

"But—"

"Now," intoned the bearded man quietly but firmly as the acoustics caused his voice to reverberate into an echo that was repeated several times, eventually fading into the distance like disappearing thunder.

"I will not forsake you!"

At that instant, as though responding to a signal, the fog began to swirl again, faster this time. The figure in white dissolved into the pastel fleece, and Hollister felt himself being propelled back along the passage away from the light to which he had been so strongly drawn earlier.

The friendly light faded into the swirling mist behind him, and Hollister was carefully moved to a horizontal position. He began to revolve in a whirlpool of haze, effortlessly but rapidly.

He felt great disappointment that he could not continue toward the distant light and renewed his protestations.

Please let me go on. I must reach it. The light promises peace. Love. Comfort. Serenity.

Nevertheless, he continued the disturbing downward spiral, unable to change his course, not unlike a leaf caught in a fast-moving mountain stream. The velocity of the wind whistling past his ears increased alarmingly as did his speed in this frenzied descent. There was a definite urgency to his return.

In a moment, he could again see the tiny figures in the emergency room. He closed the gap on the hardworking medical people until he was once again hovering above them.

Ever so slowly then, he was lowered by the unseen force until his spirit image once again merged with the body on the emergency room table.

His feeble resistance continued. His overwhelming desire was to return to the glow of happiness he had discovered earlier.

I don't want to leave, he pleaded, thoughts still focused on the beautiful light which had promised him total contentment.

"I don't want to go."

"You're not going anywhere, darling. You're back with me!" cried the sobbing voice of Joy. "Thank God. You've made it, my sweetheart.

"You've been unconscious for three days. It's a miracle, but you're back!"

Hollister struggled to open his eyes and could dimly see Joy leaning over him. He was indeed back and no longer a transient between life and death.

"Did the terrorists take any hostages?" he inquired.

"No," came the voice of Bill Wildig, bedside. "You and yo' guys prevented that. There were casualties on our side, but between you and the Masaad agent, all terrorists have been killed or captured."

His mind flashed momentarily to the enrobed figure and the object that was placed in his palm.

Forcing his eyes downward to his right hand, he slowly and laboriously uncurled his tightly clenched fingers. He was clutching a tiny glowing Miraculous Medal!

As Joy leaned over him and lovingly took his hand in hers, a tear fell from her eye and onto his cheek. It felt nice.

It's good to be back, he decided.

What he did not know and would not know until much later were the events that had led to his ultimate salvation by the gorilla of a man who had promised at one time to make him the "catch of the day."

But what were the mysterious unfinished tasks he was returned to perform?

He was to puzzle over that statement throughout his recuperation. Only time and God would reveal the nature of those tasks.

Epilogue

If man is the ultimate creation, why is it that he constantly finds newer and more horrible ways to kill his fellow man?

Can a way be found to stop the rape and carnage we have been heaping upon each other since time began, or is man condemned to forever repeat his mistakes?